Olives

Alexander McNabb

Copyright © Alexander McNabb 2011

The moral right of the author has been asserted.

All rights reserved.
No part of this publication may be reproduced, stored in a retrieval system, or transmitted, in any form or by any means, without the prior permission in writing of the author, nor be otherwise circulated in any form of binding or cover other than that in which it is published and without a similar condition including this condition being imposed on the subsequent publisher.

All characters in this publication are fictitious and any resemblance to real persons, living or dead, is purely coincidental.

International Edition

ISBN-13: 978-1466465718

If the Olive Trees knew the hands that planted them, their oil would become tears.

Mahmoud Darwish

My father slipped from us all, his mind increasingly leached away by dementia. My one enormous regret is that, back when he'd have understood what I was on about, I couldn't have put this book in his hands and said, 'Hey, Dad, I've written a book.'

This is for him anyway.

Chapter One

To be honest, this was not one of my finest moments. I waited for something to happen, picking flakes of paint from the wall and cracking them between my fingernails before letting them fall. The only sound in the police cell was the ambient roar of emptiness with the occasional dry snap of paint.

Anne, my landlady and my lover, had cried seeing me off at Heathrow. It always made her nose go red. She cried the day I came home and told her I was going to move to Jordan for a year. It was our first row in two years together but as we finally went through the act of leaving there was only terrible sadness. I promised to call her every day. As I rounded the corner into the security hall she called my name out. I turned and she mouthed 'I love you'.

I blew her a kiss as the shuffling queue took me out of sight.

The flight was overbooked and they upgraded me to business class. I made liberal use of the free champagne, trying to convince myself of the sense of what I was doing. For the first time I confronted the thought I might lose Anne, twisting it in my mind like a knife as I sipped the cool drink and watched the clouds below.

My black mood lifted as we bounced through the turbulence above the black desert approach to Queen Alia International Airport, the champagne adding to my feeling of recklessness. I was still light-headed when I met the lugubrious hotel driver, a beaten-down man called Amjad who sported a great soup-strainer moustache as he stood in the arrivals line, listlessly displaying my name on a sheet of paper. We walked out to the car park and settled down for the drive to the Intercontinental Hotel. The Grand Hyatt was out of bounds since my last, first, trip to Jordan. My publisher, Robin, had set fire to my room with a cigar celebrating the Ministry of Natural Resources contract I was now coming to Jordan to fulfil.

Amjad asked if this was my first time in Jordan, a question I remembered from my last trip, along with the familiar honorific '*seer*' and the faint reek of cigarette smoke. He was delighted when I replied no, I had been before. The stands of trees flashed past, the brown land dotted with pale stone-clad houses and patches of cultivation. Every few hundred metres, someone at the roadside hawked steaming canisters of coffee or great bunches of radishes, rows of gleaming beef tomatoes and stacks of huge, green and yellow mottled watermelons.

He offered me a cigarette. I didn't object when he opened the window and lit up. I was in a happy place thanks to the champagne and giddy newness. For now, my tearful parting from Anne was forgotten.

About halfway to the city along the King's Highway, Amjad startled me, wailing and hammering on the wheel. A cop stood in the road ahead, waving us down. We pulled over and a second cop strode up to the car and wrenched the driver's door open. They forced Amjad out of the car, shouting. I watched him colour and push away the second copper's hand on his shoulder, getting a mighty shove back that made him lose his footing. I'd normally have stayed out of the way in the car, but their bullying made my blood rise, the champagne lending me the courage to act.

Now my hope and nervous anticipation about starting a new life overseas was mired in this drab little cell. I shivered and pulled the grubby blanket tight around me against the damp. The sunset glowed balefully through the window high above. My movement brought back the dull headache from the cop's massive return punch, my cheek still raw from being ground into the gritty tarmac as they pinioned my arms.

I had never had freedom denied me before. I had never been held against my will. They pushed me into the cell and slammed the door and I railed and pummelled at it, hurling obscenities at the uncaring silence. My hands reddened and bruised, I finally slumped down on the mean little bed and waited for something to happen, playing the scene by the highway over and over in my mind, trying not to think of Anne and what she'd make of my idiocy.

One thing was certain. I had blown things in a big way.

They'd taken my watch, so I lost track of time. It seemed like hours before I found the little crack in the paint and started to break off tiny chunks and snap them. I'd cleared the paint flakes off a couple of square feet of wall by the time they came for me. It was dark outside.

I tensed at the sound of heavy footsteps echoing down the corridor, the clatter of keys on steel. The door was opening to my shame. I felt sick. A surly policeman stood aside for a silver-haired man in a brown suit and heavy beige overcoat. He cast an incurious glance around the cell, brushing at his moustache with his fingers and wrinkling his nose.

'Paul Stokes?'

A smoker's rumble. I nodded.

'I am Ibrahim Dajani. You must come with me now.'

I stood, steadying myself against the wall. 'What's happening?'

He smiled. 'You are being released. Come.'

I followed him, the slam of the door and chink of keys echoing with our footsteps along the corridor. We burst into the bright neon light of the reception area and a woman in her late twenties rose to her feet, her kohl-accented eyes flickering uncertainly.

'Hello, Paul. Are you okay?'

I'd met Aisha Dajani when we had signed the magazine deal. She and I had talked on the phone since, finalising my secondment to the Ministry.

'Yes, I think so.' I shivered violently. 'I think I've been stupid.'

I felt Ibrahim's hand on my shoulder, caught a hit of sandalwood from his cologne. 'You will be okay, Paul. You are lucky. The driver reported back to the Intercon and they rang Aisha.'

'My luggage?' The question seemed daft even as I asked it, the threat of tears pricking my eyes.

'The hotel has it safely,' Ibrahim said. 'Come. There is some paperwork which we cannot avoid but I think you can put this behind you. We have some influence.'

He led me into an office where a stout man in a braid-laced uniform slumped behind a tatty desk. We sat on chairs set sideways against it and separated by a coffee table as Ibrahim chattered to the man in Arabic. I recognised the word Amjad the hotel driver had used for journalist, *'sahafi'* being used several times. Ibrahim lit a cigarette and offered one to the policeman, who took it and lit up from Ibrahim's lighter. They seemed to be negotiating something. The officer fell silent, pulling a pad from a drawer and painstakingly inserting carbon paper into the multi-part form before filling it out, his lips pursed in deliberate concentration. He passed the form across to me, tapping it with his pen for me to sign.

'What's this?'

Ibrahim lowered his voice confidentially. 'It is the charge sheet, Paul. It is formality, but they want you to sign before they will release you. We have agreed they will not press charges but they say you were drunk and abusive, that you tried to assault a police officer. This is serious offence.'

'What about my passport? They took my passport.'

'We will get it back. For now, you should sign this form.'

'It's in Arabic.'

He smiled, his brown eyes on me. 'You are in an Arab country, Paul. I think you should sign it and we can follow this up with our good friend Captain Mohammed later on.'

I signed.

The policeman took the form back and placed it in a file. He stood, his hand on the file, and shook hands with Ibrahim, who said something to him in Arabic. They both laughed before Ibrahim led me out of the office. Aisha joined us as we went outside to Ibrahim's car, the street lights glittering on the Mercedes' paintwork.

The stony ground crunched as we pulled away from the police station. We turned out onto the main road and Ibrahim glanced at me. 'The hotel driver said to thank you for trying to help him, Paul. *Bass* you have landed yourself in a lot of *khara*... Aisha?'

'Hot water?' I could hear the amusement in Aisha's rich voice behind me.

Ibrahim frowned. 'Yes, this is polite. Hot water. If the Ministry found out about this problem they would be forced to take the action, perhaps to cancel the contract with your company. They would at least, I think, ask for your replacement.'

'I didn't mean to actually punch him. I just reacted because he was bullying the driver. I don't like bullies. Anyway, I missed. I never even connected.' I hated the querulous tone in my voice.

'It's lucky you didn't,' Aisha said. 'But you've still caused a lot of trouble for yourself.'

'I know, I know. Thank you for helping me.'

Aisha sat back. 'What else could we do? I'm responsible for you and I'm supposed to be helping you with the magazine. I've got to try and make sure you don't screw up.' She waited a few seconds before delivering the shot. 'It looks like it's going to be a big job.'

I refused to snap back at her. 'I didn't mean to cause all this. I just didn't think—'

'*Khalas*. It is over now,' Ibrahim said. His eyes were on the dark road ahead, the lights picking out the central reservation and concrete margin. 'Try to remember you are in a foreign country, Paul. Things are not always simple as they might seem. Stop worrying. We will get you to your hotel and settled. You cannot tell anyone about this, not your office in London and surely not anyone in the Ministry. We will, *Insh'Allah*, let the charges to be dropped in time. As far as the world can see, this did not happen. You understand me?'

He glared across at me and for a second the gloves were truly off. I nodded back at him. 'I understand. Thank you both.'

Aisha sighed theatrically. 'Don't worry about it, Paul. I guess it's all in a day's work.'

It was past eleven by the time I got to my hotel room. I slung my bags onto the bed and headed straight for the shower, where I scoured myself. The damp stink of the cell clung to me, a dirt inside me as well as on my skin and in my hair. Eventually I ran out of little bottles of shampoo and gel and just stood under the hot stream of water, letting the blessed torrent run over me as plastic bottles rolled around my feet.

I forced myself to make two phone calls, lying to both Anne and my mother so they wouldn't worry about me. I put my mobile on to charge then sat on the bed in my hotel dressing gown. Eyes closed, I rocked back and forth, reprising the day and my own stupidity, grateful beyond words for my freedom.

I was about to discover freedom is relative.

Chapter Two

I woke, disoriented, to the insistent chirruping of the bedside phone – Aisha was waiting down in the hotel's reception. I told her I'd be ten minutes, splashed water over myself and shaved, a puffy-eyed thirty-something gawping back at me in the mirror. The misty apparition nicked me in his haste. By the time I was done, three or four dots of toilet paper decorated my face.

I tore my clothes out of my bag, catching my foot in my jeans and hopping around like an idiot. I crossed the room and snatched open the curtains. The sight of the city spread out in front stilled me for a moment, the ragged ribbon of cars glittered in the early morning sunlight, snaking between the stone buildings stacked on the hillsides. A wave of vertigo forced me back. The realisation this was my new home made my stomach churn.

Aisha sat on the round velvet sofa in reception. I was hot from rushing around and my laptop bag dragged my open-necked shirt halfway across my shoulder. I let it drop, feeling awkward and silly.

'Look, I am really sorry about yesterday, Aisha. I know I've caused you a huge amount of trouble. I honestly don't know what to say.'

'Just drop it, okay, Paul? Just don't mention it to anyone. Ibrahim will take care of it. He has influence. We say *wasta*. Okay?'

I'd come across the word before. *Wasta* is a powerful thing: it says more about you than American Express ever can, a full-on 'not what you know but who you know' deal.

I nodded. 'Sure, okay.'

She gazed up at me neutrally, a pause to let her point sink in before she stood and slid her handbag onto her shoulder. 'Come on then. Let's get you to the Ministry.'

We walked into warm sunshine. Aisha's high heels clicked on the flagstones. I took in the crisp air, a welcome change from England's damp autumn.

Aisha delved in her jeans for coins to tip the valet. She turned to me, shading her eyes against the sunlight. 'Settling you in has been a problem. We've been looking for flats over the past couple of weeks but it's been hard to find something for the budget your company specified. I think I've found somewhere, though. Do you feel up to looking at it later on?'

'Yes, yes I would. That's great. Thanks.'

I'd assumed from her husky voice she was, in common with Ibrahim and the rest of Jordan, a smoker. But if so, she didn't do it in her Lexus, which smelled faintly of leather and her rich, musky perfume.

After a twenty minute drive through Amman's jostling rush hour traffic, we arrived at the shabby-looking building housing the Ministry of Natural Resources. Aisha took me to the third floor and showed me to my desk in the surprisingly modern open plan interior. The window looked out over the city.

'The Minister's travelling right now, but I thought you'd probably want to settle in quickly. Abdullah Zahlan has just taken over as communications director and he wanted to meet with you when you're ready. Can I tell him twelve?'

This was news to me. 'New director? What happened to Shukri?'

'He moved on. Part of the reform program. So, twelve?'

'Sure. No problem.'

She paused. 'But not a word about yesterday to anyone. Okay?'

'Yes, okay.'

My gratitude was starting to give way to a sense of mild unease at the constant reminders of my indebtedness. I decided to focus on work. Thanks to the sales skills of my boss – publisher and wanker extraordinaire Robin Goodyear – the Ministry had contracted The Media Group to produce a monthly magazine and that was precisely what I was going to get on with doing. I started working on the editorial outlines for issue one which needed approval by the Ministry before we could get the project off the ground. I immersed myself in my magazine, thoughts of police cells and assault charges banished for the moment.

I couldn't shake the feeling it wasn't over yet. The police had kept my passport and I hadn't had the heart to ask Aisha about it that morning. I resolved to bring it up next time I met her.

Robin called after two, just as the Ministry people were knocking off for the day. As usual, his faux-posh voice was disgustingly cheerful as he brayed at me.

'Stokesy. Hi. It's me. You have a nice weekend? All settled?'

The bastard had booked me on a Saturday flight so I wouldn't miss Sunday, a working day in Jordan. When our call was over he'd be off down to the pub then back home to Sunday roast and a pissy, red wine-fuelled row with his poor wife, Claire. The thought of Sunday pubs brought a wave of homesickness and the strong temptation to whinge to him about just how badly yesterday had gone. Ibrahim and Aisha's exhortations to silence won the day. Just.

'Fine. No problems.'

'You meet with the Minister yet?' Robin asked.

'No, he's travelling until tomorrow. I met with Abdullah Zahlan earlier, he's the new communications director, he's taken over from Shukri. He's feeling out of the loop and causing trouble. I've got a lot of changes to the planning and he's complaining about the lack of a Web element to the project.'

'He'll be okay. Shame about Shukri. Top bloke. Just give the new guy some love, Paul. Hurry up and finalise that outline, there's a good boy. We've got a mag to get out by the fifth.'

How did Robin always manage to jangle my nerve endings? I smiled so he'd hear my happiness on the phone. 'I just need to get email up and running and make these changes and it'll be with you. Give me until tomorrow morning your time, yeah?'

'Time waits for no man, young Paul. Hup hup.'

'Just cut me a little slack would you, Robin? I need to get settled. I'm supposed to be looking at a place to live this afternoon with Aisha.'

'Aisha? Oh, yes? The Dajani bint, ya? The one with the big tits? You got in there quick, didn't you laddie?'

I held my breath and concentrated on keeping my voice steady. Robin's casual, drawling sexism was infuriating.

'She's been assigned to get me settled in and to help us with the magazine, Robin. You know that.'

His tone slid to treacly and cajoling. 'Whatever, Paul. Look, I'm right behind you. I understand you're feeling a little at sea right now, but we've got to get moving on the project fast. We need the client committed, you hear me?

We need to pull together on this one. It might be the last real magazine you ever work on, you know?'

I was feeling sorry for myself but I could expect little sympathy from Robin. It was one thing for him to get drunk after signing the Ministry contract on our last trip and set fire to my hotel room as he blundered around with his stinking cheroot but quite another to have the editorial staff punching coppers. If Robin had to deal with the consequences of my brush with authority, I'd be standing outside The Media Group's smart Richmond offices with my final pay check minus deductions in seconds flat.

I knew he'd hear the resignation in my voice. 'Yeah, okay.' My final obeisance: 'Thanks, Robin.'

'Anytime. Give big tits a kiss from me.'

Bastard.

Aisha was chattering away in Arabic on her mobile as she navigated one-handed through the jostling traffic. I tried to mask my anxiety, but I'm not a good passenger at the best of times. I aligned my laptop bag with the seam of my jeans.

The radio was tuned into Sawa, the American-funded station that mixes funky beats with skewed newscasts in an attempt to win over the 'Arab street'. The Jordanians listen to the music and turn it down during the news. She finished her call, waving the mobile at me, her attention charmingly diverted away from the road and the random, lane-swapping traffic all around us. I focused on the seam/laptop occlusion.

'My cousin. He's been helping me to look for houses. He has some good ideas, maybe.'

I managed to look up. 'Where are we going?'

'To a place near the first circle. Amman is built on seven circles, they are roundabouts. The first circle is the old area of the city.'

I was in her debt, no doubt about it, but I worried about my passport. I had trusted Ibrahim when he had told me the case wouldn't go further and I had signed that stupid form without really knowing what it was. I felt ungrateful pushing it, yet I had to know. I pressed my hands together and looked across at Aisha. 'Has Ibrahim got any idea about where my passport is?

She smiled as she drove, her eyes on the road. 'Don't worry, Paul. Ibrahim can manage these things. It will maybe take a little time is all.'

I gazed out at the rainbow mosaic of shop fronts flashing by, immersed in the bustling strangeness of it all and wondering how much 'a little time' is. I checked the seams of my jeans and the laptop bag were still aligned.

We stopped at a traffic light and I was startled by a tap on my window. A small, dirty-faced child stood by the car, tears carving pale streaks down his cheeks as he held up his hand in the Arab gesture of supplication, his thumb and first two fingers pressed together in a little bunch. He pulled an exaggerated needy face.

If his appearance had taken me aback, the outburst from the seat next to me threw me even more. Aisha dropped the electric window, barking a stream of violent, guttural Arabic. He backed away sullenly. The lights changed and we pulled off, leaving him glaring at me in the wing mirror.

I shook from shock and anger, glaring sightlessly out of the window before twisting to face her.

'There was absolutely no need for that.'

Her eyes stayed fixed on the road ahead. 'He's begging. They're a problem.'

'I'll ask if I need someone screamed at. He was just a poor Palestinian kid.'

I caught the paleness of her knuckles on the wheel. 'We are Palestinian, but we are not beggars. Whatever we lose, however desperate it becomes. It is bad enough we have to beg the world to understand we have had our land stolen from us, to beg to be allowed to return to our houses. Better we save our begging for these things than wandering the streets for pennies.'

We drove too fast and in silence down a tree-lined street dotted with embassies, passing my hotel before turning right and dropping down into an area of older, more ornate buildings. Everything in Amman is clad in the same pale stone, the older buildings exuding a quaint colonialism.

Aisha finally spoke. 'Look, Paul, there are a lot of these beggars in Amman and they're organised. They are gypsies, *Bedu*. You'll get the picture; they hassle people. Life here can be harsh sometimes. We're not all wealthy and settled in nice middle class homes.'

I talked to my hands. 'No, look, it's my fault. I'm sorry. I just got a shock, that's all. I'm a bit nervy right now. There's a lot of strangeness to get used to.'

'It's okay. Forget it.'

Aisha took us downhill into a leafy avenue of fine old houses before she gestured, her wooden bangles clacking. 'This is the First Circle, the centre of old Amman and it's becoming fashionable for cafés and bars. There's a place here that may be within your budget, but it's unfurnished. It's just up the street from the Wild Jordan Café, quite a popular place that the Americans built as a gift to Jordan. They like to give us little gifts.'

I stayed quiet as she pulled the car to a stop in front of a flight of stone steps leading up to a house standing apart on the hillside, ornate wrought-iron railings protecting its windows and a vine trailing on the pergola in the garden to the front of it. I found myself following the swing of her hips as she led the way up the steps from the road. She turned abruptly at the top, caught me looking at her bum and raised an eyebrow. I felt my face redden. She pulled a soft pack of cigarettes from her burgundy handbag and offered them.

'I don't, thanks.'

'Suit yourself,' she said, lighting up and inhaling hungrily. Her lipstick left a dark red mark on the white filter. As she raised her head to let the smoke go, I noticed she had ink on her fingers, like a naughty schoolgirl, an incongruity in someone so sophisticated. 'It's owned by a lawyer and his wife. It's on two floors, there's a Swedish guy who rents the upper floor. You would get the ground floor and the use of the garden area.'

She opened the door and waited for me to go in. It wasn't huge, a traditional house built maybe in the thirties or forties and clad in pale Jordan stone. A green-painted door led straight into the cool, terracotta-floored kitchen. I wandered around the echoing rooms before going back outside and standing in the lush little garden. I looked out across to the Jordanian flag flapping merrily atop the Citadel, the central hill of Amman. The pale stone buildings carpeted the city around us, glowing deep orange in the sunset. I listened to the sound of a cricket in the bushes, taking in the fresh breeze and wishing time would stop and leave me with these feelings forever. All thoughts of police charges and cells were gone, chased away by my joy at this little house. I heard Aisha's step behind me and caught a whiff of her cigarette smoke, looking round to catch the glow of the setting sun on her golden skin.

'I want to live here,' I said. 'This is beautiful.'

'*Alhamdulillah.*'

'Sorry?'

'It means thanks to God. Why do you look so worried if you like it?'

'How am I going to furnish it?'

'I can get the landlord to defer the first three month's rent if you agree to leave the furniture behind you when you go.'

I glanced at Aisha, her brown eyes alive, gauging my reaction. I took in the garden again, the trellises and the wooden table and chairs under arches of vines. She ground the cigarette out under her foot. I blurted, 'Of course I will. Christ, it's ideal. Idyllic. Who's the landlord?'

Aisha sashayed toward the car. 'Come on, I'll take you to your hotel.'

I laughed, persisting. 'Who's the landlord?'

She stopped and turned, grinning. 'My cousin.' Then she flicked her hair at me and carried on down the steps.

Wasta.

Chapter Three

My first job the next morning was to finish the editorial plan and get it approved. I had a meeting with Zahlan to go through the update and he complained bitterly once again that The Media Group wasn't providing a microsite, blog or even an online newsletter version of the magazine. I resolved to talk to Robin about how we could get around what was obviously going to be a big problem for us unless we could find a way of addressing Zahlan's digital inclinations.

Scanning email got me a travel warning from the Yanks for Jordan: present danger despite the peace deal, terrorist threats against US and other allied nationals, extreme caution, yadayada. Great. Looking up the Foreign Office resulted in, as usual, the suggestion that Brits might like to wear a hat if walking through Gaza at midday as the sun can be tiresome. The website suggested, in a mild sort of way, British nationals in Jordan might want to drop into the Embassy and register if they fancied. I fancied, deciding to do just that later in the week.

I did my online rounds and scanned Facebook, Twitter and Gorkana but my heart wasn't really in it and I settled down to working on planning the magazine to escape from the nagging thoughts of police charges. They filled my every quiet moment, driving me to constantly seek out noise, activity and bustle.

The magazine was intended to highlight Jordan's resource issues and look at the initiatives the Ministry of Natural Resources was putting together to try to make the most of what little the country had to offer. Although

I'd done a lot of online research, I had conversations with as many people as possible to try to understand the Ministry's work and give myself a grounding in the issues. I wanted to create a magazine that truly reflected the Ministry's work with quality and insight. Robin, of course, was only concerned with revenue, his reading never going further than spreadsheets and expensive restaurant menus.

At four in the afternoon I surfaced, blinking, to find Aisha standing against my desk wearing a fitted black dress with a wide, burgundy belt that brought Robin's comments back to me. He might be a sexist bastard but he did have a point: Aisha was a very shapely girl. She looked every inch the Arab. Her nose curved slightly, her eyebrows were heavy and her lips full with unnerving sensuality.

She smiled. 'Who is Robin?'

'The guy with me last time I was here. My boss, my publisher. Why do you ask?'

'You were growling his name under your breath.' She clicked her fingers softly. 'Oh, wow, I remember. *Him*. Are you actually *friends*?'

'Robin? No, he's my boss, not my friend. Actually, he's the bane of my life.' I remembered him trying to make a clumsy pass at Aisha during our last trip to Jordan. Robin only did clumsy passes, although usually drunk at parties and in front of his weary wife, Claire.

Aisha shot me a quizzical glance. 'Bane?'

'Bane. Problem, irritation. Obedience, bane of all genius, virtue, freedom and truth, makes slaves of men. Shelley.'

'Shelley,' she deadpanned.

'Nineteenth century English poet. Percy Bysshe Shelley. The Revolt of Islam and all that.'

'Right.' She rolled the 'r' and crossed her arms. Her right hand bore an expensive-looking ring and a schoolgirl ink stain but her left was bare. The fine hairs on her brown arms were dark.

I sat back in my chair. 'Zahlan said you'd be fixing contacts for interviews.'

'Yes, I spoke to the Secretary General about it. Do you have an idea of what you want to focus on? I've already got interviews lined up with a couple of key players the Minister told me about, one of them is the potash extraction company.' She laughed. 'They're Brits, so I thought that'd be a nice easy start for you.'

'I've just finished the contents, actually. You want to grab a coffee and have a look over it?'

'Sounds good. Let's do it after work.'

'Starbucks?'

She shook her head. 'No. God, no. Anything but that. Starbucks is the bane of coffee. Is that right? Let's meet at the Four Seasons. Five?'

'Done.' I smiled at her, inwardly quailing at the thought of what five-star Four Seasons coffee at five would cost me.

I took a cab to the Four Seasons, where we were stopped by security scanning the car with what seemed to be a divining rod. The cabbie chuckled throatily at the performance.

'This little stick he find bomb too much, *seer*. Too much.' He gestured with his thumb at the uniformed guard walking up and down balancing his little dowsing stick. I was still shaking my head at the strangeness of the whole rigmarole as I walked through the airy lobby, past a huge display of flowers and grasses arranged in ranks of tall glass vases. I found Aisha in the sumptuousness of the yellow-carpeted piano lounge, sitting at a big round table and tapping away at her MacBook.

She smiled up at me. Her bag covered the seat next to her, so I took the next available space and took out my own machine.

She pulled a face. 'A Dell?'

'Don't start. It's a tool, not a religion.'

A waiter came over and we ordered coffee. I pulled up the flatplan and we started going through the magazine contents and discussing how we were going to set up interviews and shoots with the people I needed in the Ministry and in the big world outside. The coffee came, a little theatrical presentation of porcelain on silver trays with cafétieres and dainty biscuits. By the time we reached the end of the planning, two hours had passed and we were on our second round of coffee. Aisha's bag had moved and we were sharing my computer.

Aisha pushed her chair away and stood, stretching. She leaned on the back of my seat. 'This is really good, Paul. People are going to love this.'

I grinned. 'Thanks. I hope so.'

'Zahlan's concerned it's all on dead trees. You know that, right?'

I nodded. 'Yes. He made it abundantly clear. He wants an online version as well as what he calls "more interactivity" but that wasn't really part of the plan. We did discuss that carefully with Mr Shukri when we signed the deal.'

Aisha sat back down, this time sideways with her legs crossed towards me and taking sips of coffee, her red nails rich against the white and gold porcelain. 'Yes, but Shukri's old school. He wouldn't know the Internet if it came round and bit him on the ass. I think your Robin sort of took advantage of it. But Shukri's gone now. Zahlan's in charge and he's shaking things up. He's very good you know, Paul.'

I leaned back, stretching my tired muscles. 'I'll talk to Robin. I'm sure we can spin out a PDF version of the magazine and I can certainly put the content up for someone to use it on a website, but I can't see him agreeing to a whole social media program. The Ministry's going to have to resource that.'

She frowned. 'You're the ones making the money out of this.'

'Not enough to start building whole online campaigns. That's not fair. We signed up to a magazine, not to a whole Web campaign.'

She paused, thinking, the cup to her mouth and the dark coffee lapping against her lips. 'Well, I guess it's not our problem, anyway. Zahlan and your Robin can work it out.'

I snorted. 'He's not my bloody Robin.'

She put her cup down and pressed her napkin to her mouth, a little smear of red on the crisp cotton. 'So tell me, why did you volunteer to come to Jordan?'

'I didn't volunteer. Robin gave me the choice of this or the doghouse. I've done a couple of short term overseas secondment jobs with TMG before and I fancied the challenge of something completely different. I'm not sure I was ready for how different this has been.'

'Are you worrying about the police thing still?'

I shrugged. 'Of course I am. I can't get it out of my mind. Why wouldn't I worry? I've just made the biggest move of my life and started it with the biggest blunder of my life.' I checked myself. 'Well, almost.'

She was fast, her face a picture of innocent enquiry.

'Almost?'

I kicked myself mentally. I hadn't even told Anne about my career-ending screw-up at the *Herald* and here I was telling an almost complete stranger. For some reason I couldn't hold back or evade the enquiry in Aisha's brown eyes. Her mouth was turned up in a quizzical smile.

I took the plunge. 'I made a mistake once when I worked on a local newspaper in the UK. I had just started my first stint as a reporter. It cost me the job and meant I could never work on a newspaper again. And newspapers is all I ever wanted to do since I was a kid.'

Her smile faded and she leaned forward. 'That sucks.'

'It's a while ago now and I enjoy the stuff I do at TMG generally. It's not hard news journalism, but it's writing and writing is what I do best. Well, apart from screwing things up.'

'You shouldn't beat yourself up about it, Paul. Ibrahim will take care of it. Look, what about we finish up here and grab something to eat?

'Sounds good. Where?'

She grinned. 'Anywhere.'

It was past midnight when I opened the door with my key card. I lunged for the chirping hotel phone, flashing red in the darkness.

'Paul? Is that you?'

'Hey, Annie.'

'Paul, your mobile's been off all day. I've been worried.'

Oh no. 'I swapped out the chip for a local one this morning, Anne. I didn't have time to text you the new number, I'm really sorry. It's been busy here.'

'How are you settling in?'

I tried not to think of the police cell and 'our good friend Captain Mohammed' pushing his charge sheet across the scarred desktop for me to sign. 'Really well. I've got a few problems with one of the big bugs at the Ministry who wants us to do more online stuff, but it's nothing that can't be handled. I'm sure golden boy Goodyear will talk him round. I've found a house to rent here, a really nice one in one of the old parts of the city and I'll be out of the hotel at the weekend if everything goes to plan. It's nice here, Annie, you'd like it.'

'I'm glad it's going well. How's your mum?'

'I haven't talked to her since I arrived. I'll give her a call tomorrow. How're things with you – do you miss me?'

'You know I do Paul. It's cold here without you. I sort of don't know what to do with myself in the evenings. It's been raining and I've got the fire on, but I need a glass of red wine and a warm Paul.'

Anne was a Leo, constantly basking in what little heat England afforded. I thought of Paphos and the fine blonde hairs on the coconut-scented warmth of her flat brown belly, a million years ago on a beach so hot the air shimmered above the sand.

I smiled. 'I'm going to come back at Christmas. Can you wait for me?'

'You know I will. I'd come out to you, but you know how it is with the practice right now. I can't take lunch off, let alone a long weekend.'

Busy Anne the professional high-flyer, the BlackBerry-toting practitioner of international contract law. I often wondered what she ever saw in a scruffy journalist with a distinct distaste for big business and its corporate values. Her work and clients were something we didn't talk about anymore because it inevitably led to rows.

We chatted a little, whispering sweet nothings before we kissed air above our handsets. I undressed and drew a hot flannel over the drawn face peering back at me in the big bathroom mirror.

I lay in the dark for ages, comfortable in the puffed warmth of the hotel duvet but kept awake by memories of Anne and the nagging thoughts of dank prison cells. I flailed myself in the silent room with thoughts about what the police would do now, peeling back the layers of false reassurance like onion skin until there was nothing left but the certainty of jail before disgrace. I found myself wondering how I would survive weeks or months in an Arab prison, although Jordan was now my prison – I'd never appreciated how much actually having a passport in your hand meant, how that silly little document meant the freedom to walk out, to turn your back and just leave.

Sleep finally came and wiped away my cares, bringing dreams of home and being a kid again, playing with Charles before he left for university – a rare moment when he'd had time for his kid brother. My dad was there, too. Which was nice, if somewhat fanciful. He was never really there, even before he took his last walk out of the house without saying goodbye, leaving my mum sobbing on the sofa with the side of her face red and swollen.

Jordan takes a Friday/Saturday weekend and my first Friday I stayed at the house taking deliveries of furniture and fittings. Aisha came around to help, hauling two friends along with her, a fussy little bird of a girl and her friendly, lumbering boyfriend. They were good people and we were instantly at ease working away cleaning, shopping and arranging my new possessions. I was humbled by how helpful and hospitable they were to a complete stranger, particularly when I found out they were actually packing themselves because the guy was moving to Kuwait for better money than Jordan could ever have offered him. She planned to follow him one day.

Saturday afternoon I checked out of my hotel and into my new home. Aisha arrived soon after I did, banging on the kitchen door so hard I thought one of the glass panels would smash.

I opened the door and she burst into the kitchen, grinning. 'Here. A present for you, from Ibrahim. He says not to do anything stupid, he had to put a deposit against this.'

We were supposed to go out for drinks with the couple who had helped me move in. Aisha, normally a conservative dresser, wore a low-cut top with a pashmina draped around her shoulders.

I opened the brown envelope and my passport slid out. My relief was electric, the little burgundy document giving me the option of escape home. I felt ashamed of the thought. Ibrahim had acted as my guarantor and if I pulled a runner he would have to face the consequences. And yet, at that moment, I knew I'd skip the country if it came to facing a return to jail. I stammered my thanks but Aisha waved dismissal.

'It's okay, Paul. He said to tell you there's no formal charge yet. He's still negotiating with Captain Mohammed and hopes to have the case dropped completely.'

'Please just thank him for me, Aisha.'

'No thanks needed, Paul.' She smiled at me, her big eyes on mine. 'You're a friend of the family. Come on, let's go meet the guys.'

The bar was a two minute drive uphill from my new home. Decorated in Arabesque, its red-tinted ambience was an escape from the chill night. Everyone seemed to be smoking, chattering over the funky *Arabi* chill-out backbeats.

We sat together in a corner and talked about the Ministry and my initial meeting with the Minister earlier in the week. Harb Al Hashemi, the Jordanian Minister of Natural Resources, was one of a small band of reformers trying to introduce liberalisation and foreign investment in the face of an increasingly conservative parliament. He had been shockingly frank about Jordan's problems during our meeting.

Aisha laughed at that, hitching up the shawl around her shoulders. 'We all like to talk about how bad things are. Harb's probably glad of the chance to talk to someone from outside about it.' She played with her wine glass, frowning. 'He has a hard time trying to get these reform programmes pushed through, but Jordan desperately needs them. We need to cash in on the peace dividend. If they have truly reached a lasting deal in Palestine, Jordan has a new chance to build and grow. The water privatisation is really the most important job we've undertaken at the Ministry and Harb's negotiating his way through a social and political minefield. But Jordan simply doesn't have enough water.'

Aisha's friends arrived, weaving their way through the crowded bar. We ordered food, Aisha chatting in English, occasionally forgetting about me and lapsing into Arabic. Soon enough I found myself immersed in the conversation, revelling in the warmth of readily offered friendship and laughter.

Leaving the bar at the end of the evening, we stood on the pavement and waved Aisha's friends goodbye, our faces reddened by their rear lights. I could see my breath in the air.

Aisha turned to me. 'Do you want a lift?'

Her shawl had slipped, exposing the small mole on the rise of her right breast. I looked up to find her eyes on me. The uncertainty on her face amplified the little thrill in me, the urge towards her broken only by an instant's thought of Anne.

'No, no thanks. I'll walk down,' I gabbled. 'It's only a few minutes away and I could do with clearing my head. Will I see you at the Ministry tomorrow?'

'Of course, bright and early. Look, you don't even have a fridge in the house yet. Why don't you come around to my place tomorrow and have dinner? My mum's been dying to meet our new Englishman.'

'I'd like to very much. Thank you.'

The valet brought Aisha's Lexus and we said goodnight. The cold night air on the walk back brought a resolution to spend what little remained of my first month's overseas salary on warm winter clothes. I hadn't expected English winter weather to winter nights at home – strolling back from The Two Badgers arm in arm with Anne, huddled close together for warmth and tipsy from the insanely expensive bottle of red wine we'd shared over dinner in the little back room restaurant. Striding down the hill to my little Jordanian home, the wash of homesickness made me hunch up, my hands deep in my pockets against the foreign coldness slinking into me, making my bones ache.

Chapter Four

Aisha had arranged an affordable hire car through a cousin and I managed to strike my way through the jostling traffic over to the British Embassy without any major incidents.

The Embassy's reception area was quiet and smelled faintly of antiseptic, like a school. I asked the fussy, grey-haired woman about registering as a British national and she handed me a form, explaining they had a warden system to keep everyone 'in the loop.' The Americanism seemed slightly odd in her plummy, Joyce Grenfell voice. She made a note of the area I lived in before asking what had brought me to Amman. She handed me a card with my warden's name and mobile number and asked me to wait while she copied my passport for their records. Giving it up to her brought back a strong memory of the police cell. I took a deep breath of clean air.

She left the room and I stood reading a faded leaflet on the joys of the Norfolk Broads. I was considering going to look for her when she returned, followed by a dark-haired man in shirtsleeves. He was a handsome-looking fifty-something, with a catlike surety of movement. He strode up to me, hand outstretched. 'Hi. Lynch. Gerald Lynch. I'm the assistant commercial secretary here, Mr...'

Two could play the Bond game. 'Stokes. Paul Stokes.'

He was sweating and I caught a hint of stale alcohol under the supermarket aftershave. His accent was Northern Irish softened, I guessed, by years away from home. He knew my name perfectly well, he held my precious passport in his hand.

Olives – A Violent Romance

'Yes, that's it. Stokes. So you're a journalist.'

'Of sorts.'

'Excellent. Good man. Well then. Welcome to our little expatriate enclave. Sheila here tells me you're settling in for a long haul.'

'A year.'

'Too long for some by half.' He laughed, alone, but I noticed the laughter didn't quite reach his slightly teary, drinker's eyes. 'Settled in yet?'

'Yes. On the first circle.'

'You know your way around already.' He turned to Sheila, who was pecking at her terminal. 'Fast lad, Sheila, eh? Settled in less than…' Then to me. 'Two weeks isn't it?'

'Yes.'

Lynch patted my arm, a touch as welcome to me as his brittle geniality.

'Just pop this way a second, then, Paul and we'll get you sorted out.'

I followed him down a corridor and into a small room. Lynch gestured to the seat in front of the desk and sat behind it, rocking back on the cheap office chair.

'So. TMG. The Media Group. Didn't you people get a Queen's Award last year?'

'Yes, I believe so.'

'Grand. Her Majesty's Government delighted at your contribution and all that. You know what they say, two Queen's Awards and a flagpole before they go bust. Best not to go for the second one, just to be safe. Eh?'

Another lonely laugh from Lynch, one of those people who find themselves funnier than everyone else does. His dark hair was cropped short and receding at the temples. He needed a shave.

'You've been to Jordan before, I see.' He stated.

'I only came in here to register as a British national.'

'Sure, don't I know it. And a good move, too.' He gave his nose a conspiratorial tap. 'Difficult times, always best to be safe. Especially after peace has broken out. You can't go trusting the locals now. Not when there's Peace Breaking Out.'

It sounded like 'Piyuss breykin ayt.'

I crossed my arms and sat back. 'So what do you want?'

His bushy eyebrows met above his snub nose and framed his blue eyes, making his direct stare somehow unnerving. He was rumpled, his shirt too big for him and it had a grease stain on the collar. Women would like Gerald Lynch, they'd want to tidy him up and care for him and he'd be a bastard to them in return.

'Nothing in particular, my friend. It's nice and quiet right now our pals the Yanks have brought everyone back to the table for the latest love-in. Camp David Three, isn't it?' He didn't wait for an answer. 'Sure an' it's not every day we get our hands on a real live journalist, let alone one working with the government here, you know what I mean? It's always handy to touch base, you know, try and help out. That's the old job description, see? Building export earnings and so on. Helping you Queen's Awards types. And maybe you could keep an eye out for us, too. Give us a few hints and tips, like.'

'Just commercial stuff, right?'

Lynch sat back and smiled. 'That's right.'

I stood up. 'So what if I told you I'm not interested in being a provider of low level intelligence for you or any other outfit?'

Lynch's Northern Irish accent thickened, mangling the vowels. 'I'd say you were being a very foolish young man. Our interest is purely in building commercial links and information for British companies doing business here. And you need friends right now unless you want to find yourself being sent down for assaulting a Jordanian policeman.'

I put out a hand to steady myself as Lynch sat back, his hairy hands together in a steeple. He gestured to the chair and I sat down, my palms sweaty.

'How did you know about that?'

He ignored my question. 'So, you've been beavering away on your magazine. Ministry of Natural Resources, eh? They've got some job on their hands, that lot. Jordan's not an easy place to reform. The water privatisation, for instance. That's going to change a whole lot of vested interests, isn't it?'

'I suppose.'

'I met the Secretary General the other day, and that's a fact. Emad Kawar?'

'That's his name, yes.'

'You meet up with him yet?'

'No.'

'You've met the Minister.'

It wasn't a question. 'Yes.'

'Nice bloke, the Minister. Harb Al Hashemi. They say he's going in the next reshuffle though.'

'Do they?'

'It's what they say. Be interested to find out what the view inside the Ministry is. Might affect the whole privatisation programme. Be a shame, for instance, to invest in bidding for a programme that's not going to be taken seriously, wouldn't it now?'

'I'm sure it would.'

Lynch sat forward, his neat forefingers paired over his mouth, his thumbs under his chin. He wore a signet ring.

'Come on, Paul. Let's work together. I've been asked to scout out some background information for a couple of British companies who are interested in becoming involved in the privatisation bid. No big deal, but you're working on all that stuff and it would save us time and heartache.'

'And you're offering to help out with the police in return.'

Lynch beamed at me, sitting back. 'Aren't you the smart lad, eh? Well, yes, that's precisely the deal, Paul. I'll help you stay out of prison if you can give me a hand. Nothing more, just a hand.'

'And how do I know you can deliver?'

'I have precisely the same question. We'll just have to trust each other. Now isn't that a quaint notion altogether?'

Lynch pushed my passport across the desk to me. 'I'll be in touch, Paul,' he said, standing. He opened the door and I didn't look around as I went down the corridor, but I could feel his gaze on my back. I left the Embassy wishing fervently I'd never gone there in the first place.

I found a stranger reading a book and drinking beer at my garden table when I got home, my mind still in a spin from the surreal meeting with Lynch. Wiry and tanned with a sweep of blond hair above a high forehead and sporting a goatee beard, he stood and offered his hand.

'Hi. Lars Anderssen. I live upstairs. I'm sorry to steal your garden, but I sort of shared it with the last guy and hoped you would be open into the same arrangement.'

'Fine by me,' I said, responding on autopilot – Gerald Lynch and what he did or didn't know about my nasty little secret dominated my thoughts.

Lars offered me a seat at my own table and picked a beer out of the cool box next to his chair. I took the dripping can from him, wiping my hand on my jeans. 'Isn't it a bit cold to be drinking chilled beer?'

He grinned. 'Not for a Swede.'

Smiling back, I found myself putting Lynch away in a mental cupboard and focusing on my charismatic neighbour. Working with a local telephone operator on secondment from a big Swedish equipment manufacturer, Lars had been living in the upstairs flat for a couple of years. He'd been travelling for the past ten days, a job in Saudi Arabia nobody else could or would take on, so they'd sent mad boy Lars in. He'd come back that morning and was now embarking on the process of getting splendidly drunk.

'I haven't seen a fucking drink in ten days. We've got a compound in Riyadh that swims in this stuff, but this damn job was in Khamis Mushait. You ever been to Khamis Mushait?'

'Nope.'

He raised his tin to eye level in a bobbing toast. 'Well, then you take my advice. Don't. It's a flybowing shithole.'

I corrected him automatically.

'Flyblown.'

Lars' smile was infectious. 'That's the one.'

'So how have you found life here?'

'Ya, it's a good place, for sure. The people are crazy maybe and the government's rubbish mainly. The women are beautiful, but too much of this *hijab* thing. The ones that aren't wrapped are crazy. The wrapped heads are not so fun.' He waved the tin at me. 'The local beer's shitty, but I think you can't have everything.'

We sat and chatted for a while about settling into

Jordan, about the Ministry of National Resources and my magazine. Lars knew of the Ministry.

'It's a new Ministry, you know. They formed it two years ago. They realise finally they're causing problems by not regulating the extracting industries. You say extracting?'

'Extractive.'

'Okay, so. The extractive industries. They went crazy licensing it all off before and they're having problems with over-working some of these natural resources. You can't replace the potash, or the Dead Sea mud, you know?'

I nodded. 'That was my understanding from the Minister. I had a meeting with him the other day. He's an impressive guy. They're trying to bring it all back under control. And the water's a problem, too.'

'Yah. They lost most of the water they had in '67. It's all Israeli now. You should go up there and take a look at Lake Tiberias. It's huge and they just lost it in a crazy war they were never going to win. They're like that. Crazy.'

I sipped at my beer. 'Well, I'm off to see the potash people later this week. It's all down by the Dead Sea, apparently. I've got a fixer from the Ministry to hold my hand.'

'The Dead Sea's some place. You'll like it. Who you are working with at the Ministry?'

'Aisha Dajani? She works with the secretary general there, Emad Kawar.'

'Yah, I've heard of her. Her family owns this place, you know?'

I soon realised Lars had a massive network of friends and followers and was totally plugged in to the beating heart of Amman's social scene. 'Yes, she found it for me.'

Lars nodded sagely. 'Makes sense. It's a big family,

spread across this whole area. They're Palestinian. A lot of money. She's the pretty one? Drives a Lexus?'

I shrugged. 'I guess so.'

He raised his can, his index finger pointed at me. 'That's big trouble. Big family, big money. I tell you, Arab men are crazy jealous. Stay away.'

I laughed lightly. 'I'm nowhere near. I've got a girlfriend back in the UK.'

Lars was thoughtful. 'These guys here,' he gestured at the house. 'They had big problems early last year. A cousin got involved with Hamas, blew himself up in an Israeli bus full of kids. Usual thing, bomb belt and a green bandana, a goodbye video and all. You know about it? I think he would have been the brother of your girl with the Lexus. The other brother got lifted up by the security people, but I think they let him go.'

I took a long pull of beer before answering him. 'I don't know. I've not heard anything about that before.'

Lars threw me a calculating look. 'It was a big deal for the family. It made the papers, which they would have stopped if they could, I think. A suicide bomber. Big fuss. The other brother, he runs the family business now. The father died, too, a few years ago, you see? A lot of deaths in the family, these people. A lot of trouble. You want to watch out. Renting a house is one thing, but that is close as you want to get, no?'

I could hardly believe a wealthy Jordanian family like Aisha's would have nurtured a suicide bomber and Lars must be wrong about Aisha's father – Ibrahim seemed pretty much alive to me. I finished my beer and stood.

'Well, look, it was nice meeting you. I'm actually supposed to go to their place for dinner, so I'd better smarten up a bit,' I said, standing. 'Thanks for the beer.'

'Anytime man. What's your mobile number?' I told

him and he left me a missed call. 'There. Lars as in bras, not as in arse. Call me anytime.'

I saved the contact, shook hands and went indoors to brush up for dinner. I felt apprehensive about meeting Aisha's people, despite the prospect of getting an update from Ibrahim about my police case.

I'd never met a suicide bomber's family before.

Chapter Five

Aisha arrived at half seven to pick me up. She wore a white woollen dress under a red coat and a rich, spicy scent. I had managed to scrape together an open-necked shirt, jeans and a favourite, perhaps slightly over-worn, linen jacket — pretty much all that remained of my clean clothes from the hotel. I stank of supermarket deodorant.

'So who's going to be there?' I asked as we walked down to her car. I'd thought we were having a family tea at the kitchen table, not a big dinner party.

'Oh, just family. Uncle Ibrahim and Aunt Nancy, Mum, my brother Daoud and my sister Mariam.'

I'd never thought to question the relationship between Ibrahim and Aisha until Lars mentioned her father dying. I stared at her, startled. My seat belt clicked into the clasp. 'Oh. I thought Ibrahim was your father.'

Aisha laughed at my confusion. 'No, Paul, Ibrahim is my uncle. My father died a little over five years ago.' Her face darkened and her voice became gentle and sad, her eyes following her finger as it traced a path on the top of the steering wheel. 'I still miss him. I sometimes feel I miss him more each day rather than less.'

'I'm sorry. You sound as if you were very close.'

Her mouth tightened for a second before she raised her chin and smiled sadly at me. 'Oh yes, I was very much Daddy's girl. He used to call me his *'Ferriyah.'* It means "little bird". He was always spoiling me. All my life he was there for me, close to me. And then one day he just wasn't there anymore.'

'How —'

Aisha reached out and touched my arm before

turning the engine on. 'Come on, Paul, let's go. Leave the past for now, it'll just make me sadder.'

I nodded and sat silently as we drove across the Abdoun suspension bridge, looking at the houses in the *wadi* below and thinking about Aisha's father and the loss she still felt. I had never missed my own father, although he wasn't technically dead, just gone from our lives. Dad was still around somewhere, messing up some other woman's head the way he messed up Mum's. I wasn't sure how I'd feel to be told of his death, especially now I had a stepfather I actually admired.

Ken had stepped into my mum's life a few months after my dad had stepped out. He ran a small engineering company. A decent man who doted on her, he had insisted on paying for Charles' university place and had quietly slipped me a thousand pound cheque 'to help you settle down' when I'd left home, making me promise not to tell my mum about the gift: 'She'll only fuss, lad.'

If I'd accepted the two grand Ken tried to give me to help me settle down in Jordan, I might never have taken the little house near the Wild Jordan Café. For the second time, for all the right reasons, I was glad I had refused his kind generosity and made my own way. And yet it made me more grateful to him, I think, than if I'd accepted.

The Dajani house was in Abdoun, the wealthy part of West Amman. Aisha stopped the car at the top of the long, sweeping driveway and I tried not to stare at the huge villa with its pillared entranceway and imposing double doors. I felt like a slob.

A woman stood in the doorway. 'You must be Paul. Welcome. I'm Nour, Aisha's mother.'

She was in her late fifties, slim, elegant and pretty and I liked her instantly. Nour slipped her arm into mine and walked me into the house to meet the family, her manner easy and intimate. Aisha's sister Mariam was giggly, just seventeen and studying computer science at a private university. Ibrahim greeted me like the prodigal son and brushed away my attempts to thank him again for his help. He had a nasty Marlboro habit and I quickly discovered he made a natural comedy act with his wife Nancy, a wisecracking lady whose deep-etched laughter lines were somehow at odds with her sad-looking eyes.

I was mildly surprised to be offered a beer: When Aisha and I had gone to dinner together, we had shared a bottle of red wine. We had been wrapped up in Ministry talk and I hadn't asked her about when or how she drank. I had assumed her life at home, as a Muslim, would be teetotal.

My health was enthusiastically toasted with a heavy-based crystal tumbler of Black Label by Ibrahim before Nour sat me down on a huge, tasselled sofa and interrogated me with such charm that I had pretty much told her my life story in minutes. She was joined by Nancy, who flicked cigarette ash randomly into the wide selection of ornate ashtrays around us as she demanded to know what a nice boy like me was doing all alone in Amman. The talk turned to an upcoming exhibition of Aisha's work in a gallery in Amman. Nour was every inch the proud mother. I was forced to confess I knew nothing about Aisha's life as an artist.

'We've been so busy with Ministry stuff,' I explained. 'It never really came up. Although I noticed she always has inky fingers.'

Nour laughed, 'That's Aisha. I can't believe she didn't tell you about her sketches.'

She called over to Aisha, whose head was thrown back in laughter at the finale of some scandalous story of Ibrahim's, her hair tumbling down over her shoulders. She came, still laughing.

'Yes, Mum?'

Nour gestured fussily. 'Why haven't you told Paul about your sketches? You're too secretive. Show him the ones you're taking to the gallery.'

'Fine. Come on, Paul.'

I followed Aisha into a room adjoining the entrance hall. It was crammed with pen and ink sketches on paper and canvas, pads stacked up on the surfaces, a desk in the centre strewn with brushes and pens. The tabletop drawing board had an angle poise lamp to the side.

I stood, awed. 'Why didn't you mention this?'

She smiled; Gioconda. 'You didn't ask.'

I ambled over to a charcoal sketch of an old Bedouin woman, scanned the portraits forming a series around it. They were vibrant with contrast, the craggy lines of their sun-hardened skin scored in deft, lifelike sweeps.

'These are the ones I'm showing at the Lines Gallery next month,' she said, holding up a large pen and ink sketch. 'They're a celebration of life in the Eastern City.'

A man and boy walked hand in hand through a shabby street, the washing hanging out of the windows and cables strewn between the rooftops. It had an air of tragedy; there was a fierce pride in the man's bearing that contrasted with his battered, desperate air.

'It's stunning. You're an inky-fingered genius.'

She laughed. 'Right. Come on, let's get back to the family.' She turned by the door, a serious look on her face. 'I'm really glad you like them, Paul.'

I followed her out of the studio. To tell the truth, I was really glad, too.

I guessed the man who walked into the living room just after Aisha and I rejoined the family was her brother Daoud. Nour stood as he came in and so did I. He was in his late thirties and handsome, but there was a quiet intensity about Daoud Dajani that dampened the mood in the room briefly. He wore a tight polo neck and I could see his build. He moved like a boxer.

His eyes bored into mine as he took my hand. 'Welcome. You are Paul Stokes.'

A statement of two facts, unsmilingly delivered. I could feel myself tripping over my words before I spoke them. 'Yes. Thank you. You must be Daoud.'

He held my hand, a grip of steel. His temples carved deep incursions into his slicked-back hair, his dark eyebrows and strong chin carried an air of belligerence. He wore a slim gold chain on his neck and another, thicker one on his wrist which rattled when we shook hands. He continued to hold his grip after mine had relaxed, looking into my eyes with a force that brought heat to my face. There were only two of us in the world, a moment of paralysis, then he smiled and took my arm in his other hand, squeezing it in a fleeting gesture that could be friendly. Or not. I knew uncertainty showed on my face and forced a smile I suspected looked more like a salesman's grin. Nour was standing with us, her light touch on us both and her voice gentle.

'Come on. Dinner's ready.'

I found myself back in a space filled with laughing people. Ibrahim had finished another story and Nancy's voice was mock-shocked.

'How can he say these things? He is a fantasist. Thirty-five years married and not a word of truth in all of them.'

Dinner was a procession of dishes brought in by the

maid from the kitchen, each introduced to me and piled on my plate by Nour: stuffed courgettes, vine leaves, houmos flecked with grilled lamb and toasted pine nuts, roasted chicken on saffron rice, salads scattered with pomegranate seeds, shards of fried Arabic bread and tiny purple grains of bitter *sumak*. Nour insisted I try it all, pressing second helpings of everything on me. We talked about England and Iraq, about Jordan and the punishing Royal travel schedule and, of course, about the peace.

It was like a mantra, everywhere I went. Eventually all conversations turned to it — the peace, the peace, the peace. The new deal the Americans had finally brokered between a reluctant, right-wing Israeli government and the tired, broken down remnants of the Palestinian administration had at least brought the hope this would, against all the odds, be the *one* peace. The deal to lead to the long-awaited 'two-state solution,' the first hope since the disastrous collapse of the jury-rigged Heath Robinson compromise of Oslo.

The conversation turned to Palestine in the past, to *Al Naqba*, 'the catastrophe', the formation of Israel in 1948 and the end of the British Mandate in Palestine. When I asked Ibrahim whether he had ever gone back there, his bushy eyebrows shot up in astonishment.

'Go back? Of course we go back! As often as possible. It is not always easy.' He laid his forearm on the table as if he were about to give blood, palm up. He looked across at me. 'Sometimes they are like this on the border. Sometimes like this.' He balled his hairy hand into a fist. 'When it is like *this* you are turned back or made to wait for hours while they play with you. Sometimes before they make me kneel on the path in front of them. That is hard for a man like me. I am old, I have become used to having the dignity, you know?'

The hubbub around the table died down as Ibrahim's voice rumbled on. 'Mama Mariam is too old now. She keeps our farm alive with Hamad, my brother, because she is too damn stubborn to leave it. We are all grateful for her. We know what will happens if you leave your land there. They will take it. There are many families in Jordan and Lebanon who still have the old iron keys to their farms, but they cannot return. We still have it, the place where we all came from. She keeps it alive for us. We all do what we can to help. Some money, some supplies when they will let us take them across. The power there is bad, the water is hard to get sometimes – especially for the trees. We often have to use *wasta* to get things through the border. You know *wasta*?'

I nodded, 'Yes, yes I do. It was the second Arabic word I learned in Jordan.'

Ibrahim grunted. 'Our tragedy that this should be the case. The first word, Paul?'

'*Insh'Allah.*'

Ibrahim's laughter boomed around the table, infectious and all-consuming before he finally descended into a fit of coughing, wiping the tears from his eyes.

'My God, Paul, but you know us in two words!'

Nour smiled at me, her arm around her younger daughter. 'Mama Mariam is certainly some lady. We named Mariam here after her.'

I caught Aisha's sad, small smile. The maid brought coffee.

'Paul, Paul,' Ibrahim grinned. 'Here you are just arrived in Jordan and we are boring you with our problems.'

'No, no. Please. It's not boring. I understand so little about it all. I've only seen the violence in the Middle East on TV. It's always there on the news. You know, Iraq,

Afghanistan, Palestine, Pakistan. I'd never thought about it all in terms of people living in farms trying to get by. We miss the humanity of it when we just take in the headlines.'

'Ah, but this is all we all are. Farmers. Before we had over two hundred *dunums* of olive groves on the farm. Now there are less than twenty. The others are on the wrong side of the wall. Hamad crosses over when he can, but they always close the gates when it is time to harvest so the olives become spoiled or the settlers take them. Now they are even limiting the water we are allowed to keep the trees alive. Our family used to live on the money from the olive oil, like so many others in Palestine. Now they make it too hard for us. We live on trading instead. We will be the people who pay for this peace with our land, and yet what else can we do?'

And so you bomb them whipped through my mind, a momentary and unworthy thought shaming me as the light over the table caught the moisture in the old man's eyes. A feeling of being watched made me steal a glance at Daoud who was, indeed, gracing me with a steady, neutral gaze.

Aisha broke the silence. 'One day *Insh'Allah* we'll have our farm safe, Uncle.' Everyone around the table murmured, '*Insh'Allah.*'

Daoud stood. 'Have you ever seen an olive tree, Paul? Come with me, I'll show you the grove of olives we keep here in Abdoun.'

Nour pushed back her chair, taking Mariam's plate and beckoning for Aisha's. 'Yes, go on. We'll clear up the table. Aisha, give me a hand in the kitchen.'

I followed Daoud, hoping my reluctance didn't show. We stood together on the veranda looking out over the dark garden – a couple of acres of prime Abdoun real estate. He flicked a switch by the kitchen door and I saw part of the garden was laid to lawn, but the hilly rise to one side accommodated a small stand of olive trees.

'Ibrahim and my father brought these trees from our farm in Qaffin and planted them here over thirty years ago. Back then it looked like we were going to lose everything from over there, so they thought they'd keep at least this much.' He led the way down the steps to the trees. 'Smoke?'

'No thanks, I don't.'

He grunted, then lit up a Marlboro Light. 'These trees are everything to the farmers. They are tended like fine grape vines, the olives are pressed like wine. The first cut is virgin, the finest. The olives weep the purest oil when they are first squeezed. We press them until they can weep no more, then we feed the remains back to the land, to the animals. We still press oil over at the farm on the old stone press. It is not much, it is not enough to keep the place running, but we help out, as Ibrahim said. It is the finest oil you will ever taste. It is a symbol for us too, you understand. Of hope.'

I held a bunch of the smooth, silvery-green leaves in my hand. I didn't know what to say to him. He stood in among the trees, the faint pall of smoke from his cigarette making my nostrils widen.

'Ibrahim said the security wall cuts the farm in two. Will the peace uphold that?'

'Yes. The wall is the new border, not what we hoped, the 1967 border. We demonstrated against the wall, like the other farmers. But there was nothing anyone could do. Some of the hot-headed ones got themselves beaten and arrested. The world looked the other way. Always it looks the other way. And so they built settlements, they took land, they burned crops, they inched their way into the water. Now the peace gives us the absolute minimum and gives Israel the absolute maximum. Of our land.'

I didn't know what to say, surrounded by these trees and the family's loss. 'I suppose at least you still have the farm.'

Daoud shook his head. 'Now, after all these years, they are starting to cut the water to the farmers, both over there and here in Jordan. The olive groves are starting to die. These trees are the heritage we must take with us into the future. My company is investing in the water because we believe it will be critical for the future. Not just for the trees but for our people to live. We are bidding for the privatisation of Jordan's water resources. You have heard of this?'

'Yes, the Minister told me about it. Is it really such a problem, the water shortage?'

'We are already suffering from the lack of water. We will suffer more, our crops will fail and our farmers starve. It is critical to our future to find a better way to share the water. The Israelis steal the water from us every day. I want to steal it back.'

I let go the bunch of leaves and glanced across to Daoud, who was looking down at the glowing tip of his cigarette.

'How?'

I felt his eyes burning in the darkness. I shifted uncomfortably and so did the conversation.

'You like Aisha?'

I tried not to react to the abrupt question, taking my time and listening to the faint traffic noise carried on the cold night air. I replied cautiously. 'She's been great to me, Daoud. The Ministry's lucky to have her. I couldn't have settled in the way I have without her. She's a smart girl.'

A crowd cheered in my mind. Just right. My breath was coming out in misty puffs.

'She was my father's favourite.'

The cheering died down. 'She's a very good artist. You must be proud of her.'

'Yes. Yes I am. I would not like anything to happen to her. She took his death badly, as I suppose we all did. She is still perhaps,' he searched for the word, 'vulnerable.'

Fucking hell. Enough already. I kept the smile going, but it was getting hard to maintain. My cheeks hurt from the effort. 'Jordan is a beautiful country, Daoud. I'm glad I came here. I'm sure my girlfriend will like it here, too. She's a lawyer. She practises international contract law, actually.'

Not strictly true, the line about Anne liking it in Jordan. I hardly expected her to turn up. Workaholic Anne never took leave and we didn't anticipate seeing each other until I went home for Christmas.

Daoud seemed lost in thought, leaning against the trunk of an olive tree and drawing on his cigarette. Finally he spoke.

'The Israelis have taken everything from us, Paul. Our land, our dignity. They took my father, too. My brother. Now they're taking the water. We've lost too much.'

He pushed the cigarette butt into the sandy soil with his heel, then put his hand on my shoulder, a quick squeeze and a pat, a very Arab gesture of finality and yet somehow accepting. 'I won't let the olives die. Come on, let's get back inside. I'll get you a bottle of our oil. At least when the olives weep, we are enriched.'

Aisha took me home. I sat in her car, a little dark bottle with a gold label clutched between my legs.

She broke the silence first, 'Was it okay with Daoud?'

'Laugh a minute. I've always enjoyed the heavy-handed approach, you know? Toucha my sister I breaka your neck. Loved every second.'

She winced.

'I didn't know he was going to do that,' she said.

'Yeah, well he did. Sorry, Aisha, but I'm a nice little English boy with a nice little English girlfriend and I really didn't need that kind of heavy shit.'

We pulled up outside the house and sat in the car together. Aisha switched the engine off and the windows started to fog.

'You have to give him a little time, Paul. He's been through a lot.'

I nodded. 'I'm sure he has.'

'He took my father's death badly. He runs the businesses now, but he's very,' she paused, searching for her word, 'passionate.'

I shifted to face Aisha, the leather creaking underneath me. 'It's not just that, is it? Daoud got into trouble last year, didn't he? How did he take your brother's death?'

Aisha gripped the wheel, her knuckles pale, before stretching her fingers out. I had never noticed before, but the little fingernail of her right hand was bitten. Her red nails were perfectly manicured, which made the bitten one even odder.

She talked to the windscreen. 'How did you hear about it?'

'I just heard. Which is a shame, because I'd rather you had told me.'

Aisha stared silently out of the windscreen, her face eerily illuminated by the splashes of blue and orange light from the dashboard LEDs. I waited for her to say something, to explain, but she just looked out into the night. I pulled the door handle, the noise making her flinch.

'Goodnight.'

Aisha didn't move. I got out of the car, closing the door with more force than I intended and striding up the steps to the house. I turned as I heard her start the engine. I waited by the front door for her to pull away, but she just stayed with the engine running.

I went inside and devoted a little quality time, with the help of a bottle of crappy dry red wine from Bethlehem, to thoroughly disliking myself.

Chapter Six

Way past midnight, I heard Lars staggering past the French windows. His insistent knocking on the front door forced me to drag on a pair of shorts and T-shirt and fumble through the kitchen to answer him. He stood framed by the light, grinning and speaking with slow, painstaking precision.

'I am drunked.' He was unsteady on his feet. His eyes were bloodshot and he was focusing on staying upright and stable. 'And I thought to myself, "Lars, what would be an perfect Englishman's nightmare if not to see a drunkeded Swede at midnight?" So here,' he tottered a little, hiccupped and grinned broadly, 'I is.'

He fell over.

I eventually managed to sit him safely at the kitchen table. I made him a strong coffee and got a scotch on the rocks for myself. He took a little milk, pouring it from the plastic bottle with the wobbly concentration of a three-year-old stacking building bricks.

'Did I wake you up?'

'Nope, still watching the news,' I lied.

'Good.' He sat back heavily. 'How's your girl?'

'She's fine.' I realised he meant Aisha and so did I. I had forgotten to call Anne. I frowned at him. 'She's not my girl.'

Lars sipped his coffee and pulled a face. 'Any sugar?' I got up and rooted around in the cupboard, finding a packet. Lars stirred two spoonfuls into his coffee and asked, 'How did dinner go?'

'Fine. They're good people. Her brother took me in the garden and gave me the heavy chat about his sister, which I could have done without.'

Lars shook his head and wiggled a roguish drunk's forefinger. 'I told you about Arab men, didn't I?' He sat back. 'I asked friends about that side of the Dajanis. Stay away, Paul. They're the bad news. I was right about this brother, he was a suicide bomber. He exploded himself with a busload of kids in Haifa. People say he did it in revenge for his father. The father was killed by the Israelis, you know?'

No, thanks Lars, but I didn't know. And was becoming more and more certain I didn't want to know. But he was unstoppable.

'They killed him with a missile. A helicopter attack in Gaza against a Hamas guy.' Lars wagged his finger at me again. 'Now what would any decent man in the rightness of his mind be doing in Gaza talking to Hamas people, Paul?'

I sipped my drink, grateful for the coldness. 'I don't know, Lars.'

'So they kill the father and then the brother falls off the rails, starts keeping the wrong company. He's all the time at the mosque and then he disappears. Everyone's out looking for him when the news comes back there's been a big bomb in a school bus in Israel. And then he's on the news, they've made a video of him.'

I hoped I could stop Lars somehow, stem the flow of unwelcome information when I noticed my wish being granted, his head dropping.

'Come on, let's get you to bed,' I said, standing up. 'You're fucked.'

I helped him up the stone steps. I found the light and switched it on, while Lars slumped back against the wall by the door as I looked out over the large room, so different to my place downstairs. It had been opened out, the internal walls removed to leave a space more like an art gallery than a house, with beech flooring, white walls and halogen lamps dropped from the ceiling. There were pictures hung at intervals on the wall, each lit by a lamp. At the far end was a desk with a pair of screens on it, surrounded by racks of electronics and keyboards. The chairs were steel and black leather. An impressive display of expensive minimalism.

'You'll be okay now?' I asked him.

Lars teetered on the edge of consciousness. 'Thanks.'

I left him to it and went downstairs to bed. I was tired and perhaps a little confused, but lay awake for hours thinking about helicopter gunships in Gaza. About grubby-faced children playing in the dust between crumbling buildings pock-marked with bullet holes, lines of threadbare washing flapping a slow dance to the thump and crack of gunfire and the sky-sweep of black smoke from burning tyres. The whump of rotor blades high in the air. The hiss of rockets. The white-out.

I didn't see Aisha at the Ministry at all the next day. I wrote up my interview with the Minister and Googled some background research on potash. Journalism means picking up an intimate knowledge of all sorts of strange things, although sometimes it can come in handy. You never know when you'll be stuck in the kitchen at a Chelsea party with a potash magnate, able to wow him with your subtle knowledge of the intricacies of his business.

Having learned all about Jordanian potash and the British-led consortium holding the extraction license, Petra-Jordanian Industries, I called Robin and found out that, yes, Petra-Jordanian was an advertiser with a ratecard double page spread booked across all twelve issues. That meant kid gloves and an interview laced with platitudes. Great.

I could hear talking and the chink of cutlery on porcelain in the background. Robin must be 'doing lunch.' He was, as usual, all bluff bonhomie. 'How's the rest of the editorial shaping up, young man?'

'Good. You didn't come back to me about Zahlan and the online stuff. I'm taking a lot of heat about it. What are we going to do?'

Robin tutted. 'We signed up to do a damn magazine, Paul, not develop their website for them. Tell him we'll help them to repurpose the editorial and stuff for online, but we're not going to start developing websites unless we can negotiate an addendum to the contract.'

I emailed a meeting request to Abdullah Zahlan.

I called Anne when I got back home, flopping onto the bed.

'Hi.'

'Paul. Where have you been? You haven't called all week.'

It was Monday and we'd last talked Thursday. A miserable, guilty chill ran through me.

'I'm sorry, Annie. I moved into the house over the weekend and it's been pretty hectic. I ran out of credits on the phone yesterday too. I'm sorry.'

'You promised me you'd call or text every day.'

'I know. Like I said, I'm sorry. But things got on top of me here. It's been really busy, babe. Look, how're things with you?'

'I'm fine, thanks. It's busy at the office, too. Rory and Chloe are going to get married.'

'Really? Great. When?'

'Next year, January. In Scotland.'

'It'll rain.'

'They've planned for it. They're calling it a wet wedding.' Ha ha. I hated Chloe, although Rory was alright. She was a snob in window dressing or something in Knightsbridge. Chloe, 'dahling,' drawled.

Anne's well-to-do City friends enjoyed having a slob around. It gave them someone to patronise. I was thinking about her in the past tense, which shocked me a little.

There was a silence as if Anne were debating something. For some reason I didn't have the small talk to fill it, but waited for her. There was a faint hissing noise on the line.

'Paul?'

'Here, Annie. Sorry, wandered a bit.'

'Paul, I've got some time off. Brian's cancelled his leave next month and I can take four days, maybe even a week.'

'Great. What are you going to get up to?'

The awful realisation hit me an instant too late for me to recover. Her voice was small, breaking the little silence.

'I thought I'd maybe come and see you, Paul.'

Fuck. Fuck. Fuck. I overcompensated, my voice too eager, too bright, silly words tumbling over each other to fill the gaping void. 'Wow. Fantastic news, Annie, that's great. I'll put flowers in vases and stuff and fatten up some cows or something. We can play and go around and just see the sights and everything. Hey. Cool. Oh, brilliant.'

But the damage had been done and we were quickly reduced to small talk and big silences as we tried to want to be on the line together. Finally, the merciful click ended the call.

I spent a couple of minutes sitting in the kitchen, torturing myself by replaying the conversation in my mind with an embarrassed squirm over how totally dumb I could be.

I poured a beer and sat on the cold stone patio steps looking out onto the garden and listening to the busy crickets. The city glowed, a faint halo of purplish light framing the houses and trees uphill. For the first time in my life, the urge to smoke a cigarette came over me. I remembered Aisha had left a pack in my car and so went into the house, got my keys and wandered down to the street to get it. Everyone in Jordan smoked, it seemed. Everyone except me. I walked down the walled steps onto the street and saw a dim light by my car, parked up over the road. My reaction came automatically, London boy to the fore: I shouted out.

A dark figure detached itself from the shadows around the car and ran down the street. I dropped my beer glass and it shattered on the pavement, the beats of my running steps slapping wet echoes from the houses around me. He dived to the left, down one of the many stairways dropping steeply between the houses on the hillside, and I smashed painfully into the far wall as I made the top of the stairway too fast to turn. Winded, I tracked the figure skittering down the steps. He darted to the right a hundred metres or so below me and danced madly down into the warren of buildings. I leapt down the steep flight of steps past a blue-lit coffee shop, a blur of curious faces looking out at me. I made the right turn and caught a flash of movement ahead to my left. I stopped at the next turn, confronted by a steep, empty stairway plunging down into darkness.

I took a couple of uncertain steps down, gripping the cold metal handrail running down the centre of the stairway. Standing still for a moment, the smell of coffee and the faint sweet-sour tang of tobacco smoke from *argileh* pipes in my nostrils, I listened to the faint sounds of the sleepy city, the low chatter of voices, the clink of china from the coffee shop and, from nearby, the ragged breathing of an unfit man.

I advanced another step but stopped when a hand thrust out of the darkness to my right, the cold-looking blade flashing with his upwards gesture.

'*Yalla.*'

I didn't move. It wasn't bravery, I simply didn't know what to do. His voice sounded coarse. '*Yalla, ya hmar.*'

I stepped back and he slashed at the air with the knife, snarling, '*Yalla.*' Walking slowly backwards, I turned the corner and waited for a second then turned and headed for home. I wasn't going to get into a knife fight. I felt a coward.

I couldn't make out any damage to the car in the dim light. I poured a scotch and sat outside. My hands still trembled lighting up the cigarette, which I hated and put out after a couple of puffs. Going to bed, sleep evaded me for ages, the tobacco taste in my mouth. Thoughts of knife-toting thieves and what I'd have done to him if I were a braver man raced around in my mind.

The road from Amman to the Dead Sea drops down from the city, twisting through villages and farmhouses clinging in ones and twos to the steep hillsides as the road descends to the lowest point on earth. Driving, I found it hard to focus on the twisting road and the scenery at the same time. We saw the sparkling expanse of water slide into view below us, the misty blue shores of Palestine and Israel framing the far side of the immobile expanse of water. The road straightened out into the plains around the sea and we slowed as we reached an army warthog, a temporary checkpoint, the soldiers examining my passport and Aisha's ID card. She chatted them up in Arabic, laughing with them, her eyes flashing and teasing.

We drove along the coast of the Dead Sea.

'What was all the checkpoint stuff about?'

'Security. That's Palestine over there across the water. And Israel.'

'I thought you were at peace with the Israelis.'

She looked askance at me, an eyebrow raised. 'Jordan is. Apparently there's a government event on at the Conference Centre. It's up the road here. That's why security is tighter than usual.'

We passed a tall, square metal tower overlooking the flat expanse of lifeless water. I gestured toward it and asked, 'Lifeguard?'

'Gun position. They're not usually manned these days, but when they are they turn the guns away to face inland. So does the other side. Peace, you see?'

She flicked through my passport before handing it to me. 'Cute picture. They're usually very bad. You'd want to look after a face like that rather than being a hero and chasing robbers.'

My account of the knifeman in the depths of the city's stairways the night before had broken the ice between us. Aisha had been astonished I had been brave or mad enough to have given chase and had nagged me not to try and take the law into my own hands like that again.

'You don't get it, Paul. The Eastern City is dangerous and it starts at the bottom of the hill outside your house.

Leave things be at night, please.'

The whole episode seemed as if it had taken place in a dream, particularly as we drove along the coast in the sunshine, the Dead Sea shimmering beside us.

I reached out my hand to grab at Aisha's ID card. 'Let's see yours then.'

'No.'

'Come on, give it over. You've seen mine, show me yours.'

She laughed and pulled away from me, the light making her eyes sparkle. 'Here, then. You're not to laugh.'

She handed over her civil ID card and of course I did laugh, because the picture was truly awful. 'You look podgy.'

'I am never talking to you again, *ya* Brit.'

We reached the dusty moonscape around the potash complex, laughing and teasing each other, the angry silence of the night before a distant irrelevance. We tracked Clive Saunders, Mr Potash, down to his office.

He was perhaps in his late fifties, silver-haired and florid, his open-necked shirt exposing a little tuft of curly white hairs. He came around the desk to meet us, his hand out and grinning a welcome. He cleared a pile of magazines from one of the pair of chairs in front of his desk and waved to us to sit.

'Good to see you both. Here, take a seat. Not often we get visitors from the press!'

An Egyptian tea-boy brought *chai suleimani,* black, sweet tea served in little gold-rimmed custard glasses, and we settled down. I took my voice recorder out.

'Okay if I use this?'

'Go ahead.'

I switched on the recorder and Saunders sat forward,

his hands clasped in front of him as he considered my questions. We talked about Petra-Jordanian's bid for the potash extraction contracts, the uses of potash, the benefits for Jordan and so on. Saunders made a big fuss about how close to the Minister they were, how they all shared common goals and a vision for the future of Jordan and I soon found myself drifting away, looking around his untidy office. Books, magazines and documents covered virtually every surface, from his desktop to the low cabinets behind him. As he droned on about sustainable resources, talking more to Aisha than to me, my gaze wandered to a map of Jordan's Rift Valley pinned up on the wall and covered in coloured push-pins and lines. It was next to a whiteboard marked up with co-ordinates and a table of numbers.

Saunders talked himself to a momentary halt and I pointed to the wall display.

'What are those all about? That doesn't look like potash.'

Saunders looked up to his left at the map, blinking owlishly as he adjusted from droning about potash to answering my question.

'Oh, that's planning work for the water privatisation. We're the lead member of the Anglo-Jordanian Consortium. You've heard about the privatisation, haven't you?'

'The Minister's talked about it, but we hadn't planned to cover it in any great depth in the magazine.'

'Well, you should. It's important for Jordan. Right now, the country's in a state of drought. Water has to be taken into Amman by tankers, there's little piped water infrastructure and it's mostly ancient. Jordanian farmers are suffering from very severe restrictions because there's simply not enough water to go around. The Yarmouk

River's being depleted left, right and centre, the Jordan River's going brackish and the Israelis are holding back on the volume they're meant to be providing from Lake Tiberias. The country's damn close to crisis and we believe we can help to manage those resources effectively into the future.'

'Can I quote you on that?'

'Okay, but please don't go into any technicalities. Our bid is complicated and we're using some pretty groundbreaking technologies and approaches to water resourcing, management and distribution.'

I took notes in shorthand to back up the tape, finishing the sentence before I looked up into Saunders' blue-eyed, frank stare. 'What's the scale of the problem?' I asked.

'Massive. Jordan has one of the world's lowest levels of water resources. The country's supply stands at less than a quarter of the accepted global water poverty level. And a huge amount, something like twenty-five per cent of that water, is currently coming from over-pumping unsustainable resources. Experts are forecasting the water supply will be a potential humanitarian disaster within fifteen years or so. Personally, I think it'll come sooner.'

'What's the government doing?'

Saunders reached behind him and pulled out a thick, spiral bound document. 'This is the National Water Strategy. It was adopted in the late nineties and outlined any number of approaches to the problem but at the end of the day it didn't result in concrete action. That's one of the reasons the Ministry of Natural Resources was formed, to unify the government's response. And that's why they're going into this privatisation process. It'll likely be the single largest privatisation the country's ever seen. It's critical to Jordan's future.'

Saunders paused and I sensed the inevitable spiel to come. I wasn't disappointed. He laid his hands flat on the desk and leaned forwards, brows knit in intense sincerity. 'And we at Anglo-Jordanian believe we have the solutions Jordan needs.'

Right, of course you do. I asked because I had to, 'What's the privatisation worth?'

'No comment.'

Saunders got to his feet. The interview, it seemed, was over. I picked up the tape and whipped out my camera for few snaps, making sure for the last two that the map and whiteboard next to it were nice and clear behind Saunders' proud, out of focus, face.

As we were leaving, he asked me for a copy of the text before it was published and I smiled at him, my heart black, and assured him Aisha would send it across to him. Anything as long as I didn't have to do it myself. I'd encountered this before working for Robin on a project in Singapore – people in power who think they have the right to demand to see interviews before they're published. A real journalist would tell them to get stuffed but I worked on contract published titles and had already found out a refusal to comply resulted in a complaint to Robin who would invariably uphold it on behalf of the advertiser. Every time it happened, it reminded me of the loss of my independence and self-respect as a journalist resulting from my fall from grace.

We drove back towards Amman, passing the cluster of Dead Sea spa and conference hotels to the left of the road as it wound its blacktop course through the rocky, arid landscape, twisting around the banks of the flat expanse of torpid water. I counted the hotel buildings facing the road, betting myself that if the total was an even number I would get off the police charge. It was odd. We passed the Dead Sea Conference Centre and I added it to the total even though it wasn't a hotel.

We neared the head of the sea. Gnarled trees started to line the road and occasional splashes of roadside colour against the sandy background revealed themselves as men squatting by the roadside selling coffee and knick-knacks. We reached the curve of the road as it left the Dead Sea and snaked up to Amman. Aisha took the u-turn.

'There's something I want to show you.'

'The baptism site.'

She looked wide-eyed at me. 'How did you know?'

'I read the signpost.'

She arched an eyebrow and tutted. 'Clever, *ya* Brit. This is the Bethany, the place where John the Baptist baptised Jesus. I thought you'd be interested. The Dead Sea is rich in human history. The whole Rift Valley is.'

We turned right off the dual carriageway. The road narrowed into barely more than a single track and we stopped at the gate and waited for it to be opened for us before we drove to a partly covered car park next to a cluster of low, beige buildings. There were a couple of other cars there.

'This is new, they opened it a few years ago when the peace with Israel looked like it would last,' Aisha said. 'It's very busy in the summer.'

Aisha changed her smart patent leather shoes for a pair of flip-flops. We crunched across the gravel together as a figure detached itself from the shade of one of the buildings. He was dressed in Bedouin fashion, his head covered with a wrapped black and white checked scarf. Aisha exchanged greetings in Arabic.

'This is Abdullah, he's a guide here. He works part

time for Ibrahim.'

'*Wasta.*'

She nodded.

'*Wasta.*'

I said hello to Abdullah and we shook hands before he turned and led the way through the buildings and down a stone-flagged pathway. I spotted a city in the foothills across the valley on what must have been the Israeli side of the border.

'What's that?'

'That's Jericho. It's part of Palestine now.'

Jericho. I remembered it from primary school – being forced to sing about Joshua and his army, marching around parping away at trumpets to break down the city walls. I screwed up my eyes against sun's glare and watched the far-away city walls, the buildings little more than white dots in the shimmering air.

We struck into the wilderness and were soon surrounded by bushes, delving deeper along the path into the thick growth of twisted trunks and dusty branches. Aisha was close behind me, chattering alternately to Abdullah and I, a stream of Arabic and English that often threatened to combine in a linguistic emulsion of oil and water.

She reached out a hand to brush against one of the pale green spiky-leafed branches. 'This is tamarisk. It thrives on the salty ground here. This path was the one Jesus took.'

I was surprised. 'You believe in him?'

'We believe he was a prophet. He's revered in Islam. The Prophet Mohammed took the last word of God from Gabriel, but we believe in the same one God. Many of our names come from the Bible. Daoud is David, Issa is Jesus, Sara is Sarah and so on.'

'What's Aisha?'

She grinned at me. 'It means healthy and alive. It was the name of the wife of the Prophet Mohammed. His favourite wife. Aisha bint Abu Bakr.'

We walked along the pathway, the tamarisks binding together to form a shady bower. We came out into the open by the bank of a river. There was a stone church to our left and decking that stepped down to the river.

'This,' said Aisha, dramatically, 'is the River Jordan.'

I'd expected something big and Cecil B. DeMille, but the dull green river was narrow and lifeless. A white building on the opposite bank impressed me more than the small wooden structure we were standing in. Decorated with crosses, the white complex had stone steps running down its side to the far bank of the river.

'What's that?'

'That's the Israeli side and the old Christian baptism place. This is the new one.'

I dipped my hand into the font, the cool water bringing goose bumps to my forearm. I dried it on my jeans, reflecting how typical it was that the Israeli side was so much more impressive than the Jordanian.

'We built the other side, of course,' Aisha said, 'but the Israelis took it over in 1967. It hasn't been used much since then.'

I looked again, more closely, and saw the gun emplacements on the hills behind the building and noticed that the stone was breaking down, that the steps were covered in debris. She had a point. It looked like a wreck, while the Jordanian side was obviously being used a lot.

'Why don't the Israelis use it?'

'They don't like Christians any more than they like us.'

I'd never had much time for religion, let alone the intolerance and bigotry that invariably comes with it.

'That's playground politics, Aisha. Nothing's that simple.'

She turned away from me with a 'tut,' the sound the Arab World uses to denote all shades of denial.

I noticed Abdullah wasn't with us. 'Where's Abdullah?'

'Abdullah? Oh, I don't know. Maybe he's gone to see if the church is open. Come on, let's go up there.'

We strode up from the river towards the little stone church, but the door was closed. We waited in the shade of the door for our guide to reappear. A couple of minutes later, he arrived, walking purposefully from behind the building and spoke to Aisha, who turned to me and laughed nervously.

'A call of nature, you say?'

'We say.'

We wandered back silently through the tamarisks and said our goodbyes to Abdullah. I wanted to give him some money, but Aisha would have none of it. We drove back out and through the checkpoint, then up towards Amman. The sun sulked low on the horizon and a slow orange light filled the hills with a luxuriant play of contrasts and long shadows. I stopped at the top of the climb and got out to take some pictures looking back over the Dead Sea. I sat in the car and saw the empty back seat.

'Your bag. Your bag's gone.'

Aisha looked worried for a second before relaxing. 'It's okay, I've got my mobile with me and there were just a few books in it. I'll call Ibrahim. Some of the guides are, how do you say, opportunists. Abdullah will get it back.'

I was surprised at how cool she was about it. I

remembered locking the car.

'They must have picked the lock.'

She laughed. 'And got a couple of books on potash and a few rough sketches for their troubles. Don't worry Paul, I'll get the bag back.'

She called Ibrahim and was still talking to him when we joined the Amman highway to go home. It was clear something was wrong, the tone of Aisha's voice changing from chatty light to what seemed to be confusion and shock. She ended the call and I waited for her to explain, but she kept her eyes fixed on the road.

'What is it, Aish?'

I watched the tension in her neck, her lips pressed tight. She didn't look at me. 'Ibrahim has heard from the colonel in the police he has been talking to. The policeman is insisting you injured him. They're not going to drop the charges against you. There's nothing more Ibrahim can do with the police. It will go to court.'

I slumped back against my seat. An overwhelming sense of my impotence quickly turned to intense sadness. The game was up. I had no choice but to start the process of confession that would end my life in Jordan.

I found my voice, but it felt like someone else's mouth shaped the words. 'Well, if you could thank him for me anyway, that'd be great. I'm sure he's done everything he can.'

'They have set the court date, Paul. You will appear before the judge in October. Ibrahim is still trying to fix this. He has powerful friends in the Ministry of Justice.' Aisha reached across and squeezed my hand. 'It's a setback. But don't worry. 'brahim hasn't given up and neither should you.'

'And what do I say to people now?'

'Say nothing. There's still hope he can get you out of

this.'

To my horror, my eyes started to prickle. Turning away from Aisha so she wouldn't see, the dusty hillsides stretching out beyond the roadside planted with olives and cypresses blurred with the tears I tried to blink away.

'I didn't hit him.'

'I know, Paul.

We passed a faded green water lorry jangling with battered metal decorations and I wiped my eyes. I now had little choice but to meet Gerald Lynch of the British Embassy, a meeting I swore wouldn't take place. Being beholden to the Dajanis was one thing; being in Lynch's debt was quite another. Something told me his help would come at a high price, but I had already resolved to pay it.

Chapter Seven

I arrived home from a long, lonely day at the Ministry spent brooding over my impending court case. Aisha hadn't returned my calls. The warm day was cooling fast and I stood looking out over the uniform pale stone of the city below me, watching it darken from umber to aubergine and wondering how I'd get through a trial in an Arab court.

I went inside, switched on the TV and undressed to take a shower. I came out of the steamy bathroom wearing two white towels, like a pilgrim to Mecca. I caught the image on the TV screen, frozen for a moment before it played out in real time before me, water dripping on the stone floor.

Glass, blood, sirens. A man's hand poking out from the debris, its fingers curled, the forefinger pointing, an oddly Raphaelesque gesture. Women crying, dust and desperate screams of loss. Palestinians. The skeleton of a bombed out jeep, the torn wreckage of a checkpoint behind it. Men in uniforms, guns and a distorted commentary over a videophone, the journalist's voice breathless and over-excited. It wasn't the news of a bombing that stilled me, or the fact four Israeli soldiers had been killed in the attack on a military checkpoint.

It was the name flashing across the bottom of the screen, white on red.

Jericho.

I remembered the whitewashed buildings nestling across the Jordan when I had stood next to Aisha looking at the city over the muddy green river. Joshua marching around the walls with his army tooting away on their trumpets. Joseph and his Technicolour Dreamcoat.

I went to the kitchen and poured a whisky then sat down in my towels to watch the news again, hopping between channels to catch each brief mention of the Jericho bombing, snippets sandwiched between the smaller concerns of the world at large.

Aisha wasn't there when I turned up at the Ministry the next morning and her mobile remained switched off. I sat at my desk looking blankly at the news on the screen and sipping at the *chai suleimani* the tea boy brought to each new morning arrival. Someone laughed across the room from me, a girl carrying too many bags, bustling and bitching about the traffic.

Something nagged at me about Aisha's stolen bag. The news about my trial had pushed it out of my mind, but now it seemed increasingly odd. The man by my car the other night, Abdullah the guide disappearing for no reason and coming back from a 'call of nature' out of breath. I cursed my overactive imagination, always making connections that weren't there, the product of a lonely childhood spent pretending trees are tanks and sheds are submarines. It had left me with some funny habits, including one of predicting outcomes through random events. If the red car lets me cross the road then I'll get off with Sonia Smith. That kind of thing. Besides, the bag wasn't big enough for a bomb. How big *was* a bomb?

Real time searches for Jericho were pulling up small snippets of information and loads of chatter, twittering and the like. I found precious little insight but then the news had already moved on to a political scandal in

Germany and soon the chatter had turned purely local, mostly in Arabic.

Someone walked past my desk and I caught a whiff of stale cigarette and aftershave, a pat on my shoulder and a good morning, *'Sabah al khair,'* that I returned, a new habit, *'Sabah al noor,'* a copy of The Jordan Times dropped on my desk. I reached out for the paper. The report added nothing to the online stories, didn't say how big the bomb was, only that it was 'big.' Two Palestinians died, one instantly and one in hospital. Four Israeli soldiers dead, two seriously wounded.

How big is big? Big enough for a knapsack? As big as a lawyer's suitcase?

Aisha called me back as I finished my tea.

'Hi. Sorry I didn't call earlier.'

'Hi. Are you okay?' I asked.

Her voice sounded uneven. 'Umm, I've been better. You saw the news about Jericho?'

'Yes.' *I'm wondering whether you helped to do it, actually, Aish.* 'Yes, I did.'

She took a deep breath before the words tumbled out of her. 'I've taken today off. My cousin was killed in the bomb. He died in hospital this morning. I've known him all my life. I went to school with him. They tried to save him but he was terribly wounded. They said he screamed all through the night. Nancy's gone there.'

My voice came to me as if it were someone else's as my hand tightened on the handset. 'Nancy? He was Ibrahim's son?'

Aisha stammered. 'No, no. Nancy's nephew. He worked for Ibrahim. His name was Rashid. Look, Paul, I'm not too good right now. Could we maybe talk later?'

'Yes, sure. I'm sorry, Aish. Please tell them I'm sorry.' I didn't have the words to deal with the situation and hated that a platitude came so readily to my rescue. 'I'll call you later on.'

'Okay.' She drew a deep breath. 'Thanks.'

Leaning against the warm window frame and looking out over the rooftops, I felt like a shit for letting my imagination run away with me, for thinking she could help to do something like that. Growing up, I had always wanted to be there, to be one of the men standing by the carnage and flames, reporting back to the world. I had made heroes of the 'greats,' the Simpsons and Adies, the Woodwards and Bernsteins. Now events were closer to home, I began to realise how deep the wounds cut – not just there and then, not just at the event itself, but into the people around who have to live without those they have lost.

I tried to do some work, but eventually I left the Ministry building early, saying I had an interview. I didn't drive straight home, but parked up near the market, the old town area of East Amman, walking down through the streets and losing myself in the choking traffic and the flows of people in the grimy streets. I leaned against a rough stone wall and watched the groups of men selling tired-looking birds in plastic cages. For the first time since I'd moved in to my own home, I felt like an utter stranger in this ancient oriental city, remembering the sick feeling of alienation that gripped me as I first looked out of my hotel window across Amman, the morning after Aisha and Ibrahim had got me out of jail.

Aisha's news about her cousin made Jericho real in a way news reports somehow never were, forcing me to confront a new relevance, a new immediacy where I would normally have been cushioned by the distance between the viewer and the events being broadcast around the world. Now I was, literally, in the picture, an actor in the tragedy, one of the constant stream that flickers past us, our screens refreshing fifty times a second and touching, yet never actually embracing, each new unfolding event.

A balding man selling canaries called out to me, '*Salaam y'sidi.*'

Startled, I could only grin stupidly and mumble back at him. His smile died and he turned back to the children in front of him. As I shambled away, the man pulled the cage open for one of the children handing over a coin.

I walked into the kitchen. Lynch called on my mobile.

'You got any plans for the weekend, Paul?'

For some reason the sound of his Northern Irish voice made the hairs stand up on my neck. 'No.'

'Good. Let's meet up for a chat. Tomorrow morning, say eleven at the Citadel? You know the Citadel, right?'

'Why should I meet you?'

'That bomb in Jericho. Very nasty. They traced the explosives back across to Jordan, you know. Smuggled over the border, so an' they were. The Israelis are making quite the fuss about it, in a diplomatic sort of way you understand. You might find you need a friend or two in the weeks ahead. You know, what with court cases, bombings and all that. You seem to enjoy a, how should I put it, a colourful life.'

I brought my racing mind under enough control to speak without stammering. 'What's Jericho got to do with me?' But I was speaking to a dial tone.

Jericho, the biblical city across the River Jordan. I'd stood on the banks of the river with beautiful Aisha, the daddy's girl who had lost her *baba* to the Israelis and whose brother had blown himself up on a bus full of children.

The girl unworried by her bag disappearing from a locked car in a remote place near Jericho, separated from Israel by a few feet of brackish water.

Chapter Eight

I took a shower, made myself a large orange juice and soda then sat in the living room watching the news. Jericho was yesterday's bomb and there was only a small piece on Jordan TV confirming one of the wounded Israelis had died in hospital.

I opened my laptop, shifting the empty whisky bottle and glass out of the way. I didn't have a great deal of time before my impending encounter with Lynch and the nausea rolled over me in slow waves, making it hard to focus. I searched for the Dajanis, Daoud, Ibrahim and the names of the people I knew of at the Ministry. I sketched out likely connections on some sheets of paper, searched for those and connected some more. I looked up whois records for the owners of websites, scanned the scant news reports on the Dajani scandal and the extensive news coverage of the Jericho bomb. I searched blogs, forums and business databases. Close to three o'clock, I'd sketched a patchy map of the relationships I'd encountered, trying to tie them together into what I knew of the family into some sort of tree.

Aisha's brother, Daoud, was a powerful man but his Uncle Ibrahim was more powerful by far. I understood why Aisha had brought him along to spring me out of chokey. Ibrahim Dajani had clout. I could only find hints of the whole: Arabs are strangers to the word transparency. Whatever I could dig up on the Dajani family's business interests on the Web would only be the tip of the iceberg. Still, I found a string of companies across the Arab World, a network of relationships stretching back decades.

A complicated web of ownerships and investments span out from a central holding company, Jerusalem Holdings. Aisha's father, Emad, had founded the whole empire and his name came up in connection with Arafat's people, from Kuwait through to mentions of him in Lebanon during the seventies. His death brought a stop to the thread, killed in an Israeli rocket attack on a house in Gaza five years back. The target of the attack, according to the Israeli press, had been a big Hamas man called Mohammed Eftekhari. Nobody in the little house in Gaza had survived the rockets, which had killed twelve people in all, three of them children.

I sat back, trying not to think of the nagging question. *Who is Aisha?*

Lynch picked me up when I walked into the Citadel, Amman's central hill topped with the ruins of ancient civilisations and one of its big tourist attractions. The guide hassling me to take a tour melted away when Lynch appeared. The Irishman strolled casually beside me as if he'd been there all along.

We walked up the hill until it flattened out onto the top of the Citadel, stopping by the Roman columns that overlook East Amman in its blue, hilly haze. The Roman amphitheatre was below us, the colourful shops and tenements of the Eastern city spread out crazily around it, stretching up into the hills beyond.

We stood together in the warm breeze. Lynch lit a cigarette. 'You been here before?'

'No. Never got around to it.'

He puffed out smoke. 'They've done a good job here. They excavated it in layers, preserving the best of each age. Roman, Byzantine, Muslim. It's all here. Thousands of years of history on a single hilltop.'

'Can we get down to brass tacks?'

Lynch turned to me, his eyebrow raised. 'Sure, Paul. I'm just after some information in return for helping you out with this court case you've landed for yourself. Simple as that.'

'Bollocks, Gerry. You're beyond information. You're playing War Against Terror with all the other little spies and I really don't want to get involved with any of you, if that's all the same to you, thank you.'

I wanted him to react, to try to defend himself, but Lynch wasn't going to give me the pleasure. His accent seemed stronger, an image of the murals on the Falls Road popping incongruously into my mind as he faced me. 'That's Gerald, if you don't mind, Paul. I've been twenty years getting away from Gerry Lynch.'

I scanned his angry countenance, surprised by his violence. 'Um, okay. But it doesn't change the fact. I don't want to play your games.'

Lynch talked to the Citadel. 'You know, I had a hunch that you'd meet up with Daoud Dajani. You've been spending a lot of time with his sister. He'd want to meet you. Have you met him?'

'Yes. Why do you ask?'

'He likes to be in control, does Daoud. He's not a very nice young man, you know.'

'No, I don't. I've only met him once.'

'Did he ask you to do anything for him? Carry anything, talk to anyone?'

'No. Why would he?'

'Oh, no reason, just wondering.'

Carry anything? Like a bag to the border area near Jericho? No, officer. I packed it myself.

Lynch's face was screwed up against the sunlight, his

shabby jeans and brown corduroy jacket seemed designed to let him blend in with the crowds in the city's streets. He strode off again and I followed him.

'Look, I know Daoud Dajani's got form, that he was in trouble last year because of his brother,' I said, my hands in my pockets. 'I know his father was involved with Arafat and even Fatah, and he was helping to fund Arafat in Kuwait, okay? But so are a lot of business people in the Middle East, particularly Palestinian ones. You going somewhere with this or are you just fishing around?'

Lynch stopped walking and looked at me, blinking. A palpable hit. Oh, thank God for the Internet. 'How did you know about all that?'

'Aisha told me.' Which wasn't true, but I certainly planned on giving her the chance. 'So what's your interest, MrLynch from the commercial section?'

'Like I said, just interest.'

'Gerry, don't fuck around. Can you help me or not? And if you can, what do you want from me?'

Lynch smiled at me. 'I told you before, it's Gerald. I won't tell you again. You could use a rethink about your attitude towards authority. You're due in court to answer a serious charge against you of assaulting a police officer and pissing me off will just make things a great deal worse. I'm not going to argue with you about what I do or don't do. Take it or leave it. Just don't dress me up as something fancier than I am. I know you hacks, you've got overactive imaginations. But I thought we could share information, you and I. You've got access to the Jordanian government, you're working within the infrastructure. We'd like to share some of the inside track. Particularly on the water privatisations. There's hundreds of millions of pounds at stake, some key British companies are involved and it's a strategic play for us. You've met Clive Saunders, you know Anglo-Jordanian are going for the water. It's in our interest to help them out in any way we can.' Lynch turned and looked at me, his eyes glittering in the sunlight. 'Legally, of course. Always legally. So there are my cards, Paul. There they are, right there on the table.'

I sulked. 'I'm flattered by your interest in me.'

Lynch paused by a huge stone-lined hole in the ground, a hundred feet across. Steps curled around the inside wall of it down to a layer of green water in the bottom. A pillar of cylindrically cut stones rose in the middle.

'This is a Roman cistern,' he said. 'One of their reservoirs. Clever chaps, really.'

I looked down into the hole, my eyes following the steps down, a little thrill of vertigo ran through me, reminding me of the day I had looked out over Amman from the hotel window. It seemed like months ago.

Lynch kicked a stone over the edge. 'You want to be careful of Dajani, you know. We don't know for sure he was behind Jericho, but we do know he was involved, and both his father and brother were involved with people we would rather not see wandering around the streets of Tel Aviv, let alone London or New York. We've got a hunch he might be funding more of the same. The family likes to fund things. Daddy used to fund things, like you said. But Daoud's bigger. He's got enough money and enough legitimate business interests to stay moving around between places that we'd rather he wasn't mixed up with, to be honest. And now they've lost another one of the family, a cousin of Daoud and Aisha's. He died at Jericho, but not in the blast.'

Aisha's hesitant voice on the telephone came back to

me. The boy who had screamed through the night from his injuries before finally welcoming the cool, dark relief of death. Aisha taking huge gulps of air as she talked through her grief.

Lynch stared at me, his face expressionless. 'The Israelis shot the kid. That's been kept out of the news. They don't seem to be able to remember *quite* why or how they shot him, so we can't *quite* link him to the bomb. It just happened in the confusion. We're keeping an eye out, though. I'm not a great believer in coincidence. You could help us to keep an eye out, too. I'm not asking you to do anything more than have the occasional chat over a drink, to keep your eyes open. It'll be kept confidential. Like you journalists, we're always looking for a second source, for corroboration. And I'm not asking you to carry a micro-camera or a Walther PPK around with you, it's just low level fill-in stuff. Really. Local colour, call it.'

'So you want me to spy on Daoud Dajani for you. This isn't about the Ministry at all.'

'Daoud Dajani's a worry. He's seen as something of a visionary here, you know. Moneyed Arab visionaries are trouble. Look at Osama Bin Ladin. God rest the poor bastard.' Lynch bent down and picked up a stone before flinging it into the cistern where it clicked and skittered off the downward leading stone staircase into the empty depths. 'We've had research requests from the Israelis about Daoud. They've got something on him, but they're not sharing. It'd be nice to know quite what he's up to, Paul. That's all. Is he just commercial or is he playing a bigger, nastier game? We'd love to find out but we can't get close enough. Now if you could let me know you'd be up for helping us out, just by keeping on your toes, so to say, it would be very much in my interest to keep you out of the slammer, wouldn't it?'

Lynch raised his finger as he faced me, the violence in him making me step back. He may well have been too fond of the sauce, but I didn't want to get into a tussle with Gerald Lynch. 'The water and Daoud. You're close to two things sitting in my little file of unfinished business, Paul. It's in my interest to help you. If you'll help me.'

My mouth was open to reply, but Lynch was on the move again, his hands in his jacket pockets as he struck out ill-naturedly through the ruins. He stopped by an excavated area, a low wall around a foot high, the size of my living room at the house. There were bits and pieces of mosaic tiling poking through the hard, dry earth.

'So. You going to play, Paul?'

'If you can help me with the court case, I don't see I have much choice.'

Lynch smiled. 'Right. Sensible. Good man.'

He nodded towards the mosaic, his hands in his pockets.

'This is Byzantine, by the way. Dates back to the dawn of Christianity. There's an older one at Madaba and another at Nebo. The Madaba church contains the oldest surviving mosaic map of the Holy Land. It points to the place where Lot escaped to and holed up with his daughters, a cave above the Dead Sea. The girls conceived their father's incestuous children there.'

The depth of his knowledge surprised me. I hadn't expected sensitivity from the man, let alone lectures on theological history. Lynch kicked a stone into the entrance of the excavated outline of the church and it smacked off the low back wall and clattered along the mosaic floor. He pulled a sour face. 'Bunch of dirty fuckers, if you ask me.'

Chapter Nine

Aisha invited me to dinner with friends from her salsa group. I had already refused at least three invitations to go along to their dance classes, much to her amusement. We agreed to meet up at my place before joining the rest at a trendy bar in the posh Abdoun area. The weather was cooling fast, so I lit the old stove in the kitchen.

She arrived wearing a fur-lined coat over a light brown knitted wool dress, which clung to her down to just above her knees. She draped the coat over a kitchen chair. Turning, she caught me looking at her and smiled. I felt myself colouring.

'Sorry if it's too warm,' I stammered. 'Lars showed me how to use the stove. I thought it was just decorative but it's turned out to be a secret Jordanian blast furnace.'

Aisha laughed, holding her hands out in front of the roaring glass-fronted stove.

'Red okay with you?'

Her bangles jingled as she nodded. 'Perfect. Thanks.'

I poured a glass of wine for us both before sitting, picking a chair opposite her at the table. I needed a barrier.

I took a deep breath and plunged in. 'Aisha, I wanted to talk to you.'

Her smile died, her eyes flickering between mine, trying to read my face. 'Sure. What's up? Is it about the court case?'

I hesitated, unsure how I was going to approach this, but knowing I had to face it for my own peace of mind. The meeting with Lynch had shaken me and I'd spent the rest of the day worrying about Aisha and her family's connections. She had become a central part of my life in Jordan and I had been a little shocked when it hit me Aisha was creeping into my thoughts more than Anne.

Some heavy clicking on Amazon over the past few weeks had resulted in a growing collection of books of Middle East history, helping me to learn enough to appreciate I would never truly learn enough. Aisha's history, her very self, formed part of the larger picture, shaped by it and somehow completing it. I could no longer escape the fact that I had to find some way of reconciling her story with the things I was hearing about her family.

I sipped some wine and watched her. Long, dark hair with highlights she'd had put in at the weekend, brown eyes fixed on mine, her brow creased and the last remnants of a smile dying on her full lips.

'I'm really sorry about your cousin.'

She relaxed. 'It's okay, Paul. The funeral's over, life's back to normal for everyone. You have to move on, you know.' She laughed, a bitter little laugh, flicked her hair back. 'You even start to get used to it after a while.'

'That's what I wanted to talk to you about.'

She tensed again.

I looked at my glass. 'About your father and your brother.'

'Oh,' she said. I watched her shoulders hunch and her hands come together on the table, a barrier. 'Why does that matter?'

I ploughed on. 'Because other people are telling me about it and I wanted you to tell me first.'

'It doesn't concern you, Paul. It's...'

Go on, I thought. *Tell me it's none of my business*. She looked down at her own wine glass. I saw her eyes were moist, the warm light from the stove sparkling in them.

'It's not something I like to talk about very much.'

I tried to be gentle but heard myself whining instead. 'I wanted it to be open between us.'

Paul Stokes, bumbling prat. The man who takes his conversational gambits from third rate soap opera scripts. If I had a low opinion of the human race in general, at least I had the grace to put myself at the bottom of the heap.

Aisha looked away from me, reached into her bag for her cigarettes and lit one. I got the ashtray I kept for visitors, grateful for the excuse of movement to break the tension.

She talked to the table, her voice low. 'My father was born on a farm in Palestine in 1946, outside a village called Qaffin. It's the farm we have today. My grandparents left during the troubles in 1948, what we call the *Naqba*, the disaster. You know this, right? The *Naqba*?' I nodded. 'When the Zionists threw my people from their land and declared Israel a state. They had a saying, you know, "A land without a people for a people without a land." But it's a lie.'

Aisha slowly twisted her lighter between her thumb and forefinger. 'My father met my mother in the camps. He was just another urchin in the streets there, but he was smart and started selling fruit on a street corner, grew it into a business by employing other kids so that eventually he could open a shop of sorts in the camp, made of cinder blocks. He was a good businessman and soon opened a proper store in Amman. He opened more of them. He started to trade with the Syrians and the Iraqis before he left the Amman business in Ibrahim's hands and went to the Gulf in the seventies, to Kuwait, with my mother. The Gulf had oil and needed food, steel, concrete, cars. He did deals with family traders, earned a name for being able to get things nobody else could get, ship things nobody else could ship. Ibrahim found the supplies, my father sold them. My parents moved back here after I was born.'

'And he met Arafat in Kuwait.'

Aisha's eyes widened and she took a pull on her cigarette, staring at me, the lighter twisting in her hand, the shaking tip of the cigarette glowing momentarily as she inhaled. 'Yes, he met Arafat in Kuwait. Through Kaddoumi. And he supplied Arafat. My father believed in Arafat. His family had lost everything, including my grandfather. My father believed that we had to try and fight to return to our country, to our land.'

'But Arafat was a terrorist.'

She was trembling. 'No. *Abu Ammar* was a unifier. There was no Palestine, no Palestinian people, no Palestinian identity. We lost everything, you see? Arafat brought us the dream that one day we could go back to things we had lost, that one day we could become a nation again. What could my father believe in other than this? We are lucky, at least we still have some of our family land, but only because we are on the border, only because we had an Arab Israeli lawyer on our side. Back then, there was no hope for any Palestinian other than Arafat offered.'

I was watchfully silent. Aisha gestured with a wide sweep of her hand. 'My people lost everything they had, living in camps with rusty keys and English title deeds that meant nothing. The world stood by and let it happen. Who else offered any hope to the Palestinians except Arafat and the people around him? Who else was helping us?'

Aisha ground her cigarette viciously into the ashtray. 'My father supported Arafat in the early days, but he turned away from them after the problems in Jordan. He stopped believing in Arafat's way. Both he and Ibrahim became closer to King Hussein, then the King threw the PLO out of Jordan. We stayed here.'

'Why did they leave Kuwait?'

Exasperated, she spat out her answer. 'Because I was born.' She recovered herself with a long silence, her voice shaky when she spoke again. 'I was my father's favourite. He was always very close to me. We used to go on little adventures together, especially after I learned to ride. He was an accomplished horseman. I remember once we went riding with His Majesty. It was such a special day, the horses groomed until they were shining and HM chatting with us while we hacked along the *wadis*. He asked me what I wanted to be when I grew up and I told him I wanted to be a princess. Can you believe it? My father told the king I was already a princess and they both laughed at me. My father was a very gentle man.'

'But he was with a Hamas man when he died,' I blurted.

She recoiled as my words shattered her reminiscence, catching my gaze for an instant, her eyes flickering around the kitchen, casting around for something from inside. I waited for her to calm and speak. She took a deep, shuddering breath and spoke to the tabletop in a small voice.

'Yes, Paul. My father was in a house in Gaza that belonged to one of his old business contacts from the Gulf days. Another man was visiting, an important man in Hamas. The Israelis attacked the house with missiles. They killed my *baba* and took him away from me forever.'

'Was he involved with Hamas?'

I had spoken as gently as I could but then I saw, to my horror, the splashes on the tabletop. The tears brimming in Aisha's eyes ran down her cheeks as she looked up. Her chin was puckered, her words halting as she fought for control of her breathing. 'My father... was not a terrorist. He was... not an evil man.'

She held onto her lighter so tightly the blood drained from her fingers and her hands shook. She dropped it, sniffed and wiped at her cheeks with her fingertips.

'He was not accused, tried or found guilty of a crime. He was in the wrong place at the wrong time, just like the young mother in the shopping mall when the bomb comes. He was killed by a state formed by bombing and violence, founded by terrorists who threw my people off their land by murdering them and driving them away with fear. By the people that killed the villagers of Deir Yassin and hundreds of Palestinian villages like it, the people that killed thousands when they smashed into Gaza and poured phosphorous on it from the sky like rain. There was no judge, there was no jury. He was murdered in cold blood.'

Aisha delved into her bag for a tissue and wiped her eyes, shaking her head as she looked out of the kitchen window, away from me.

'I don't want to think about this, Paul. I prefer not to live with it in my mind every day. I have a life to live. As Palestinians we have to put this behind us and *live*, because we can't afford to spend every single moment focusing on the tragedy and death that is around us, inside us.'

She drank from her wine, her reddened eyes on mine over the fine rim of the glass. Her mascara was smudged.

I broke the long silence. 'So is that why Hamad did what he did? To revenge your father?'

Aisha glared at me, placing the wineglass on the table with agonising slowness, her eyes on me as she pushed her chair back. She turned to hook up her coat. My chair rattled as I leaped to my feet. 'Where are you going?'

'I don't need this. You don't need Daoud lecturing you, but I don't need you questioning me, either. You just go ahead and believe what you want to, listen to what you want to. I will not be *interviewed* by you. I'm going home. Goodbye, Paul.'

I was incapable of movement, shocked by the realisation of my own immense stupidity and crassness. I saw her chin pucker again as the light caught the side of her face, but she didn't look back as she closed the door gently behind her. The kitchen was quiet, apart from the soft background grumble of the wood burning in the stove and the electronic tick of the wall clock. It ticked four times before resolution rescued me from stasis and I ran out after her. I caught her opening her car door, about to get in. I called across the road to her as I stood at the bottom of the steps that led up from the road to the garden: 'Aisha.'

The tears were streaming down her cheeks as she turned to me, shouting, her face contorted and her voice echoing down the dark street.

'Fuck off, Paul. Fuck off and creep about in the garbage of someone else's life. Leave mine alone.'

I was still standing there ten minutes later when a truck full of red-painted gas bottles drove past, blaring an ice-cream van jingle out of the speakers mounted on the cab. The gasmen waved at me, but I didn't wave back. I shivered in the cool of the evening. I blundered back into the house. For the first time in years, I felt utterly alone. I sat in the kitchen and drank my wine, listening to the tick of the clock and replaying the conversation, twisting the knife in the wound just so I could feel the pain of it.

A little later, I drank hers too, matching my lips to the lipstick mark on the glass. It tasted waxy.

Chapter Ten

I didn't see Aisha for the next three days. She sent messengers down from the Secretary General's office with arrangements for interviews or with information I'd requested. The magazine was coming together and we were preparing to send it to press by the end of the week – I just had to get the final pages signed off by the Ministry. I took the printouts up to Abdullah Zahlan, who liked them but suggested I show them to Aisha for the Secretary General's approval.

There was a heavy crystal paperweight in the shape of the Al Aqsa Mosque on Aisha's desk and a furry toy monkey with big, dopey eyes sitting on the top of the cabinet by the wall. She had a visitor, a veiled woman with whom she was chatting animatedly. She barely looked up at me, her voice cool.

'Thank you, Paul. Just put them down on the side table there and I'll return them to you this afternoon.'

I bit my tongue and went back downstairs, stopping halfway down the dingy staircase to smack the gloss-painted wall with my fist. I sat at my desk, calming down and gazing into my screen for a couple of hours. I'd been spending my time drinking with Lars, missing Aisha's company but keeping myself busy socially rather than having to sit down and think about what a total idiot I'd been. I felt guilty about prying into her life and about hurting her with my stupidity and selfishness. She had been kind to me, amused but tolerant of my ignorance and patient with my constant questions and demands. I had repaid her by digging into her pain, gouging away at the wounds until I'd forced her away from me. Stokes the lonely journalist who can't switch off the desire to interrogate people, to indulge the driving curiosity that wrecks trust and renders everything down to the cold, hard facts that lie at the centre of all weakness. Pity poor Paul.

Aisha strode up to my desk, the page proofs in her hand. She wasn't smiling.

'This stuff is approved. You're going to buy me a drink at the Blue Fig tonight at eight o'clock.'

I looked up at her. Her face was serious, but her eyes were flickering between mine uncertainly.

I nodded, fighting to keep the astonishment from my face. 'I am.'

She left without another word but when the phone rang a few seconds later, I answered it giddily, 'Stokes Precision Engineering and Victorian Toy Repair Service.'

'Paul?'

'Oh, hi, Robin. What gives?'

His plummy drawl sounded relieved. 'Sorry, thought I'd got a wrong number there for a second.' His braying laughter jangled down the line. 'Look, just called to make sure you got those proofs signed off okay.'

'Signed off, Robin. The whole thing's ready to print.'

'Good work. We've broken target by 10k and forward bookings are looking great. We've hit bonus.'

Ah, Robin, Robin. 'We've hit bonus' was code for Robin Goodyear has hit bonus. Paul Stokes would remain scrabbling around in near-poverty in a foreign country while the CEO, Michael Klein, joined Robin for drinks in his converted Kentish barn or maybe down the road at the BMW-lover's pub, the Morgan Arms. They'd stand there at the bar in their Aran sweaters, telling each other just how well the whole Jordan thing was going and how clever they'd been to think it all up, then drink their beers and go back to Robin's for an impeccably cooked Sunday roast prepared by Claire who would have drunk too much because she'd been entertaining Mousey Hilary, Klein's plain little wife. Claire, a secretary at TMG before Robin 'rescued' her, knew full well Klein spent most of his time in the office pushing as much of himself as he could into the various openings offered by Lynda, his bumptious and yet decidedly pneumatic personal assistant.

I imagined Robin naked and crucified upside down and managed a smile. 'Good. I'm glad you're pleased, Robin.'

'Keep it up, Stokesy. Hear Anne's coming out to visit you. Do you good to get your end away. Oh, wait a minute – haven't you been servicing that Dajani bird?'

Anne and Robin had always got on, often chatted. They moved in the same circles.

'Just been waiting for Anne, Robin.'

How I hated myself for not slamming the phone down on the bastard.

'Good show. Well, must get on. Toodle pip.'

Toodle pip my arse. I wrapped up and went home, too appalled at Robin to be mad with him. How on earth people like him survive, let alone climb to the top of their little dung heaps, constantly amazes me. I was angry when I got to the house and stomped up the steps to Lars' place.

Lars answered the door in a sarong, gesturing me towards the fridge as he fiddled with the mouse and closed whatever strange online session he'd been absorbed in before he turned to me.

'What's new?'

'I'm meeting Aisha for drinks tonight.'

'Okay. So it's back on.'

'What's back on? It's not as if we're anything more than friends.'

'Like friends sulk when they don't see each other for a couple of days? Huh? You sulk if I'm not in when you get home, English? Hmm? I think not. Surely you're friends. Look, just go to her. You're crazy, but go anyway. Stop being a puppy sick. You say puppy sick?'

I laughed despite myself. 'Sick puppy, you silly sod.'

Lars sat back, contentment on his handsome Scandinavian features as he raised his can in a toast. 'Yes, like this. Go with her, Paul. Be happy. Be careful. Here, I have a present for you. Watch it if you like, don't watch it if you like.'

Puzzled, I took the memory stick he offered me. 'What is it, Lars?'

He smiled grimly. 'It's Hamad Dajani's goodbye video. A friend of mine in Jordan TV got it for me. Like I say, watch it if you like.'

When I had finished my beer with Lars, I went downstairs and stood in front of the TV for a very long time before putting the memory stick down by the screen and going to the bathroom to wash.

The Blue Fig is a funky art-house café bar in the wealthy Abdoun district owned by a couple of Jordanian bigshots, all wooden flooring and antiqued steel trimmings. It's a popular meeting place – in the summer it heaves with rich, pretty young things come back from the Gulf. Even now, early in the cool autumn evening, it was becoming noisy. I spotted Aisha in a quiet corner away from the bar. She wore the brown woollen outfit again and I couldn't help my grin.

'I thought we'd try starting again,' she said, standing

to meet me as I walked up to the table.

There was a second's hesitation – her hand wasn't held out. I leaned forward and kissed her cheek, my hand resting lightly on her hip. It felt like the most natural gesture in the world. She smelled of warm spice.

She handed me a little blue plastic bag. 'Here. I brought you a little something.'

I opened the bag. It was a delicate pen and ink sketch of a bunch of olives on a branch. I wanted to cry.

'Listen, Paul, I owe you an apology. I'm sorry. I guess it was too soon after my cousin to start talking about all that family stuff and I just flipped out. I'm really sorry. I thought an olive branch was appropriate.'

An uncomfortable, burning sensation seared my throat. I managed to swallow and keep the tears out of my eyes.

'Thank you. It's beautiful.'

She smiled. 'The salsa girls won't forgive me. I stood them up.'

'Aisha, I'm sorry.'

She leaned forwards, put her finger to her lips. 'Shush. Enough.' She put her hand on mine and squeezed it, an electric moment of soft warmth. I felt myself falling into those gold-flecked eyes, our long gaze driving a thrill through me, a feeling close to fear and yet ecstatic. Aisha broke the moment first, taking her hand away to reach for her handbag and fuss for her cigarettes.

I looked down at the table rather than meet her eyes. I tried to force a light tone, but just sounded manic. 'I've got my own troubles anyway. Anne, my girlfriend, is coming out from England to visit me at the end of next week.'

She froze for a second, her hand still in her bag. I had told her about Anne long before, but my girlfriend hadn't been a topic of conversation between us precisely because I had avoided bringing it up.

Aisha looked up at me and I cursed myself as I saw her strained face, her smile as bright and brittle as her voice.

'You must be pleased. How long is she staying?'

'For the week. She'll go back just before the court case comes up.'

'This will be her first time here?'

'Yes. I honestly didn't think she'd come at all. She's very busy with her work.'

Aisha lit her cigarette and puffed the smoke high into the air.

'You never told me what she did.'

I fought the urge to steal a smoke from her. I couldn't believe Jordan was doing this to me. I'd never smoked in my life, although my father did. When he left, my mother threw out all the ashtrays and suddenly smokers weren't welcome at home. Smoking never bothered me, one way or the other, although I tended to avoid smoky rooms just because of the smell it left on you. And I'd avoided smoky girls because it is, when you come down to it, just like kissing an ashtray. Which got me thinking about kissing Aisha and so I blew it and took one of her cigarettes with a shaky hand.

'She's a lawyer.' I said as I lit up. Aisha raised an eyebrow, but I shook my head. 'Contract law, not criminal stuff so no, I haven't told her about the court case. She's very good at it.'

'Did you live together?'

'Now you're just being nosy.'

The spark was back in her eyes and she flicked her hair back. 'You'd know about that, wouldn't you, *ya* Brit?'

I winced. 'Okay, yes, we lived together but not, well, not quite like that, not at first. She was my landlady and things sort of developed. But I still paid her rent up until I left her. I mean, left England.'

Aisha's face was serious. 'Do you love her?'

Did I? Anne the golden girl. Anne of the fiery temper and the 'yah set' friends. Anne the determined career girl with the Saab Aero and a flat in Balham pronounced 'Barm'. Bling bling Anne. Anne the lover who liked to be on top. Anne of a million years ago, another continent. Anne who hadn't changed since I left England, while I was becoming another person. Anne who didn't belong in this life of mine, this new life. Dreams of Anne and home drifting away.

I scanned the busy bar. Three guys in open-necked, square-patterned shirts stood by the beer taps smoking cigars; a group of six girls two tables away looked through a photo album, shrieking with delighted laughter; a big, boisterous table at the other side of the room chattering, two young men standing up and slanging each other in loud, laughing voices, their body language exaggerated as they accused each other of being liars.

I nodded. 'I think I did, yes.'

I walked Aisha home. It was getting chilly and her heels tapped shorter steps than mine on the uneven pavement. The plastic bag bumped against my leg and I folded it around the little picture to hold it in the crook of my arm. She spoke into the cold distance ahead of us.

'You asked me if Hamad was revenging my father.'

I started to interrupt her, to tell her I didn't want to know anymore, but she silenced me by taking my arm.

'No, it's all right. I want to tell you. Hamad took my father's death badly. I don't mean that any of us took it well. It was a very bad time. But Hamad was always an angry man and his reaction to *baba* dying was furious. I think he learned how to focus his anger into hate. He was always very religious. He won prizes for reading Koran at school. My father was never strict like that, but he was a quietly devout man in his way. Hamad became more explosive as he got older, more...' She paused as she searched for the right word. 'In Arabic we say *borkan ghadab*. More than a, volcano, yes? He was angry always. He would go a lot to the East of the city, he had friends there. My father used to worry about him. After father's death he used to be away from home for days on end. He drove my mother half-mad with worry, but he would always turn up in the end, usually in a very bad state, half-starved. He wouldn't talk to Mum about himself, but he was always close to Daoud. He lost a lot of weight over that time.'

Aisha stopped walking and pulled her cigarettes out. She lit one and offered them to me. I hesitated but took one. We stood together and Aisha gestured down the street towards her house, her eyes shining in the sodium light.

'I heard them arguing one night, out in the garden by the olive trees. Daoud was telling Hamad to stay away from someone or something and he was hissing back at Daoud. They were arguing in whispers, but of course they became louder as the argument became fierce between them. After this, Hamad was gone for a month. Daoud used his business contacts to try and keep track of him. But Hamad had disappeared. Daoud heard he was in Lebanon and finally he drove up through Syria and across to Lebanon to look for him. It's not a long drive.

We have some business in Lebanon and the people there tried to help Daoud, but of course it was too late. Hamad was in the south and had gone across the Israeli border.'

'You don't have to go on,' I said, as gently as I could. 'I'm sorry for asking you in the first place. You know that.'

'No, no. It's actually good to talk about it.'

She reached into her handbag, smiled up at me and dabbed at her eye with a tissue. I felt awkward, wanted desperately to put my arms around her and tell her it was all right. I didn't because I come from a cold place and the coldness was deep in me. Because I didn't want to betray Anne with my body as I had already betrayed her with my mind.

Aisha's heels clicked as we walked. 'He killed himself. They had strapped a bomb to him. He was wearing a green headscarf. He left a video dedicating his life to father and God.'

Yes, I know. I watched it. She couldn't see me blushing in the darkness, thank God.

Aisha wheeled around, her face shadowed by the streetlight, her hands balled into tight fists and her voice tight. 'My father didn't want his life, Paul. And I don't think God did either. I don't think God wanted the lives of the twelve Israelis on the bus with him, the lives of the little children. But he took them all to God with him.'

I reached out to her and put my arm around her shoulder. I squeezed, feeling her arm warm around my waist.

We rounded the corner of the street to Aisha's house.

'What did Daoud do?'

'The *Mukhabarat*, the secret police, arrested Daoud at the Jordanian border. They imprisoned him. It was two days before Ibrahim could get to him. They beat him.

Ibrahim had him released.'

She looked up at me defiantly. 'There were no charges. He hadn't done anything wrong. But he's been different since then. Quieter, more intense. More driven. He's never told us what happened to him in there. But Daoud is a good man, Paul.'

We walked up to the front door together in silence. Aisha turned to me in the light of the doorway, her troubled eyes looking into mine. 'I don't think you can ever properly understand. I don't even think it's fair to expect you to.'

I shook my head. 'No, you might be right. I suppose I can at least try, but it's a different world to the one I'm from, isn't it?'

She nodded, her lips tight. 'When Anne has left, after your court case, will you come to the farm in Palestine with me? I'd like to show it to you. You never know, it might help you understand.' She grimaced then smiled apologetically, 'If you want to, I mean. I have no right even asking you to try to understand us.'

'Yes,' I said, and in one word confirmed life after Anne. 'Yes, I'd like that. Thank you.' An unwelcome thought hit me like a bucket of freezing water, sucking the warmth and pleasure out of me. I stuttered as I spoke, looking down at the stone steps. 'If the court leaves me free to, of course.'

'You will be free, Paul. I know it.'

She smiled and I wanted to kiss her for her smile, for everything behind it, the sadness and pain in her. For her bravery and beauty. Our eyes locked together and in that instant I saw the certainty I was feeling mirrored in her eyes. A thrill, a delicious sensation of falling and joy went through me as I looked down at Aisha's beautiful face, raised to mine. Her lips were slightly parted.

The front door clicked open as the porch light came on, leaving us blinking and disoriented. The moment fled and I tried not to look guilty as hell and failed. Daoud's face was impassive.

'Hello, Paul, nice to see you. Aisha, you're out late.'

Aisha smiled, a little nervously I thought, but then she was probably going through the same as me – trying not to look guilty because we weren't, but knowing it hadn't looked good when Daoud saw us.

'Paul walked me home. It's okay.'

'Come in, both of you.'

I decided to do the decent thing and run for it. 'No thanks, Daoud. I'd better get going myself. I just wanted to make sure she was home safe.'

'Of course. Thanks, Paul.' Four words and Daoud managed to make them say 'You lying bastard.'

I scrabbled around for something, anything to say to him. Daoud spoke first, 'Another time, maybe.'

I forced a smile to my face. 'That'd be great.'

I tipped a finger to my forehead and had turned to leave when I heard Aisha call out to me. 'Paul.'

I turned back. 'Aish?'

'Thank you for tonight. You will come to the farm, won't you?'

'Yes. Yes I will.'

Aisha pulled the door to behind her as she stepped down to meet me and kissed me with a suddenness that took my breath away. She was back in the house before I could react, leaving me with the fleeting memory of her light, soft lips pressed on mine and her rich scent wrapping me in its warmth. I strode down the dark street, pulling my coat around me against the cold. I wondered how I was going to get through Anne's visit now I knew with absolute certainty I loved someone else.

Chapter Eleven

Anne's flight landed on Saturday afternoon, halfway through the Jordanian weekend. I'd taken the week off work, the first issue of the magazine having gone to the printers and the Web-formatted content alongside a neatly laid out online newsletter duly placed in the hands of the Ministry's digital team.

Robin didn't know about the extra effort I'd gone to. I saw no reason to tell him.

Anne didn't have the ten Dinar visa fee I had warned her to have ready for immigration and so she had to change money and queue again, by which time the queue had doubled. The airline lost one of her bags and she waited by the carousel for an hour before reporting it missing, tracking it down just in time to walk into a bored customs officer who spent an enjoyable half an hour rooting through her underwear and personal effects.

By the time she came around the corner of the partition in arrivals, red-faced and scowling, I had spent two hours nagging the BA duty officer to death. A wave of relief, tenderness and sheer delight washed over me and I ran to her and scooped her up in my arms, laughing and talking gibberish. We pushed her trolley, arm in arm, to the car park.

Anne slept in the car as we drove back to Amman and I took care not to wake her until I switched off the engine outside the house. She glanced around, disoriented. Her skin was pale and there were dark smudges under her eyes. She put her hand on my arm, as if to steady herself, and peered up the steps to the house above us.

'Is this it?'

'Certainly is. Come on, I'll give you the grand tour.'

It was an unusually warm day for autumn and Lars sat in the garden taking in the rays with a couple of friends from work, a French guy from the phone company and a Canadian consultant working with the Ministry of Information and Communications Technology.

Lars got up, grinning and held out his hand to Anne. 'Hey, hey, hey. You must be the famous Anne. It's nice to meet you.'

Anne glanced sharply at me before taking his hand. I had never mentioned Lars. 'Sorry, Annie. This is Lars, we share the garden. He lives on the first floor.'

Anne smiled dutifully. 'Well, it's nice to meet you, Lars.'

Lars' expression was mock rueful. 'Paul's been keeping me a secret, obviously. He's too scared I will steal away your heart. Anyway, I'm glad you're here. At least now he'll have to behave and stop being drunk, coming home late from the clubs and keeping us responsible citizens awake all night with his parties.'

Lars was obviously under the impression that he was being hysterically witty and had earned himself a sharp bark of laughter from the French guy, but Anne wasn't looking amused. I hefted her bags again.

'Well, thanks for the character reference, Lars, but we're going to get Anne settled in. Maybe we'll catch you later.'

Lars let go of Anne's hand, to her obvious relief, and we went inside. Anne frowned as we walked through the house. 'What was all that about clubs and parties?'

'It's just Lars' sense of humour. He's okay, but he can be a bit Scandinavian sometimes. And his English can be odd.'

'But you said you'd been working late all the time.'

I turned to face her and took her hands in mine. 'And I have. Look, this is the bedroom.'

I opened the door and followed her in. I had spent all morning preparing my bower and it was a vision of terracotta, wood and white linen. I had even put some twigs in a vase in the corner. The dappled sunlight streamed through the French windows, splashing highlights across the bed.

Anne barely glanced around the room before turning to me. 'So why would he make so much fuss about drinking and parties?'

'I don't know, Annie. Sarcasm. Swedish humour. I don't know.'

Anne passed her hand over her tied-back hair, frowning at me. 'And who is he anyway? You've never mentioned anyone called Lars on the phone.'

'Haven't I? I suppose because he's not really very important.'

'He seemed to know you pretty well.'

'We've been out together a few times, is all.'

'Drinking and going to parties.'

I let her bags drop. 'Why's it such a big deal, Annie?'

She had wandered over to the window and was looking out to the garden, her arms crossed. I heard something bump upstairs.

'Anne?'

Her voice was small and tight. 'Oh, nothing Paul. I suppose I feel a little disconnected and I'm very tired. Where do you want me to put my things?'

I showed her the cupboard and the bathroom, then went to the kitchen to get a coffee while she freshened up. When I eventually went back to find her she was in a dressing gown, curled up asleep on the bed.

Later on, I cooked dinner and we went to bed. I reached out to her but she murmured, 'No, not now,' and turned away from me.

I woke late to the sound of my phone. It was Robin telling me about an advertisement holding up the magazine at the printers. He wanted me to sign off the machine proofs and make sure everything was okay. Anne went into the bathroom as I whined to him. I went to tell her we would have to go down to the press on our way out sightseeing but she'd locked the door. I shouted out to her but she didn't want to visit any printing presses, so I went alone.

I came back three hours later, the magazine duly saved, to find Anne watching the news. She glanced up as I walked into the living room, but didn't smile. She wore jeans and a white blouse, her feet tucked under her on the sofa. I sat down beside her, stroking her leg.

Her voice was listless. 'Did Lars call you? He came looking for you earlier.'

'No, I'll call him later. Look, I'm sorry, Annie. There was nothing else I could do, they'd screwed up the pagination and everything. It's done now. Come on, let's go and see the sights of glorious Amman.'

She shook her head, her straight blonde hair flicked over her right shoulder. 'It's too late to go out, Paul. Let's do it another time.'

'Nonsense. There's a couple of hours at least before sunset. We can go up to the Citadel and watch the sun over the city. Come on, Annie.'

She turned the television off but talked at the screen. 'No. I said no. I don't want to go out now.'

I didn't really know where to go next. I got to my feet. 'We could go down to the Wild Café and watch the sunset over a drink?'

Anne smiled tightly up at me. 'No, no thanks.'

'Anne, it's not my fault I had to go out today. Why take it out on me?'

She fiddled with the remote control in her hands. 'I'm not, Paul. I just don't want to go out.'

A wave of unreasonable irritation took me, then: a hot surge of anger. I stood over her. 'So what the hell *do* you want to do?'

She sat back on the sofa, her hands gripping her arms. 'Who is Aisha, Paul?'

I must have gasped. I certainly stepped back. 'What the hell kind of question's that?'

'Who is she?'

'She's a girl who works at the Ministry. What's she got to do with anything?'

'I just asked you who she is, Paul. What's the big deal?'

'Well, I suppose I'm a bit confused as to why some girl at the Ministry would come up right now when I rather thought we'd be going out somewhere.'

'We're not going anywhere, Paul. I told you I didn't want to go out. Why didn't you tell me about Aisha?'

I had turned away but now I rounded on her. 'What about her? What the hell's got into you, Anne? She's just a girl who works there. What would I tell you about her?'

Anne got up from the sofa and struck out towards the bedroom. She paused in the doorway. 'Lars said she had found this house for you and that it belonged to her family. There's a picture in the kitchen signed Aisha. Is she the same person?'

'She helped me to settle in here. I'm sorry, but I don't

get your problem with that, Anne.'

But Anne had closed the door. It was almost nine o'clock before she came out again, taking me by the hand and leading me back to the darkness where she made silent, desperate love to me. After a time we both stopped trying and I felt her tears dropping onto my face.

I got up as silently as I could to avoid waking Anne. The sunny weather had held and I went outside to drink my coffee and read the newspaper. I listened to the susurration of the city below. Lars had left a packet of cigarettes and a disposable lighter on the table the night before. The pack was damp but the moisture hadn't penetrated to the Marlboros and the lighter worked, so I lit one and luxuriated in my coffee and the perfect morning. I gazed at the blue tendril of smoke rising lazily from my cigarette.

Anne slid open the patio window from the bedroom and stepped into the garden, sleepy-eyed and blinking in the warm morning light. She shaded her eyes and started to walk towards me. She stopped, her hand dropping to her hip.

'Paul, what the fuck do you think you're doing?'

I looked around me, the newspaper on my lap, my mobile on the table next to my still-steaming coffee, the paved area around me scattered with brown leaves. Too late, I realised. I grinned weakly. Anne hated smoking. I snatched my hand behind my back, a reflex that made me feel like a naughty schoolboy, but Anne had already turned on her heel. She went indoors without a word.

I stubbed out the cigarette and followed her into the kitchen, anxiety pricking at me and making my heart pump. If my voice was over-bright, then Anne's was dull and lifeless.

'Fancy some toast?'

'Fine.'

She was sitting on one of the kitchen chairs, one leg tucked under the other and her hands cupped protectively around a glass of orange juice.

I made coffee and toast, the kitchen filling with breakfast smells. Buttering the slices, I remembered I didn't have any marmalade. Anne only ever had marmalade on toast. I had meant to go down to FineFair and buy some for her.

'Um, there's no marmalade. Jam?'

She didn't look up. 'No, I'll just take it plain, thanks.'

Her toast stayed on the plate as I ate mine. She finished her orange juice and left the kitchen and I heard the shower as I sat, looking at the sunlight on the tiled floor and feeling sick.

I stood centre stage in Amman's Roman amphitheatre feeling the pressure of my own voice reverberating from the stone seating circled around me. I watched Anne as she walked in the flat arena, called out to her. 'Come up here and try it. It's so acoustically perfect you can hear a man talking in a normal voice even if you're sitting all the way up at the back.'

She looked up at me and smiled. 'I'll take your word for it. What's the equipment behind you? Do they still have concerts here?'

I surveyed the stage behind me. Beyond the speaker stacks I could see the shabby Eastern city climbing up the hill towards the Citadel, straight stairways set into the tightly packed buildings, reaching towards the cloudy sky.

'Yes. A big Lebanese singer played here over the weekend. Not bad to be using a venue after two thousand years, is it?'

I jumped down to her and managed to wind myself in the process. Anne laughed and put her arm in mine, her cheeks rosy with the cool autumn air. She had zipped her brown leather jacket up, her red scarf tucked into the top.

'It's cold.'

I held her closer. 'Come on, let's drive up to the Citadel.'

The Amphitheatre is on the margins of the Eastern city's poverty, the streets choked by jostling, beeping traffic. A line of desperate people sat along the front wall selling miserable scraps, their last pathetic possessions laid out by the roadside. Anne stopped by a small boy, a broken radio, a tape cassette and a pair of worn shoes laid out on the stained blanket in front of him. My mobile rang. It was Lynch insisting we meet. I walked away from Anne, hissing at him.

'I can't. My girlfriend's over from the UK.'

I turned to see Anne staring at me. The boy was imploring. Anne beckoned me.

Lynch's clipped Northern Irish vowels were urgent. 'This is important, Paul.'

'I can't just dump her in the house and go gallivanting around Amman right now, Gerald. Sorry.'

'Call me back later, so. You've got the number.'

'All right, all right.'

I dropped the line and went back to Anne, who shook her head as I pulled her away from the boy. 'Can't we give him something, Paul? It's so dirty here. These people are so poor.'

'Come on, Annie. Whatever we do here won't change that. And most of the beggars are actually professionals.'

'Says who?'

'Me, Anne. I've been living here, remember?'

She was silent until we reached the car. 'Who was on the phone?'

I hadn't thought to concoct a reason for the call. What the hell do I say now? Nobody, dear, just a gentleman from British intelligence. I opened the door to buy time. I looked across the roof at her, smiling reassuringly.

'Just one of the people from the Ministry. He didn't realise I was on leave.'

Anne's reflection on the car roof was framed by dark cloud. I shivered as her face softened and she smiled. 'Come on, then. Show me this Citadel place,' she said.

My relief at having avoided another big scene was tempered by the knowledge that the lie, like getting caught smoking and our disastrous attempt at copulation the night before, was another little wedge between us.

The Golan Heights are both notorious and beautiful, a majestic sweep of green rising up from the lowlands around Lake Tiberias, a couple of hours' drive north of Amman. Exploring the North of the country was Lars' idea – he'd made the suggestion the night before at dinner.

We stood in the ruins of the Roman City at Umm Qeis and looked out at the green swell of one of the world's bloodiest and most hotly contested pieces of land, and I was humbled into silence. Anne was next to me, her jacket collar turned up and her hair whipping her face. It was a day of clear, cool sunshine. The clouds were starting to gather, drifting across the rich blue sky and casting jagged shadows across the ruins and the hump of the Golan beyond. I heard the shouts of the *tamar* man selling his date juice in the ruins behind me and turned to see him lugging the huge, brass pot on his back, bright ribbons and pompoms decorating it.

Lars spoke to Anne, raising his voice against the breeze blowing across the black stone skeleton of the city Rome had left behind. The wind gusted through the centuries and across into Israel. 'The Israelis took it from Syria in '67,' Lars shouted against the wind. 'You could stand here at the time, apparently, and watch the MIGs dancing in the air as the land shook with the bombs. I know a guy who was here. He was crazy to have been close to it as like this. He said it looked beautiful, the explosions and smoke. The border's down there, in the valley. The Syrians used to launching the rocket attacks from the heights down onto the Israelis. Gave them more range.'

Anne shuddered. 'I think it's horrible. Why can't they just live together?'

'That is a long story, Anne,' said Lars. I could imagine him thinking 'stupid cow' as he smiled at her because, to be honest, I was thinking something like it myself.

Lars' exposition into the wind continued. 'The Arabs tried to fight against the Israelis ever since the country was founded in 1948. But they couldn't work together, the Egyptians, Syrians and Jordanians. They took the beating in '48 and took another one in '67, the six-day war. The crazy Syrians lost the Golan, tried to take it back in '73, the Yom Kippur war, but the Israelis threw them out again. Back and forward all the time, you see? It's all about the water – that's Lake Tiberias you can see over there – the Israelis took it in '67. It's the cornering stone of their water supply now.'

I was impressed. Lars had the history down pat. Although Anne and Lars seemed cordial enough over our dinner together the night before, they were not exactly destined to be star-crossed lovers. Lars had brought a pal of his along to the restaurant, a privatisation consultant. Privatisation Man and Anne had spent most of the evening swapping London stories and I hadn't even noticed she wasn't drinking until we got back to the house and she gave me a hard time for being pissed.

A real comedy of errors, except I couldn't hear anyone laughing.

We wandered through the maze of ruined buildings to eat lunch at the Lebanese restaurant hidden away around the back of the Roman city, a few wrought iron tables topped with marble mosaic scattering a patio overlooking the Heights. We ordered *mezze* and *arak* and sat, shielded from the breeze. Anne didn't like the *arak* so I ordered her a glass of dry local white wine she liked little more.

As Lars chatted to Anne, I watched the clouds chasing the sunshine across the Golan, my thoughts drifting to Daoud, driving up through here into Syria and Lebanon in search of his fanatical younger brother. Daoud must have watched Hamad changing and becoming angrier, more politicised. I could imagine his concern, his growing reservations about the company his brother was keeping, the late night meetings and the family arguments. One day Hamad hadn't come home and Daoud had chased after him, tailing him across the uncertainties of the Syrian border.

I was there with Daoud, white-faced at the wheel of the car as he raced to try and catch up with his headstrong little brother, knowing in his deepest heart what Hamad was planning. The failure, the vengeful *Mukhabarat* stopping Daoud at the border on his way back. Daoud brought low, moaning in the prison cell with the wounds and bruises from the hourly beatings, until Ibrahim tracked him down and had him released. No wonder Daoud came across as dark and intense now.

Of course, I had eventually given in and watched Hamad's last testament, the videotaped statement he had made wearing a green bandana and a bomb belt. The grainy quality of the recording couldn't disguise his strong resemblance to Daoud. I didn't have the means to decipher what Hamad was saying on the tape. But I had been mesmerised by the sight of him crowing before he marched off to kill a busload of children, his chin raised and his eyes angry and defiant.

'Paul.' Anne's voice, sharp, bringing me back to the present, the marble-topped table cold under my elbow and Lars grinning at me. 'I asked if you could get the bill please. I don't have any Dinars on me.'

The unkind thought flashed through my mind, *use your fucking Amex then, dahling*. 'Okay. Hang on a tick,' I said, fumbling for my wallet.

I called the waiter. *'Law samaht. El-fattura, min fadlak.'*

He came over with the bill.

'Yislamouh,' I said as I handed back the little black folder.

Lars turned to Anne. 'See? He's even speaking Arabic now. He's bright, your boy. Half Arab already.'

'Yes,' she said.

Anne's face wasn't exactly a picture of pride.

We left Umm Qeis and would have been totally silent on the drive back to Amman if it hadn't been for Lars the tourist guide, who kept up a constant patter from the back seat as I drove. I rather suspected he was doing it because he knew Anne didn't like him. My mobile rang and it was Lynch. I rejected the call before clearing the received call list on the phone and dropping it back in the car's ashtray so Anne wouldn't pick it up and see the last caller number. Her eyes followed the phone as I put it back into the slot in the dashboard.

When we got back to the house late in the afternoon, Lynch was sitting in the garden. I introduced him to Anne as a friend who worked at the British Embassy. Lars took Lynch's proffered hand.

'Nice to meet you,' Lars said, making it abundantly clear it wasn't. 'Paul, Anne, thanks for the fun. I am going out to meet a crazy Jordanian chick who loves me too much, so I have to make myself beautiful.' He nodded at Lynch. 'You'll excuse me, ya?'

Lynch smiled at us both and sat down again. He looked up at Anne, standing with her arms crossed.

'I just need two minutes with Paul here, if you don't mind. Maybe you'd like to freshen up a bit after your trip or something?'

Anne gasped. I saw her out of the corner of my eye, looking at me and waiting for me to defend her right to stay but my eyes were on Lynch. She snatched the keys from my hand and marched over to the door, unlocking it with a savage twist before slamming it behind her.

'You rude fucker.'

Lynch smiled. 'Do you actually like her? She doesn't seem your type.'

'That's none of your business.'

He leaned forward, his smile fading fast.

'We need your help. Dajani's confirmed to a journalist from one of the Arabic rags he's going to be bidding for the water privatisation and he's claiming he has the solution to Jordan and the West Bank's water supply problems. We're deeply concerned about what he's up to, Paul. The West Bank's none of his business and it isn't part of the privatisation as far as we are aware. The Izzies are screaming blue murder already and asking the Jordanians for clarification – and they're saying nothing, not confirming, not denying. Your Minister has clammed up tighter than a shark's arse at fifty fathoms.'

'So what am I supposed to do?'

Lynch cast his eyes briefly to heaven. 'Find out what he's up to, Paul. Find out why the Ministry's gone quiet.'

'And why should I do that? Don't you have the contacts there to do that? Since when did Israeli reaction to newspaper reports become a problem for the Foreign Office?'

Lynch relaxed, his hand on the table and his arm hooked over the back of the chair. 'Why should you help me? Because you and I are great pals, Paul. Because I can help you and you know it. My friends across the border have confirmed the Arafi boy was the Jericho bomber, by the way. Thought you might like to know that.'

'What Arafi boy? Who's Arafi?'

Lynch counted on his fingers like a child. 'Rashid Arafi. Son of Ghaith Arafi. Brother of Nancy Arafi. Wife of Ibrahim Dajani, brother of Emad Dajani, father of Daoud Dajani.'

He reached the seventh finger. 'Brother of Aisha Dajani. You've got to get used to these Arab families, Paul. They're spread out. Rashid Arafi was family and he worked for Ibrahim Dajani and the Israelis shot him running towards the checkpoint in Jericho set up next to the police station. Remember Jericho, Paul? Rashid Arafi killed nine people. He was wired up with enough explosive to bring down a house.'

I was still trying to make sense of the family tree. I

bought a little time to think. 'So what does that change, Gerald?'

Lynch leaned forwards again, peering intently into my face. His cold gaze was fixed on me, his voice a Northern Irish rasp.

'Rashid Arafi was no innocent bystander. He was a bomber and he's tied into the family you are so buddy-buddy with. He's part of whatever Daoud's up to, and it's a problem for Her Majesty's Government precisely because we don't like terrorists or the people who fund them. Any more than we like people stirring up trouble with wild schemes driving wedges into one of the most divisive political issues in this part of the world – the fucking water. Dajani's a two for one deal. He's up to his neck in both.'

He glared at me for a second, then rocked back on his chair, stretched his legs and got up with a small grunt. 'Tell me what's going on there. Find out from the Ministry. They're covering his arse, I know it.'

'I'm on leave.'

'Go off leave.'

'I can't.'

Lynch leered at me. 'Yes, you can. By the way, your case will be heard by a judge called Ayman Khasawneh. He's a powerful man, very respected. A reputation for upholding the law. A hardliner.'

Lynch stood by the garden table, flicking the flaky-varnished surface with his fingernails. 'He's a big pal of ours, actually. Big Anglophile. Loves coming over to the Ambassador's house for roast beef, so he does. The Ministry of Justice assigned your case to Khasawneh because there's a clampdown on public order offences right now and they don't like foreigners taking swings at their police. They even brought the case forward. It'll be heard next week. So you've got a deadline.'

'What if I don't make the deadline?'

Lynch looked straight at me, his blue eyes totally devoid of emotion. 'Find out what's happening with Dajani and the Ministry, Paul. The sooner you do, the sooner we can help you. Don't put anything in writing. You don't have to be James Bond. We just want to know what's going on and you just happen to be the boy to tell us.'

My heart raced, the anger and fear in me making my skin prick with sweat despite the cool evening air. I had a sudden urge to flee, to strike out at him, to take any action to affirm my right to a choice. But choices were a luxury denied little people like me.

Lynch patted my arm before he walked away down the steps to the road, leaving me standing by the garden table trying to contain my growing sense of horror and hopelessness.

I went into the kitchen looking for Anne, but found her in the bedroom, sitting on the bed by her packed bag. She had been crying. She got to her feet clearing the damp hair from her face as I came into the room.

'I've checked into the Hyatt, Paul. I'm leaving. I've had enough.'

The relief I felt was like slipping into the warm, gloopy waters of the Dead Sea, an almost sensuous feeling of enveloping calm. I'd paused outside the house before coming in, dreading telling her I had to go back to work. Standing alone in the garden with the city spread out below me darkening from the spectacular roseate glow of its sunset, it had been a huge effort to push open the door and face yet more of Anne's palpable disapproval of everything I had come to enjoy, of my new life in this city that had won my heart.

'I'm sorry, Anne.'

She sat back down again. Her face crumpled and reddened. I stepped towards her but she waved me away.

'No. Leave me alone. You're not sorry, Paul. You're not. You didn't want me here in the first place. You've changed and I don't like it. I don't want it. You're happy here, I can see that, but you were happier before I came. I'm no fool, Paul. This was all an awful mistake.'

She started sobbing, drawing heaving breaths, her nose blocked and her eyes streaming. I stood watching her snivel in front of me. She gushed simplicities, almost childlike, a jarring contrast to Anne the smart, hard international contract lawyer who negotiated like a pit bull. She reached across to the box of tissues on the bedside table and wiped at her face.

'I can't like this place, Paul, but you do. I don't want to be part of this. I should never have come.'

'Then you have to go,' I heard myself say to her, an awful finality in my voice I didn't mean to let out.

She hunched in on herself as if I had hit her, looked around the room slowly before looking at my feet. Her voice was small, quiet as she said: 'So that's it, then.'

I looked down at her.

Jericho. A checkpoint. Rashid Arafi running, little clouds of dust kicking up under his heels. Shouts. Shots. A fat, greasy-faced Ambassador wearing his napkin tucked into his collar, cutting into Yorkshire pudding and red beef, gulping down claret as the slight, neat Englishman with the blue-striped shirt sitting across from him laughed at his own joke. The cell, cracking paint in my fingers. Aisha smiling at me, playing with her lighter and her lips soft on my cheek, the coolness of a gold earring tapping my lips as I smelled her hair.

'Yes,' I said with someone else's voice. 'I suppose it is.'

I drove Anne to the Grand Hyatt in silence, getting out to help the concierge take her bags from the car. We stood by the open boot. I took a step towards her, but she shook her head. 'No. Don't come near me. Goodbye, Paul.'

The revolving door glittered with the lights from the street, spinning to release a party of young revellers in coats and scarves, their breath showing in little puffs as they chattered and laughed. Anne watched them with a thin smile. She turned to me as I reached up to close the boot.

'I hope she makes you happier than I did.'

I wrenched at the lid of the boot, bringing it smashing down.

'Who? Who's she? What she are you talking about, Anne? Does there have to be a *she* for you to rationalise it's over?'

Anne stepped back, clutching her bag to her chest. 'Forget it, Paul. You do what you think is right.'

'What I think is *right*? Who the fuck do you think you are? You fly in here expecting the world to be ordered just as it suits you, you swan around the place sniffing at every fucking thing you see, you bitch at me for days on end until every waking fucking moment is nothing but a space for you to fill with your disapproval then you justify it all by inventing someone else to carry the can for your own shallowness and intolerance. Get real, Anne. Smell the coffee. You fucked this up by yourself, it didn't take another woman.'

She stared back at me, her tearful blue eyes wide and

her fingers pressed into the soft brown bag. Her shoulders slumped as I looked around to see the cars piling up behind us.

The valet touched my arm. '*Khalas, sidi*' – 'Enough, stop, sir.' I rounded on him but there was nothing more than an expression of gentle, genuine concern on his face. I saw several hotel staff standing around us, stilled by the commotion. I turned to Anne.

'Goodbye, Anne.'

She said nothing, looking at me blankly before she turned and strode into the hotel, the bellboy with her bag following. He glanced at me over his shoulder, his expression as they went through the door, making it clear he thought I was a shit.

He had a point.

I drove home and drank whisky, wandering around the house and missing Anne terribly, the misunderstood tyrant mourning his loneliness. Ibrahim called and told me the court date had been brought forward and my hearing would take place next week. More good news, except Lynch had beaten him to it and Lynch knew more than Ibrahim.

I dutifully pretended it was, indeed, news to me and thanked him, hung up and poured more whisky into my glass, walking through the house into the garden, where I stood looking over the lights of the city. I went back and poured more until eventually, quite drunk, I held the heavy-based tumbler between my two fingers above the flagstone floor in the kitchen and let it fall, bright and scintillating in the halogen spots as it twisted through the air, shattering on the stone. A thousand reflective shards skittered across the floor. I went, unsteady on my feet, to bed where I lay in the darkness, trying to stop the room from spinning.

Chapter Twelve

I cleaned up the glass in the morning before going outside to gaze out over the city and get some fresh air. The leaves in the garden were glistening wet under the soft drizzle, the rolling clouds a patchwork of grey highlights and shadowed depths. I stood by the kitchen door and felt the freshness of the moisture, shivering in the cold and letting the water fall onto my face. My mind wandered over Paul Stokes and where he found himself.

The cold finally drove me inside and I took a warm shower before driving to the Ministry, feeling sick and wretched. I tried to call Anne but the hotel operator said she wasn't taking calls. I left a message for her to ring back.

I'd come to a decision standing in the rain, accepting I couldn't fight Lynch anymore, or perhaps just deciding it had all got so bad it didn't matter how much further I went down the path of deceit and self-loathing. I scanned my email over a coffee and went upstairs to the Secretary General's office suite with the vague notion of seeing if there were any papers of value lying around. It was early and there was nobody in as I strode through the small reception area where his PA sat, past Aisha's office into the larger office beyond. I hurriedly riffled through the papers on the big teak desk but found nothing exceptional or interesting.

I left in a cold sweat, closing the door quietly behind me and crept out through into the main corridor, my hand clammy against the cold metal handle. I pulled the outer door shut behind me with a sigh of relief, turning to find Aisha walking towards me with a colleague, chatting and laughing and carrying their Starbucks paper cups. She was as surprised to see me as I was to see her.

'Paul. Hi. What are you doing here?'

I managed a laugh, but my heart rate was stratospheric. 'Looking for you, actually.'

She turned to her friend. 'I'll catch up with you in a second, Maha.'

Maha walked past me into the office suite with an amused glance as Aisha smiled at me and said, 'I meant what are you doing at work?'

I tried to mask my relief. 'That's a very long story. Are you doing anything tonight?

'Nothing arranged.'

'Then I'll tell you later on. Right now I'm looking for some help on the content for issue two.'

'Let me get settled in first and I'll come down to you.'

'Great. Thanks.'

I left her and my heart rate started to slow. I took the lift down to my floor and hurriedly put together a contents list for the second issue of the magazine ready for when Aisha came down. She arrived fifteen minutes later, still wearing her coat and scarf.

She wrapped her arms around herself and chided me. 'It's cold, Paul. How can you sit there in your shirtsleeves?'

I took her hand in mine and, sure enough, hers felt warmer. She put her other hand on mine.

'You need warming up, *ya* cold Brit.'

I felt myself blushing like a teenager as I looked at her, bathing in the warmth of her gaze. We sat with our hands together, neither of us daring to move, until someone called across the office and we both remembered where we were. I snatched up the contents list and noticed Aisha doing the same. We agreed on the editorial plan and she left, touching my shoulder fleetingly as she went. I couldn't move from my desk for twenty minutes in case someone noticed the consequence of her touch.

A box of advance copies of the magazine's first issue arrived from the printing press. I scanned a copy. It looked good. It smelled good too – there's nothing quite like the smell of fresh print in all the world. I picked up a handful of them and made my way up to Abdullah Zahlan's office. I sat down with Zahlan and waited for him to go through the magazine. He flicked through the pages, nodding appreciatively.

I had come to realise Zahlan put on personalities, not just clothes and I had consequently begun to look forward to each change in his wardrobe. If I'd been back at home, I'd have started an office sweepstake on the next outfit. A little voice in my head was making a catwalk announcement as I waited for his verdict: *Today, Abdullah Zahlan wears tight, dark denim designer jeans and a white collarless shirt and is sporting this year's advertising agency executive look.*

Zahlan beamed. 'It looks very good, Paul. When does it go to distribution?'

'Saturday. These are just the advance copies. I'm glad you like it.'

'I do. And I really appreciate the way you came through on the Web stuff. It's not just me being difficult – our communities are using the Internet more and depend on print less each day. I can see why Shukri would have signed up to a print only project, but it's not part of the vision we have for a modern, accessible and transparent Ministry. I'm glad you understood that. You are working on the second one now?'

'Yes, I've brought you the draft contents, I've just been going through them with Aisha. I thought we'd focus on the water issue: the Minister seemed keen on that and there's apparently a big event, a conference about water resources, coming up in a few weeks' time, so we could use this to highlight some of the issues.'

He smiled at me as I got up to leave. 'A good idea. Let's do it. By the way, I thought you were off this week?'

I didn't miss a beat. I had already given the explanation to Aisha and it came more easily a second time. 'Well, my girlfriend was visiting from the UK but she had to go back early, a crisis at her office, so I thought I'd use the time to get ahead with the magazine.'

Zahlan beamed, walking around his desk to pump my hand. 'That's dedication, eh? Great job on the magazine, Paul. I'm glad we're working with TMG on this. I confess I was worried at first, but it's worked out really well. This will be good for Jordan.'

He had made life pretty difficult for me in the early days, querying every decision and making huge changes to the magazine at every step, let alone the great Internet content issue. I was delighted at the way he'd come round.

'I honestly couldn't have done it without your help and Aisha's. She's been fantastic.'

He smiled. 'Well, if there's anything else you need, you just have to ask.'

'Thanks, Abdullah. It's appreciated. I might need a hand convincing the Minister to have some photographs taken looking out over an aquifer or something. I know how valuable his time is right now, especially with the new cabinet and the whole water privatisation issue to deal with.'

'Yes, he's been really tied up, but the new cabinet's confirmed now. They'll announce it in the papers next week. He's free to get on with the privatisation. You've heard about it, then?'

Is espionage this easy? 'Yes, it seems to be the talk of the town right now. In the UK it'd be top secret stuff.'

Zahlan laughed. 'Nothing's secret in Amman, my good friend. Nothing. There's usually lots of guesswork going on and you'll find a hundred people who know someone who knows someone who heard it from someone else and has the answer. We're the opposite to your people: the reality gets shrouded in speculation here, not secrecy.'

I shrugged. 'So what is the reality?'

'Between us? The privatisation will be fought by two qualifying bidders who came through the first round. One's the British-led Petra-Jordanian Consortium and one's Jordanian, headed by Jerusalem Holdings. You know Aisha's brother, Daoud Dajani, yes? From what we've seen of his consortium's bid, it's highly innovative, uses some leading edge technology and research and has every chance of supplying Jordan with the water it needs through exploration and discovery of new resources and better access to old ones. The Brits are a little stronger on conservation and management experience, but the Jordanian consortium's work has really set people afire here. They're going to get our water back for us.'

Zahlan rose, his hand on a thick buff file on his desk. 'The fact is, Paul, water's something of a political hot potato around here. We've already been getting expressions of concern from our friends next door who are snooping around trying to find out what we're up to. They'd prefer we remained dependent on their handouts and we'd prefer not to trust them after the way they've handled reducing our water allocations under the 1994 peace treaty. So I'd appreciate you treating this as highly confidential, not even for your bosses in London. We're expecting to announce the winning bidders during the Dead Sea Water Conference, but it's pretty much a done deal already. And our friends next door are not going to like it one bit.'

'Our friends? The Israelis?'

Zahlan nodded, his fingers intertwined and his face serious. 'Yes, Paul. Who else? They took our water. Now we're going to get it back.'

'So we focus on water in issue two?'

'Yes, Paul, focus on water. And give the Brits plenty of coverage, would you? Make them look like favourites. I'll arrange some time with Harb for you so he can tell you how inspirational we find their approach is, no?'

I managed to hide my awe. The old fox had just confirmed the whole bid was as good as awarded and the Brits were going to get some lip service as the consolation prize. I grinned at him and Reynard grinned right back.

'Sure, Abdullah. Consider it done.'

I managed not to jump and click my heels mid-air as I said goodbye to Zahlan, but it was a close thing. Bond pulls it off, walking insouciantly away, the Ministry building in flames behind him.

I met Aisha at Grappa, the funky bar we'd last gone to with her friends when they had helped me move into the house. We shared a bottle of red wine sitting inside, all warmth and noise, the glowing interior fuggy with smoke. The sky had been dark all day, roiling black clouds deadened the light in the city, brooding over us all as we scurried about our business, dulling the afternoon and ushering in the cold night.

Aisha was fiddling with her lighter again. 'How did it go with Anne?'

'I told you a lie this morning, Aish. She hasn't gone home. She's still in Amman. We argued and she went to stay at the Hyatt.'

'All over? Just like that?'

I put my hand on hers to stop her twisting the lighter and left it there because I wanted to.

'It was pretty messy, to tell you the truth. Anne didn't like Jordan at all and we both found we had grown apart since I came out here. It was a disaster from beginning to end.'

'Were you sad?'

'No, not really. I drove her to the Hyatt and she said some stuff that made me mad so I ended up shouting at her in front of everyone.' I caught Aisha's troubled expression. 'I'm not particularly proud of that bit, incidentally.'

'So what did you do afterwards?'

'I drank some whisky and went to bed. I broke a tumbler in the kitchen.'

'Because you were drunk?'

'Yes, but not by accident. I just dropped it.'

'How metaphorical of you, Paul. You have a talent for drama.'

'Not intended metaphorically.'

'Hmm.' She poured us both more wine from the bottle on the table. 'So what are you going to do now?'

'I don't know, Aish. She's due to leave tomorrow. I tried calling, but she hasn't returned any of my calls. She's probably got an earlier flight in any case. Anyway, I don't know what I'd say to her.'

'How about starting with, "Sorry?"'

I sat back. 'Well, that's part of the problem, isn't it? Because I am and I'm not. I didn't want the scene outside the Hyatt to happen and I didn't want to take my anger out on her. But if I'm truthful, I'm actually glad she's gone and I can't pretend to her or anyone else I'm not. We have nothing whatsoever in common anymore and she made it really unpleasant for us both.'

'And you didn't?'

'No, I don't think I did. I tried very hard. But the harder I tried, the more she seemed to reject everything around her.'

Aisha lit a cigarette and blew the smoke up into the air. Her gaze was cool. 'And you couldn't have helped her to try and understand it, to make allowances for this little country of ours? To at least give her some time to become used to the fact you have changed?' Aisha waggled her lighter at me. 'And you *have* changed, Paul.'

'I did try. I think she'd set her heart against here from the first second which just meant she hated it and was against all of the things I've come to love here.'

'So it's over.'

'Yes, it is.'

'Simple as that. Shout at her, throw her out and Paul's off the hook.'

I was surprised to find Aisha taking Anne's side in this. I'd somehow expected her to be pleased rather than mad at me.

'No, Aish, not that simple. I've changed and she hasn't. I found myself trying to work out what we ever did have in common. I've come to realise I don't like her friends, I don't share her values. And now I can't for the life of me work out how we ever came to believe it could last. It's as if we had never shared anything more than...'

Anything more than what? A bed? Hotel room weekends with champagne and room service and so much boisterous, noisy lovemaking that on one occasion the staff had audibly tutted when we checked out? Paphos and nights of Retsina-fuelled passion? The movies, the laughter, the walks together?

Aisha was combative. 'Than what?'

'Oh, I don't know. Just anything.'

'You're very eloquent except when you're talking about your own feelings, aren't you?' She wasn't smiling. 'You can be a very cold Brit, Paul.'

I had nothing to say to her, just sat looking at my hands joined on the rough table top as her long, steady regard burned into the top of my head. I looked up but found it hard to hold her gaze and dropped my eyes first. I fiddled with my wine glass, looking at the orange glow of the lights shimmering on the surface of the liquid.

'Paul.' Aisha paused until I met her glare. 'Paul, if you ever do that to me I will find you, wherever you are, and I will fuck you up.'

Her eyes were rock steady on mine and I felt like a rabbit in headlights until she smiled and was beautiful, raising her drink to me. I clinked mine against it, sealing the past and ringing in the future with the clean, bright sound of glass on glass.

We walked arm in arm from the bar. I was still in shock as we headed downhill back to my place, my mind whirling with possibilities and Aisha's intimate proximity. I breathed in the heavy richness of her perfume, her hair brushing my cheek. Her skin was warm and soft in the cold air. I stopped and she turned to me, her face raised. The first drops of rain fell, plucking up little explosions of dust in the gutter.

We kissed.

We walked on, giggling and clutching each other but the house was ten minutes away and the falling rain strengthened. It was too far back to the bar and get a cab, too far to get home dry. The rain battered down and we split up to run. Aisha clattered to an unsteady halt, tottering in her heels. The water rushed down the street.

'Come on, we're going to get soaked,' I shouted at her.

'We are already soaked. How can you get wetter than this?' she retorted, pirouetting in the rain and laughing, her face held up to the sky so the droplets glistened on her cheeks in the streetlight. She span, dancing to her own rhythm, laughing and beckoning to me. I grabbed her hand and tried to pull her towards the house. She held back, her face radiant with laughter. I felt her in my arms and the rain didn't matter anymore as I bent to her warm lips and pressed them against mine, feeling her yield and open to me.

The water swept down the street in waves, the drumming of the rain was all around us, pattering on the leaves, hissing on the tarmac, the street lighting hazy in the downpour. We stood, our eyes locked, Aisha's flickering as she tried to read my expression.

Aisha murmured to me, 'Come on, *ya* Brit. I'm getting wet. And I don't mean in a good way. Take me home.'

She flicked her hair back over her head. Her mascara was running and blackened her hands as she brushed the rain from her face. She glared at them and wiped them on her hips, leaving two black smudges on the denim. She growled in irritation. 'Ah, shit.' She punched my arm. 'It's not funny, you English bastard.'

We reached home and wrenched our shoes and

jackets off. I fetched a towel. Aisha pulled a mirror out of her bag and gazed at herself in mock horror. 'Look at me. I'm like a clown.'

She grabbed her long hair in a bunch and pulled her hand down it, letting a little shower of droplets spatter on the kitchen floor. Her clothes stuck to her, steaming in the heat from the secret Jordanian space project stove.

'Here,' I said. 'Take a shower and throw your clothes out, I'll dry them against the stove.'

She laughed and wagged a finger at me. 'Me Arab girl, *ya* Brit. Is not zis easy.'

She put her hand on my cheek, moved towards me and we were kissing again, long, sweet warm kisses filling me with a wonderment reflected in Aisha's face as my hands slipped into her jacket and the rising beat of our intimacy become deeper and more exciting, my hands on her hips, moving up her sides and hers in my hair, drawing me to her as our tongues danced together.

Aisha broke away, her finger on my lips. 'I meant it, Paul. I have to go. Thank you, a million thank yous for tonight, but I have to go home now.'

My frustration must have been smeared across my face because she put her hand on my cheek and reached up to kiss me again. 'There's all the time in the world, Paul. But not tonight.'

Long after she had left, her perfume lingering, I stood in the kitchen reliving the feel of Aisha's nipple, hard under my sweeping thumb.

Chapter Thirteen

Abdullah Zahlan had arranged my meeting with the Minister the next day, so I found myself sitting on the leather sofa outside Harb Al Hashemi's office, drinking a little gold-rimmed glass of thyme *zaatar* tea as I waited for the big panelled doors to open. When they did, a little grey-haired man in a blue-grey suit shot out, a pile of papers clutched in his arm as he paddled a fussy wave of effusive thanks and *effendi*'s to Al Hashemi's crisp, efficient secretary, who ignored him.

'You can go in, now, MrStokes.'

I peered through the half-open door and saw Harb Al Hashemi sat at his desk. He looked up and beckoned me.

'Good morning, Minister.'

'Paul. Good to see you again. How's the magazine going?'

We shook hands and he gestured to me to sit. He was wearing a sharp grey suit with a pale silk tie, his cufflinks expensive and his hands manicured. He was precise in his movements, a man in control who could afford to be friendly and informal.

We settled into platitudes for a while before I started recording, taking the opportunity to confirm everything Zahlan had told me about the water privatisation by asking oblique questions, which Al Hashemi answered in his usual frank and forthright manner. He confided in me more than I had any right to expect, a privilege accorded to a foreigner removed from the political battles he was fighting against the reactionary forces resisting the push to modernise.

We talked for almost an hour. About the distribution

crisis, the fact that only the area of Amman I lived in actually had piped water, much of the city fed by a constant stream of little bowsers driving in from distribution points. We talked about the farms in the countryside dying because of a lack of water fit for irrigation. About the Israelis and the water assurances in the peace treaty the Jordanians believed their neighbours had abrogated. Al Hashemi was passionate as he described the crisis of rapidly depleting resources, Jordan's desperation for a solution and how the privatisation was intended to revitalise the whole network.

The interview concluded, I switched off my recorder. He removed his steel-rimmed glasses with a sigh and rubbed his eyes.

'Thank you, Minister. I've talked to Clive Saunders at Anglo-Jordanian, so we'll write it up into a bigger piece looking at the whole water issue and the solutions being proposed.'

Al Hashemi sat back at his big, oak desk. 'The privatisation has taken years to get this far, Paul. I'll be glad to have the whole award settled at the Dead Sea conference. We can get on to other items on the agenda then. And there are plenty of them.'

'Abdullah Zahlan seemed to think it's pretty much a done deal anyway.'

Al Hashemi's face darkened, his eyebrows furrowed. He brought his hands together. 'That is not the case, Paul. This is an open, transparent and fair process.'

I dropped my eyes. I thought I'd gone too far. I looked up to apologise, but Al Hashemi stared out of the window.

'Paul, we're going to be fair to the bidders, but the Jerusalem Consortium has some big innovations to bring to the table, including ways of recovering water that will benefit both Jordan and our friends in the West Bank. It's hard to compare the two bids as apples to apples. One is visionary and brilliant and one is professional but doesn't address our longer term needs.' He tapped the desk for emphasis. 'But these bids will be treated fairly and openly and honestly by a committee tasked with evaluating them.'

He stood and so did I, smiling.

'Yes, Minister.'

I met Lynch the next day. I had gone home after my meeting with the Minister and written everything down while it was still fresh in my mind. I recalled Lynch telling me to report verbally, but there was so much information I felt it best to document all thirty shillings worth: the confirmation of Al Hashemi's post and therefore the privatisation, details of the water bids from Zahlan, the strong feeling in the Ministry that the Jordanian consortium was technically so far ahead of the Brits and the fact whatever they were proposing was about extracting additional water resources and would not go down well with the Israelis. I had also added Zahlan's comment about getting the water back.

If I thought Lynch would be delighted. I couldn't have been more wrong. We sat in his car together, his hand on the manila envelope I had handed to him.

'What's this?'

'I wrote it all down.'

He held the stapled sheaf of paper, his knuckles white. I could see the edges of the paper trembling. 'Where is this document held?'

I could hear the sulkiness in my voice. I couldn't

believe the Irish bastard's ingratitude. 'On my laptop.'

'Where is that?'

'At home.'

'Did you email this anywhere?'

'No. It's just on my hard disk.'

'Did you back it up?'

'No.'

'Did you connect to the Ministry network with this document on your hard disk?'

'No.'

'Go back home now and erase it. Empty the recycle bin. Write files over it. Defragment the hard disk. This document never existed. You understand me? You report verbally, you commit nothing in writing.' He was red-faced. 'I fucking told you that.'

He turned to me, holding the wheel to support himself as he did, his bloodshot eyes unwavering. 'Do you understand me, Paul? If you get caught you're looking at life in an Arab jail and we won't lift a finger to help you. We'll drop you faster than a lead fucking Zeppelin.'

I was caught in his glare, dropping my own eyes under the onslaught. 'Yes, I understand you.'

He waited until I looked up, holding my eyes for a long time, his face impassive, before giving a tight smile. 'Okay, okay. I'll read this and call you if I've got any questions.'

Lynch dropped my report into its envelope and slid it into the door pocket. He put the car into drive and pulled out of the car park outside the Abdoun Mall, the place he had chosen for our meeting.

'I'll drop you at the Intercon, you can get a cab from there.'

Whether that was field craft or convenience was

something I never knew with Lynch. 'Fine.'

'Your case comes up for trial this week, doesn't it?'

I hated Lynch's habit of asking questions when he knew the answers. 'Yes, you know it does. Tuesday.'

He drove in silence for a while, stopping at a traffic light and looking out at the oncoming cars. 'You and the Dajani girl are an item.'

For a second my mind went into freefall as I wondered how the hell he'd known. Aisha and I had been careful not to let our closeness show in public – she was worried about Daoud's possible reaction, a worry I shared.

I kept my voice light. 'No, not really. We just get along.'

'Funny, you should be. She's a peach.'

'I told you, I've got a girlfriend already.'

'She left you.'

I struggled to conceal my irritation at his casual invasion. 'Is that commercial information too?'

He chuckled. 'Sure, it is. You seen anything of Daoud Dajani?'

'No, not much.'

We'd reached the Intercontinental Hotel. Lynch stopped the car and looked across at me, his expression earnest and intense.

'I want you to get me a copy of the Jerusalem Consortium bid for the privatisation, Paul. Dajani's bid.'

I froze, searching Lynch's face for clues he was joking. He looked straight back at me.

'I thought you didn't want James Bond stuff.'

'You've done well. You obviously have a talent for this.'

'You just spent twenty minutes slagging me off for it.'

'Paper thinking is a liability in the information age,

Paul. You don't store sensitive information on unprotected computers. Just remember that.'

'Stealing bid documents is a really big ask.'

'Have a try. It's valuable information. There's a lot riding on it in the long term.'

'Valuable? You're bribing me to do it? Is that it, Gerald? Stokes will steal for money?'

'It's on the table anyway, Paul. So I'd take it if I were you.'

'No. No, I don't think so. I don't mind giving you chickenfeed, but I'm not going to start stealing documents for you. I'm in enough trouble already. Thanks all the same.'

I got out of the car. Lynch called across the roof at me and I turned. His face was screwed up in fury as he stabbed his finger at me.

'You are being fucking stupid, Paul. You have no choices anymore. Do you understand me?' He emphasised his words with stabs. 'You have no choices.'

Monday. Another day at work, another long and pointless phone call with Robin, who considered email Satan's spawn and preferred to lock me up in pointless team building-style pep talks before dumping me with some new mad scheme his ad sales team had dreamed up. It was like red sky at morning, a call from Robin. He was being particularly solicitous so I wasn't surprised when he told me he had some nice extra work for me to do. The British Business Group had contacted TMG and asked about producing a yearbook for British companies in the Middle East, apparently. A three-year contract. Robin was, of course, delighted. They had asked specifically that I edit it and TMG had agreed. Of course, as Robin was so fast to assure me, because I was their very bestest, cleverest boy.

I wondered what would happen when my refusal to get what Lynch wanted filtered through to his contacts in the British Business Group. A *Carpe Diem* moment led me to ask Robin for a raise and, to my absolute consternation, he agreed instantly.

Aisha dropped by at my desk for a chat, a smile breaking out on her lovely face as she looked down at me, holding a file pressed up against her left breast.

'What are you grinning about, *ya* Brit? You're supposed to be in court tomorrow. Shouldn't you be biting your nails or something?'

'I just got a raise.'

'Clever boy! Listen, I have to get on. Do you fancy coming over to our house for dinner?'

I grinned all the more widely. Stokes the Cheshire Cat.

'That'd be great.'

'Nothing fancy, just family, but I thought it would take your mind off tomorrow.'

I laughed. 'I'm done worrying, Aish. It is the will of Allah now.'

'And maybe you could ask Daoud if he would allow you to take me over to see Mariam at the farm at the weekend?'

A momentary wave of concern hit me, an alarmed thought about how safe I would be, but it had been quiet since the Jericho bomb and the inevitable reprisals, a gunship attack on a car in the ruined, dusty streets of Gaza that killed four people. That had all been two weeks ago, just as Anne had left for home without a word. Two weeks. It seemed like a lifetime ago. One of my childhood games cut in: if you get off at the trial, you'll be safe at the farm.

'That'd be great. But what if tomorrow goes badly?'

She frowned. 'It won't, Paul. Ibrahim's on top of it. He says it'll be over and done with quickly. You still have your passport and you're free to travel. Don't worry. Seriously. How about eight o'clock?'

'Eight,' I confirmed, taking her hand and squeezing it. I wanted to scoop her up in my arms, but we had agreed on our 'Ministry Rules.'

'Thanks, Aish.'

She exaggerated the swing of her hips as she left me, turning and flashing me a glance that made me shiver.

I went back to brooding about my day in court. I hadn't been strictly truthful with Aisha about my feelings on that one. Robin's agreement to pay me almost eight grand more had brought the first smile to my face that day, but I had been up most of the previous night staring into the darkness and playing out likely scenarios as I tried to sleep. I was worried sick about returning to a stinking jail cell.

Nour smiled knowingly as I helped her to take back the dishes to the kitchen after the meal. 'Aisha's very happy these days, Paul,' she said, her eyes on mine as she put the pile of plates onto the drainer. 'Things must be good at work.'

'The magazine's going really well, yes. Aisha's been a fantastic help. I couldn't have got the project together without her. Honestly.'

'That's good. It's given her something to get… involved in.' She smiled. 'And you mustn't worry about Daoud.' She put her hand on my forearm. 'He's a good man.'

Well, there at least we disagreed. Daoud still worried me, his intensity and seriousness always had me on edge. The fact he had almost been genial throughout the evening was even more worrying. Daoud left the table and came over to me as I walked back into the dining room. I noticed Aisha and Mariam had left the room.

'Let's get a comfortable seat,' he said. He smiled, a new sight to me. Nour brought coffee in gold-decorated porcelain cups arranged on an ornate tray.

Daoud sat back and lit a cigarette, offering me one. I took it. Damn the Jordanians and their smoking.

'Harb thinks a lot of you. He was singing your praises the other day, wondering whether I'd met you yet.'

Harb. First names for the Minister, a member of the Cabinet, a Minister of State and a moment of sheer disassociation for Paul Stokes. I imagined myself sitting back with a fag, puffing out blue smoke saying to someone in the UK: 'The PM noticed you in the Commons today. He really loves your nails, Marjorie.'

I smiled at him. 'I like him too. He's very frank.'

'Maybe too frank sometimes. It's lonely being a reformer, even though there are more of them these days. This government's still very conservative.'

'So he said. But they seem to have committed to the whole idea of liberalisation.'

I really did have to be careful about my big and expanding head. It's a long way from being Robin Goodyear's bitch to chatting about government policy over coffee with Arab millionaires.

Daoud smiled. 'Yes, they are. We've got quite a lot riding on that right now, there are some big contracts being talked about. We're well positioned to win them. We're investing a lot. It'll be good for Jordan.'

I wondered how many salary raises this conversation

would be worth and hated myself just a little bit more. I sat and talked with Daoud about the water contracts and about the interviews I'd done with the various players, the ministry people and the consultants who were working on the privatisation project.

I found myself relaxing and chatting freely, whether a result of the whisky, Daoud's own relaxation or the comfortable warmth of the room I wasn't sure. My outsider's view of people he had known all his life obviously tickled Daoud and he laughed out loud when I told him about the disastrous interview I'd had with the Minister of Planning that morning.

'So you thought he was *haughty*? That's a good word, haughty.'

I pulled myself up from the depths of the sofa, my elbow on my knee and chopping the air with the flat of my hand, speaking in heavily accented Arab English. 'You are going too deep with this question. You will drown us with details. Focus on this good for Jordan, not always the broblems. Always you British bress you focus on the broblems. You must to open your mind.'

Daoud laughed at my impersonation, but his laughter died quickly. 'He's a good man, though, Paul. His heart is good.'

'Oh, I'm sure. But Harb is more my idea of a progressive man, a reformer. I suppose he's more... sophisticated.'

'Oh, don't underestimate Qasim. He's leading the whole reform movement. He's just a little older. But he's closer to the conservatives, to the street. He gets more done with less conflict than Harb.'

I sipped at my little cup of strong coffee. 'Do you think you can take the water bid?'

'Yes. I know we can. We're a million miles ahead of

the British when it comes to our technical bid and they know it. In fact, it's something of a worry. The British don't always play fair in Jordan, you know.'

Ah, the cunning British. The Arabs have never lost their view of the '*Breets*' as cunning, Machiavellian strategists. What I found odd was how such a bunch of muckle-headed chinless wonders with their classical educations, convictions of racial superiority and love of brown boys' pert arses could ever be seen as cunning.

I said as much to Daoud. 'Ah,' he said, smiling a rueful smile. 'But maybe we have to demonise them. Imagine, if we took your view of these people, the Storrs and Glubbs, Philbys and Lawrences. Imagine how little it would make us, to have been conquered by these creatures. We'd rather build them up to be cunning and forceful. At least it would explain how they could take everything away from us.'

Which is one way of looking at it. I smiled, but Daoud's expression stayed serious and earnest and his voice urgent.

'Paul, we have found new ways to gain access to deep water resources that will help to rebalance Jordan's position on the water map of the region. We've been using some of the most sophisticated deep geophysical mapping systems in the world, systems developed to explore for oil and gas in the Gulf. Because of our partners, we can combine that ability to see further underground than ever before with cutting edge French micro-boring technology. We know where the deep water is and where it flows and that it flows through Jordanian land. We can tap into those aquifers before they rise across the border. You see? We can keep our water, we can seize it back from them.'

I was taken aback by the fire in Daoud's voice. 'Can

you make it work? I mean, you've not only got physical constraints but political ones too.'

My question merely fanned his passion. Daoud's hand was on my shoulder as he leaned forwards, his eyes locked on mine and his fervour drawing me in.

'I know we can do it if we win the privatisation bid. I know we can make it work. Together with the backing of our government, which we absolutely have, we can do it. And it's vital, not just for the consortium but for Jordan's future. We can get back most of the water they took from us in 1967 and the same technology will let the people in the West Bank reassert their right to their own water so their farms can live again. Farms like our own, on the very border with Israel and divided by that wall, will die unless we get water. And I can give it to them, I know I can. I can make water flow throughout the land.'

He was mesmeric, his passion both contagious and persuasive. At that moment, I was with him, watching the trails of fresh, clean water sparkling between the olive trees on the Dajani farm as they brought the desert back to life. I was watching glittering droplets flying in the sunshine as children played in the cool shower.

Daoud stubbed out his cigarette in the heavy crystal ashtray and I took the opportunity to slip in my request. 'Aisha mentioned visiting the farm. She is keen for me to go there and perhaps to understand more about what shapes people in Jordan. I wasn't sure if it was…' I struggled for the right word. 'Appropriate.'

Daoud positively beamed. Paul is learning, his expression said. Paul is asking my permission and even doing it like a good Arab, slipping it in at the end of the conversation. 'I think it would be a good idea. Tell me when you would like to go. We can help to ease the crossing.'

'*Wasta.*'

'Yes.' He slapped my leg delightedly. '*Wasta.*'

'We were thinking of going at the weekend.'

'Great. I'll let Hamad know. Mariam will be delighted to meet you, I know. Don't worry about the paperwork. Selim over at my office will get you all the permits and passes sorted out.'

'Thank you, Daoud.'

Standing, Daoud put an arm on my shoulder. 'Paul, I don't want to make Aisha unhappy. I wouldn't see her harmed for anything, in any way.' He turned serious again. 'Please, Paul. Take care of her.'

Daoud was smiling, his words meant kindly and so I thanked him, as much to hide my confusion as through any sense of gratitude.

'I will, Daoud. Thank you.'

Thank you for trying. Thank you for being so direct. Thank you for smiling. Thank you for letting me know at the same time you'll break every bone in my body if I let her down without actually saying a word about it.

As if on cue, the women appeared to say goodbye. I caught Aisha's calculating glance at Daoud. An instant later she was beside me on the doorstep, a look of pure delight on her face.

'Clever Brit,' she whispered. 'Good luck tomorrow.'

Fast and light as a darting bird, her lips brushed mine and she went back inside. I was left alone on the doorstep wondering where I'd find a Lonely Planet guide to the West Bank.

Chapter Fourteen

If I had expected my court case to be a grand affair, I was to be disappointed. For weeks I'd worried about the outcome of this day and yet it seemed like any other, a little sunnier perhaps, but a cool Amman October day for all that.

Ibrahim met me outside the courthouse accompanied by his lawyer, Tariq Al Bashir. We all shook hands and made small talk on the broad stone steps leading up to the courthouse building as Ibrahim smoked his cigarette. Al Bashir had pretty impressive credentials – Aisha had told me he had managed Daoud's case after he was picked up by the *Mukhabarat* on the Syrian border. It had been Al Bashir's brilliance, together with Ibrahim's influence, that had secured Daoud's release and had the charge of conspiracy against him dropped. I could only hope the same would be true in my case.

Al Bashir's predatory stare, heavy eyebrows and curved nose reminded me of a bird of prey. I later discovered his nickname was in fact *Al Saqr* – The Falcon. He was confident the case would be thrown out on today's hearing alone but no matter what his reputation, I could not bring myself to share his certainty. I was consumed by visions of disaster, wearing my only suit, uncomfortable and sweating despite the cool breeze. Although I had prepared myself as much as possible over the past few days, I was frightened, my nerves were shrieking and my senses heightened so every touch or sound made my heart jump. I felt Ibrahim's hand on my shoulder as I mounted the stone steps. It was more of a comfort than his bluff attempts at reassuring me. An even number of steps confirmed my concern. I had banked on odd for a good result.

We stood as the judges filed in, the last of the three men and by far the most commanding. I noticed Ibrahim whispering furiously to Al Bashir. He was pale and looked shocked, stroking his grey moustache distractedly.

'What is it?'

Al Bashir leaned across, whispering, 'It is the wrong presiding judge. We understood another man would hear this case. I am very sorry. This is not what we had expected.'

'Who's this?'

'This is Ayman Khasawneh.'

I felt as if someone were looking at me and turned to catch Khasawneh's glare. He barked something in Arabic and everyone sat. My trial had started and I couldn't understand a word. I looked around the stark room as a court official got up to speak, presumably reading out the charge. I caught sight of a familiar figure sitting in the public seats, his eyes on the judge. Gerald Lynch didn't even spare me a glance.

I had never in my life felt so impotent as I did sitting in that courthouse as these men debated my future around me, their guttural Arabic echoing in the bare room. A fat, fussy little man in a beige jacket took to his feet and started reading from a sheaf of papers in Arabic as Al Bashir leaned across to me and whispered, 'This has all just been procedural. The prosecution will read the charges now.'

The prosecutor's voice droned on in Arabic for a little before Al Bashir sprung to his feat, making me jump as he slammed his hand down on the table and cried out in rage. Khasawneh shouted back at him, his hand in the air as Ibrahim also took to his feet. The prosecutor was shouting now and the judges were all standing. Khasawneh smashed his gavel into the desktop in front of him. It was instant pandemonium and I sat, bewildered and uncomprehending as the red-faced men shook fists at each other, Khasawneh shouting above everyone else before wheeling around and leaving the room followed by the other judges. Al Bashir and Ibrahim were bent towards each other, talking urgently. Al Bashir pointed across at the prosecutor, who was making a great show of playing with his papers. I spoke, my voice sounding oddly small and thin after the outbursts of furious shouting I had just witnessed.

'Would anyone mind telling me what's going on here?'

Al Bashir sat, turning to face me.

'Yes, Paul, I'm sorry. The prosecutor has laid two charges against you. One of assaulting a police officer and one of possessing a small amount of cannabis. They are claiming the reason the officer stopped you was to search you for the drugs and you resisted arrest. They are asking for the maximum penalty. It is a substantial prison term.'

I looked at him in astonishment, my mind racing to try and find some possible explanation for the charge, every muscle in my body taut and my hands clasped between my legs. My voice was reduced to a hoarse whisper.

'It's a total lie. It's not true.' I struggled for words. 'It's a fabrication. How can they do this? Ibrahim knows, he saw the original charge sheet, saw me sign it.'

'I appreciate this. The prosecutor has broken all procedure in bringing a charge they haven't notified us of and I don't think they'll be able to make the drugs charge stand in law whatever happens, but it is a very unfortunate escalation of the case. Khasawneh has adjourned the court until tomorrow. Ibrahim will make a written statement now and we will submit this to the judge this evening.'

Something snapped inside me. I sprang to my feet, my arm outstretched in accusation and shouted 'Liar' across at the prosecution lawyer. Ibrahim restrained me, his heavy arm around my shoulder and I breathed in his musky aftershave as I leaned on the table, gasping for air. The prosecution lawyer busied himself in his papers before he glanced furtively around him and left the room.

I looked over to the public gallery. Lynch had gone.

The tension left me and I collapsed against Ibrahim's shoulder, hot tears of rage and frustration shaming me as he patted my back.

I didn't go back to work, but drove up onto the Citadel, sitting on a fallen column, looking out over the bustling city below me, smoking and reliving the courtroom, reprising my memories of arriving in Jordan and being arrested, replaying the scenes again and again until I had finished the packet, leaving a scattering of white butts around me. I got up and headed for home.

I was fishing in my pocket for my key when I noticed Lars' front door open at the top of the flight of iron stairs up the side of the house. Finding my key, I was in two minds whether to mind my own business or just nip and check things out. I started up the steps, but stopped halfway and called out to him. His reply was a cracked moan of pain that had me leaping up the remaining steps and standing breathless at his door as the sound died on his lips.

His room was a mess, computer equipment and toppled racks of electronics strewn everywhere. What had been neat minimalism looked like a junkyard. In the middle of it all lay Lars. There was a lot of blood.

I ran over to him and put my hand on his arm, not quite knowing what to do. I waited as his eyes opened painfully and focused on me, helping him to struggle to a seated position. I went to the bathroom and wet a towel and tried to clean up his face as best I could.

'What the hell happened?'

'There were two guys here when I got home. I took some time off this afternoon, got here early. They were messing with my gear.'

Lars gulped twice, then turned away and threw up. I got him another towel and a bottle of water from the kitchen.

'Will I call the ambulance?'

He shook his head, painfully. 'No, don't think so.'

'So you had a go, then?'

'I shouted at them. I think they will stop or panic or something. I'm not sure what. I never been burgled before. And in daylight. There was a fat guy and a thin guy, like Laurel and Hardy. The thin guy just stayed messing with my gear, the fat guy came over to me. They were wearing face-hats. He came over to me and just beat the shit out of me, deliberate, not angry. The last thing I remember is them trashing the place and kicking me on the way out.'

'Who were they?'

His face darkened. 'How the fuck can I know, Paul? They didn't leave business cards, did they?'

'Sorry, sorry. Stupid question. But they must have had a reason, must have been after something?'

Lars gestured to the wreckage around him. 'Whatever it was, they weren't here to steal stuff. Look, you wanna fix me a whisky?'

When I got back from the kitchen holding two tumblers he'd propped himself up against the wall with his hands on his legs to support him. I righted one of his black and chrome chairs and he eased himself into it before taking the tumbler.

'Thanks. Glad you came by.'

His face glowed red on one side, his lip split and a livid bruise forming around his eye and temple. He had a gash on the back of his head and his hands were cut. The state of his knuckles told me it hadn't been an entirely one way conversation.

'You look awful. Will I take you down to A and E?'

'No, I'm okay.

I looked around. 'Why on earth would they want to do this?'

'I don't know, but like I say, they weren't thieves. This stuff is worth thousands. A thief runs, he doesn't step up to you and start punching.' Lars grimaced. 'And the guy doing the punching was good at it. Real good.'

'Were they trying to get at your computer?'

'Must have been. But why? There's nothing special about it, but the encryption software I use and the line down to your place.'

Lars had set up a flylead and a wireless link to my place downstairs – being a telecoms freak, he had a hyper-fast, multi-megabit Internet line and hadn't paid a bill for it since he had moved to Amman. He'd been kind enough to extend that privilege to me soon after I moved in.

I kept quiet, but his words hit home. There was nothing special about Lars except his connection to me.

And it had got him beaten up.

I caught his look. Lars had made the connection at the same time I had. I dropped my eyes.

'Right,' he said softly. I heard him drink from the glass I could hear his hand shaking in the clink of the ice.

'Lars...'

'Paul, drop it. It doesn't matter. Whatever you're up to with your Mr Lynch of the British Embassy, just leave me out of it. You hear? It's not my problem. The less I know the better off I will be, I think, no?'

My mouth was dry, the drink untouched in my hand. I looked up at his battered face. Lars smiled, a tight, bitter smile.

'You're a good man. Just watch your back well, you hear? These people are crazy. Hell, fuck, I'm crazy.' He grinned angrily. 'We all crazy, right?'

He drained his glass and got shakily to his feet. To my surprise, he held out his hand. I took it and we shook. He turned and slowly, painfully started to clear up. I left him without a word.

I walked down the iron stairs, the handrail cold in the evening air, but didn't go into my own house. I sat at the garden table, lit up a cigarette and called Lynch.

'Paul.'

'I've had enough. I want to meet.'

'Sure, Paul. You just at a loose end or have you got something in mind?'

'You saw what happened today. You were behind it.'

'Okay, Paul. Let's meet at TGI's, the Marriott. At eight.'

I finished my cigarette, luxuriating in the last rays of the setting sun and listening to the rustling of the vine leaves as the cool breeze caught them. I went indoors to catch the news and freshen up.

*

The bar was noisy and beery, a warm contrast to the cool evening outside. People chattered over a background of daft pop music and chose from unfeasibly large plastic-laminated menus. I sat in the corner with Lynch.

'I'll try to get the Jerusalem Consortium bid documents for you. But only if you have this case dropped.'

'I don't think you're in any position to be making demands here, Paul.' Lynch looked around the bar with a look of mild puzzlement, as if he had just realised where he was. I waited for him to come back but he looked down at his glass for a long time, gently tapping his signet ring against it to the rhythm of the music.

I had been rehearsing this for hours in my mind. The last thing the bastard would expect was I'd push back. And so that's precisely what I did, although the little Brit in my mind screamed at me to give in, capitulate, throw in the towel. I drew a breath.

'Well, you'd be wrong, Gerald. You see, I think you've pushed it too far. As far as I can make out, I'm in trouble whatever I do. If I tell you to fuck off, I'll go down for assault. They won't make the drugs charge stick. If I play along with you, you'll have me by the short and curlies for all time. And I really don't want that. So this is how it's going to be. You want the Jerusalem document, the case goes away. And so do you.'

I wondered if I'd overplayed it. I looked at Lynch to gauge his reaction but he wasn't looking at me. He was signalling a waitress for a refill. She smiled at him and he winked lewdly.

'What if you can't deliver, Paul?'

'I can deliver. I know where it is and how it's

secured,' I lied with a facility that surprised me.

He turned to face me, still leering. 'And what if I can't change the way your case is going? Had you perhaps thought of that? What if I'm not able to wander around telling Jordanian judges what to do?'

'You said it yourself, that Khasawneh was your man. You can fix it. Because you bloody broke it in the first place.'

His drink arrived and he lifted the glass, looking at me over the foamy head of the lager for a second before drinking.

'Okay, Paul. I'll have a word. But you deliver on the Jerusalem document in full or I'll hang you out to dry. In a friendly way, you understand.'

'And call off your thugs. No more break-ins.'

He was stilled in an instant, watching, wary. 'What thugs?'

'The two bully boys in balaclavas who broke in upstairs and beat the living shit out of my neighbour.'

He shook his head. 'Sorry, son, not mine. Not house style. We don't do heavy-handed stuff like that unless we're occupying military. I can't help you there. Sounds like local talent.'

I stood, tossing a note on the table to cover the beers, and left, my hands damp with sweat and my heart pumping in my chest so loudly the whole world could surely hear it.

I waited in the courthouse, my head in my hands, listening to the undisciplined noise of the place, low voices, shuffling feet and doors banging. A mobile went off somewhere in the public gallery and its owner left the room with it to his ear.

Tariq Al Bashir and the prosecution's counsel, the fussy little man I had shouted at the previous morning, had been called to the judge's chambers, the court session suspended pending the result of whatever they were discussing. All I could do was wait. Ibrahim had gone outside for a smoke and had just returned, reeking of aftershave, hair lotion and cigarettes, when Al Bashir came back. He was elated.

'Okay, here's the deal, Paul. Khasawneh has offered a plea bargain. If you plead guilty to an attempted assault charge, he'll throw out the drugs one. He won't press for the full penalty and will accept extenuating circumstances.'

'But that makes me guilty. I'm not guilty.'

Ibrahim's smoker's rumble cut in. 'Paul, this has not gone as well as I had expected. Someone else is pulling the string here and I cannot do much about it. I think you are best to accept what they have offered.'

'What's the implication, Tariq? What's the sentence?'

'The drugs charge carried a ten-year term. An assault charge against an officer would have meant at least two years. Attempted assault would be a maximum of three months, extenuating circumstances would maybe not even be a custodial sentence. We'll have to see when this gets to sentencing. But he was signalling pretty strongly back there that he just wants this out of his courthouse quickly.'

'So what happened to the hanging judge?'

Tariq shrugged, rubbing his chin. 'I don't know. There's something about this case he doesn't like and he just wants rid of us.' He laughed grimly. 'And we want rid of us too, no?'

'But what about the Ministry? The papers will carry the sentence, won't they?'

Ibrahim shook his head. 'I can deal with it, trust me. Accept the deal and this will finally all be over.'

I felt stupid, naive and trapped. I cast around me for some sort of inspiration, something to help me. I found Lynch, sitting in the public gallery. He nodded, the briefest dip of his head. Every man has his price and I had just found mine.

'Okay. Let's do it.'

Al Bashir disappeared into the door at the back of the courthouse again. After a full ten minutes spent watching the motes of dust in the sunbeams penetrating the gloom of the courthouse from its high windows, I watched him re-emerge, followed by the three judges. Al Bashir joined us as the judges took their places, the courtroom sitting on Khasawneh's signal. He started to talk to the room in general, his voice rising.

Ibrahim's smoker's breath was on me as he whispered. 'He says this case should never have come here. You should never have been arrested originally.'

He paused as the judge went on, his voice ringing out, his staccato Arabic sounding more like a Friday mosque than a judge summing up.

'He says the police work on this case was sloppy and he has, is it censored? Censored the public prosecutor?'

'Censured.'

'Yes, like this. Censured. He says valuable court time has been wasted.'

Dominating the silent court, Khasawneh turned his attention to me and I was caught in his bushy-browed, furious stare. I caught '*Inglez*' but little else as the judge gestured at me, his hand chopping the wooden surface in front of him.

Ibrahim's throaty rasp again. 'He says you were foolish and had been drinking. He does not like to think foreigners can behave just as they like in Jordan. There is a law here and it has to be upheld. Even if you are English *khawaja*. He is being sarcastic here when he says this.'

Khasawneh's voice rose in pitch, poised and dropped as his hand scythed the air.

'He says you must face the consequence of your actions under the law. You can not behave in a foreign country as if you own it. He says these days have gone for you.'

I whispered back to Ibrahim through the side of my mouth. 'These days have gone for me?'

'For the English, Paul. He means the English.'

There I sat, tried by a judge for being English while the British government pulled his strings. Ibrahim broke in on my impotent introspection. 'He says the court will sit next week to decide sentencing.'

I turned, alarmed. 'But the plea bargain.'

Al Bashir shushed me, his hand out, palm down as we stood for the judges to leave the noisy courthouse.

'Don't worry, Paul. It's going to be okay.'

I'd heard it before. And was fast learning it was Arabic for 'You're fucked.'

Chapter Fifteen

It was raining Thursday morning as I left the house, negotiating my way carefully down the slippery steps to my car. The sky was a uniform dull grey.

I stopped in horror. The windscreen was smashed. The driver's side front wing had been crushed against the tyre, which was flat. I couldn't tell whether it had been done by another car or a tyre lever. The interior was soaked. A battered yellow taxi came along the street and I flagged him down.

At the Ministry, Aisha came down for coffee and I told her about the car.

'Shit. I was hoping you'd drive tomorrow. My car's in the shop. Let me call my cousin.'

She laid the sheaf of papers she was carrying down, pulled her mobile from her pocket and made the call. I made coffee for us both and, by the time I came back, she was mid-way through an impassioned burst of Arabic. She winked at me, listening to the reaction on the other end of the line before she returned fire, waving her free hand in the air as she described what I could only imagine would be the globally disastrous consequences of not having a replacement car from Hassan's car hire company.

My eye fell on Aisha's papers. The thick document on the top of the pile was titled in English: 'Jordan Water Privatisation. Draft Recommendations of the Evaluation Committee.'

She finished the call and sat at the side of my desk, sipping her coffee and pulling a face at the taste. 'Fixed. He'll have a replacement car over at your place tonight.

It's older, but it's a Mercedes. And he'll do the same price. They'll take the damaged car away, too. It's fine, it's properly insured so there are no worries about that. He'll deal with the police.'

'Cool. Thanks, Aish. You're a wonder,' I said, touching her hand, then holding it in mine. She smiled down at me.

'Ibrahim told me it went well yesterday.'

'As well as could be expected. I have to go back for sentencing next week but Tariq thinks it's likely to be a fine. I'm not happy accepting a guilty plea, but Ibrahim and Tariq both insist it's the best course. We'll see. At least they sorted out the drugs charge. I can't work out where that whole lie came from.'

She frowned. 'What about the press? Won't they report the judgement?'

I smiled. 'Ibrahim says he's fixed it. The court reporter for Petra is a lifelong buddy of his. I can only assume it means Ibrahim's spent a lifetime in court.'

Aisha's soft, throaty laugh was a provocation in itself, her soft, full lips parting like an invitation to heaven. She growled at me.

'Down, *ya* Brit.'

I changed the subject, pointing at the pile of papers she had been carrying. 'So they've evaluated the bids? It's a done deal?'

She looked down at the documents. 'Nearly. It just needs to be signed off by the Minister, but he's travelling right now. And then they go to the financial bids. That's where this whole process will be won or lost.'

'Travelling? When's he back? He asked to take a look at the article I've been doing about the privatisation and the whole water issue.'

'I don't know. He's out this week, though. Why don't

you show the article to Abdullah Zahlan? He'll be able to sign it off.'

I shook my head. 'It's more a courtesy. Never mind, perhaps next week. I've got time. Dinner at mine tonight?'

Aisha played with the silver coins dangling from her Bedouin necklace. 'Can't,' she whispered. 'I have salsa class and then I have to pack and get stuff ready to take over to Mariam. Will you come to ours in the morning so I can load up the car?'

I hadn't thought we were going to be acting as a private aid convoy, then felt unworthy as I remembered how the family sent little luxuries over whenever they could. Luxuries I had come to think of as everyday things – candles, toothpaste, fine soap, English tea and liquorice allsorts, the latter a particular weakness of Mariam's, apparently.

'How much stuff are we taking over?'

'A couple of bags. We won't take too much in case it doesn't get through. The Israelis sometimes just confiscate the lot.'

'Okay, I'll come to yours. Nine? Can I bring anything for them?'

'Nine's fine. And yes, it'd be a nice idea to bring Hamad some sweets, maybe. Zalatimo? He's crazy about them.'

Amman's famous Zalatimo Brothers, a shop in the bustling *Shmeisani* district packed with huge trays of fine, butter-soaked filo pastry parcels filled with nuts and honey, tubes of fried vermicelli packed with pistachios, little rich cakes of cracked wheat and nuts and date-filled crumbly *maamoul* pastries, all ready to scoop up and be tightly arrayed into their distinctive dark red and gold tins.

'Done. I'll pick some up later on the way home.'

Aisha slid off the desk, her dark denims tucked into knee-length leather boots. She glanced around to make sure nobody was looking our way, then stooped and kissed me.

She walked away and I watched. She turned as she rounded the desk at the end of the row, caught me looking at her bum and stopped for a fleeting moment, hand on hip and wearing a mock-scandalised expression. I laughed, but after she had left I sat brooding. The Jerusalem Consortium water bid would be my last betrayal, my parting gift to Gerald Lynch and his spooky pals at the British Embassy. I'd stay in Jordan somehow, for Aisha, but not by sacrificing her and her family to Lynch.

I looked at my screen, seeing nothing but a blur of text and images as I mulled over the water bids and my new career as a stealer of things and professional liar. I was amazed the sister of one of the bidders could wander around with the results of the technical evaluation. And ashamed that my first thought on seeing the document was how I could steal it.

People were starting to leave for the day and I was still turning things over in my mind and gazing at an empty screen. I waited a good fifteen minutes after the last cheery, bustling figure had shouted a goodbye across to me before I went up to the Minister's office. Harb's secretary worked late when he was in town, but invariably skipped for home and quality time with her two children when he was travelling.

Sure enough, the office suite was open with nobody there. The bid evaluation document was lying on the secretary's desk and I sauntered over to it, treading softly, my laptop bag bumping my thigh and my heart hammering painfully in my chest. Silence, a clock, my blood rushing in my ears. I heard a creak as I picked up the document. Abdullah Zahlan's puzzled voice came from the doorway behind me.

'Paul. Hi. What are you up to?'

Oh fuck. Oh fuck oh fuck oh fuck oh fuck.

I stood still, the bid evaluation held in place against my chest by my elbow. Thank God I faced away from him: my shock must have been written across my features like a billboard. Worse, if I turned, he'd see a sheaf of papers in my hand held together with a binding bar and clearly, oh so clearly, marked 'Confidential' across its top.

I heard Aisha's voice in greeting. 'Hey, Abdullah.'

I caught his movement away from me in the corner of my eye and, quick as a flash, unzipped the side pocket of my bag, slipped the bid evaluation into it and pulled out the copy of the water article I had printed out earlier. I was facing Zahlan, gesturing with the printout by the time he'd turned back to me.

I walked towards him, smiling and trying to sound airy, 'I was just dropping this piece for the Minister to review when he comes back. I didn't think his secretary would have left by now. Perhaps you'd care to take a look at it for me?'

He was dressed as ad agency man again today, all black and a polo neck, carrying his heavy jacket in his arm. He took the document from me, his face still carrying an echo of puzzlement. 'Certainly, Paul. Can I come back to you Sunday? I'm just on my way out now.'

I smiled. 'No problem, I'd value your insight.' I kept moving and was zipping up my bag as I passed him. 'Have a good weekend.'

'Hang on a second,' he said.

I pulled up. My heart stopped beating.

Zahlan headed for his office. 'I'll come out with you.'

He put my article on his desk, closed his office door and slipped on his jacket before joining me in the corridor. I was sweating under my coat, a nasty hot and cold feeling.

The bid evaluation document in my bag seemed to weigh me down. Aisha took a taxi home and I took another, relieved at not having to talk to her just then.

We crossed over at the Sheikh Hussein Crossing, a relatively short drive north from Amman through the green-flecked beige expanse of rocky hillsides. Daoud's man Selim came with us to smooth the process of crossing the border. The queue at the Jordanian checkpoint snaked back from the barbed wire fences and the scattering of low buildings and concrete barriers marking the crossing point. The Jordanian soldiers were thorough and suspicious as they searched the car and checked our documents, Daoud's man Selim fussing and fixing all the way, a greasy little character who simpered and cowered, yet who seemed to be able to smooth our way through, procuring letters of this and documents of that. We were finally waved through. I found the whole process unnerving, bracing myself for the infamous Israeli checkpoint. I was already jittery passing though the Jordanian side, fear making me gabble nervously and point out silly things around us. I looked across at Aisha, but she seemed lost in her own thoughts. I noticed she was gripping the door handle.

'Are you okay?'

Her smile was taut as she shook her head. 'I never like this very much. Sorry. I usually go through the Allenby crossing and it's never good. This one I don't know and it makes me nervous. Selim is supposed to have fixed the paperwork. I hope he's done it well.'

Her face darkened as the Israeli soldiers came up to the car and asked us to get out. They were pleasant enough, which surprised me given the many tales I'd heard about their aggressiveness and the routine dehumanisation that took place at the border. They took our passports and the car permit Aisha gave them before starting their search of the car, a methodical and unhurried process that involved quite a lot of electronic hardware. My mouth was dry as I willed myself to look relaxed but I knew there were dark patches of sweat under my armpits. A dog was brought up to the car and led around it. It stopped a couple of times, once by the rear wheel and, in my state of heightened perception and fear, I saw it barking and soldiers rushing over to us. But it just sniffed the wheel and whined, then moved on.

'Cat piss,' said one of the two soldiers standing by me, in English, and the other laughed.

I wondered if he had spoken English for my benefit. I felt confused, my expectations of sneering brutality confounded by their dismissive efficiency.

We were taken into a building where we were separated, each asked a set of routine questions by indifferent, pretty women in uniforms. Where are you coming from? Why are you visiting Israel? I was asked why I decided to live in Jordan, what other Arab countries I had been to and did I have any contacts or family in the West Bank, a barrage of questions, each answer noted down before we were sat at opposite ends of the room and the women swapped over and ran through their questions again. We were finally allowed out to the car, which had been thoroughly searched while we were being questioned, our bags on the tarmac and the supplies Aisha had brought for Mariam neatly laid out, each parcel sliced open and reduced to its components in a careful, considered act of searching as destructive as any wanton act of brutal vandalism, perhaps more so for its cold efficiency. We gathered our things up and repacked the car, trying to stem the tide of tea from the sliced-open packets and repack the slippery, loose soap bars. One of the two big red, yellow and blue tins of tuna we had been carrying had been opened and the pungent oil slopped out into the car boot, soaking into the faded grey carpet.

Another soldier came out of one of the checkpoint office buildings and walked over to us.

'Come with me,' he said to me and, to Aisha, 'You stay here.' She didn't look at me, just held his gaze, her mouth turned down and her head held up. I followed the soldier past a service desk and into a sparse, modern office. A uniformed man with more badges than the others sat behind a desk: a pleasant face, slightly rounded by middle age, hair greying at his temples. He looked European.

'Hello. Paul Stokes?' I nodded. He tapped the table with his pen. 'Why are you come here?'

'I'm living in Amman. I thought I'd come across and see the other side of the Jordan. I'm travelling with a friend.'

'Yes, I see that.' His accent sounded Russian. He scratched his head with the pen. There were laughter lines around his eyes that seemed somehow out of step with the checkpoint environment and its clinical efficiencies, railings, concrete posts and razor wire.

'You know we not get many Brit come here.' He looked up at me, a sudden directness which made me avert my own eyes despite myself. 'You are perhaps a little of the light relief for us.'

'Well, I'm happy to relieve the monotony, if nothing else,' I smiled, glad of the touch of humour in his words and starting to find my ease, just a tourist in a strange land.

He flicked through my passport, a gesture for show: he must have gone through it before he had me brought in. I thought of Lynch and a similar gesture made back in the reception area of the British Embassy in Amman. He reached over the desk, my passport in his hand. I took it. He picked up Aisha's.

'How well you know the girl?'

'I work with her at the Ministry of Natural Resources in Amman.'

'You trust her?'

'Yes, I do.'

He handed Aisha's passport to me, but when I went to take it he kept his grip, leaving me leaning forwards, unbalanced over his desk. We stayed that way for a second before I managed to find my balance again, my hand still on the passport. 'You like Arabs?'

His eyes held me and I looked back at him, furiously trying to think of a response. 'I've liked the people I have met since I arrived in Jordan.'

'So you think we are bad people then, Paul Stokes? That we should be drive into sea? You agree about this?'

I let go of the passport as I sensed the traps lying in wait all around me, refusing to play a tug of war with him over the document. I tried to keep my voice mild and neutral as I responded, but I found it hard to focus, the phrase *tug of war* in my mind stopped me from thinking properly. I wanted to go to the toilet.

His question had been put in a mild, almost offhand

way, but at the same time it went directly to the heart of what many of the people I had met in the Arab World thought. That the Israelis didn't belong here, that they should never have been allowed to come here.

Dealing with it from his point of view confused me. I tried to think quickly, not so much about my own opinions, which I had taken a great deal of trouble to keep neutral, despite the pressure to join everyone else and demonise the Israelis, but about what I needed to say in response to his question. *Tug of war* running around in my idiot mind, I started to appreciate that, casual and offhand though he may appear, he was very good at his job.

'No, I don't. I haven't been around here long enough to make judgements like that. I think a lot has happened that is regrettable, but I simply don't know enough to take a view.'

'Regrettable. Yes, is regrettable.' He was emphasising the word as he repeated it, thoughtful. He moved faster than I thought possible, dropping Aisha's passport and balling his fist before slamming it down on the desk. He sprang up from his chair, kicking it backwards and leaning towards me, his finger pointing into my face.

'Regret? What you know of regret, Paul Stokes from *Great* Britain?'

I had jumped at the sound of his fist on the table but now I froze, looking at the soldier wide-eyed and lost for words. He pulled his chair back and sat again, calmly reaching out for Aisha's passport and flicking slowly through the pages, the rasp of his thumb on the paper sounding in the silence. There was a bump as someone threw a bag on the floor in the next room. I smelled cigarette smoke from somewhere, then heard low voices through the wall, two soldiers talking, laughing. I waited, watching the officer as he sat at his desk looking down at the passports in front of him, his large shoulders slightly hunched and his hands together on the desktop. He was breathing heavily.

He threw Aisha's passport across the desktop without looking up. 'Go. Get out.'

My heart was pumping as I emerged into the sunshine. I must have looked like death. One of the soldiers came up to me. 'He gave you a hard time.' A flat statement.

I stammered a reply: 'Yes, he did actually.'

'Forgive him. A Palestinian labourer stabbed his daughter, before the,' he made finger quotes in the air, 'peace broke out.'

'Don't you believe in the peace?'

He laughed, a ragged sound as he turned and walked away, flapping his hand at me behind his back, dismissing me and my peace.

Lost in thought, I got back to the car. Aisha, standing by the door, saw the passports in my hand, grinned wickedly at the soldiers and spat on the hot, dusty tarmac at their feet as I got to the driver's side. The big gates opened to let us through.

'Why the hell did you do that?' I snapped, tension making my voice harsher than I intended. Aisha glared at me but the soldiers were still grinning and one waved us through by flipping us a casual, bored digit.

We drove away from the checkpoint in silence, leaving Selim and Jordan behind. I felt my anger growing, impelled by my feeling of guilt at having barked at Aisha, my thoughts increasingly hot and hard. How Arab of her, to spit at them when she knew we were through the checkpoint, to indulge that little spite in a moment of small victory. Cringe in supplication and crow in triumph.

We drove on past the queue of trucks and cars on the other side in silent, cold recrimination. If our kissing and trembling touches had been passionate and intense, then our conflict was to be of the same order of intensity. Where we had cherished, now we would hurt. Aisha's whole form hunched in anger as she flailed herself with my reprimand. Clear of the border post and the checkpoint just beyond it, I stopped the car and got out to escape the toxic atmosphere and breathe fresh air. Aisha leapt out behind me.

'So I spit. On the dust my father and brother gave their blood to.'

'You're so fucking melodramatic. They did nothing to you. All that bullshit about the brutal Israelis, the humiliation. They just did their jobs.'

'Yah, like the Nazis did theirs.'

'Listen to yourself. You can't believe that.' I reached to the sky for the words, the inspiration to try and get through to her. 'They're just men, soldiers, the same as the Jordanians, the same as you. They're scared, they're angry because people bomb them and kill their children. The guy in the office lost his daughter because a Palestinian murdered her. What the fuck gives you the right to treat them like that? They're no different to you, don't you understand?'

'Who are you to lecture me on difference, please Paul? What is this sudden expertise in the grief of strangers? I didn't take their land, I didn't kill their children. They have killed three members of my family and tens of thousands of my people, they bomb us from helicopters and destroy our houses, make us crawl in the dirt and laugh as they point their guns in our faces *on our land*. What do you want to find here, precisely? You want to find love, Paul? Is that it? You think you deserve to see reconciliation? You, whose nation sold my people into this slavery in the first place? What exactly do you want to impose on us, Paul? Your superior fucking values?'

I banged the flat of my hand on the roof of the car, a surprisingly loud, deep sound in the quiet of the deserted road. 'Those soldiers were polite, Aisha. They didn't spit at you. Why do you want to perpetuate the pain with everything you do? Why have you got no feeling for their loss? You lost three members of your family, but didn't Hamad even up that little score for you? Didn't he kill children? Their children?'

She had rounded the car towards me then, her boots covered in the pale roadside dust, her face enraged. 'And what about our children, English? What about our pain? How much do we have to suffer before it stops? Here. You love them so much, you take the same as they do.'

She spat on the ground at my feet.

I looked down at the little congealed drops of saliva lying on the dusty ground, then up at Aisha. At her wide, beautiful brown eyes. The horror at what she'd done written on her face. She waited, scared, for my reaction, for the next escalation, wiping her chin with the back of her trembling hand. We stood under the warmth of the sun, the clouds banished from the sky as Aisha, trembling, waited for me to hit her. I saw the moisture gathering in her eyes, the shock in her face, our scared eyes locked in that long moment.

Aisha's face crumpled as the intensity of her fury passed and gave way to fear. I stepped forward and she was in my arms and I felt her salt tears on my cheek as I held her and murmured her name. We clung to each other, standing on the dusty margin of the road, whispering sorry over and again. A car raced past, sending up a small cloud of dust and beeping its horn at us cheekily and we finally found relief and laughter, standing under the warm sky, peacefully and blissfully alone together. The storm had passed.

We were stopped again at the West Bank border crossing, an altogether smaller and tattier affair than the Sheikh Hussein crossing. The long stretch of rich and prosperous-looking farmland we passed through on the road down to the crossing made the stark contrast of concrete tank-traps and metal gates seem even more obscene. Aisha had been sketching the farmland in one of the pads she had brought with her, pencil-work – now her sketch was altogether starker.

Debris was scattered around the broken-down kerbstones and a zig-zag of concrete blocks forced a slow slalom as the cameras mounted high above us looked down on our painstaking progress up to the barrier. Another set of questions, another scan of the car and we were through, this time to the West Bank itself – Palestine, as it was now to be. After a stretch of open country, we started to see the security wall to our right, the countryside less developed and more arid.

We passed through a small town and were quiet, gazing out around us. It reminded me of the villages in the Jordanian countryside, poor, flyblown and ramshackle. Wrecked washing machines, prams and rubbish littered the scrubby ground between the buildings and dirty kids played in the streets. Somewhere in an area of low, crumbling houses a tyre burned and a trail of thick, black smoke was rising up into the clear blue sky.

We drove past farmhouses by the roadside, patches of

cultivated land here and there, but nothing on the scale of the agriculture I'd seen in Jordan – or, indeed, a few minutes ago in Israel.

As we passed by him on the roadside, a small boy grinned a grubby-cheeked urchin's grin and drew himself up to salute us and I laughed at him and waved back. And then his face changed and became fearful, his eyes focused on the sky beyond us. I stretched around and saw the black speck as I heard its rotors. It was travelling parallel to us and at approximately the same speed. I turned to watch it every few seconds until Aisha noticed my preoccupation.

'What is it?' said Aisha.

'Chopper over there. Can't you hear it?'

She nodded, 'Yes, I can now. Look, it's coming closer.'

I brought the car to a stop and we got out to look at the helicopter which appeared to be heading straight for us. The side door was open and I could make out a soldier in khaki, wearing a green beret. He was armed.

The chopper dropped down towards us and I started to feel an odd stir of mounting fear. We were in an area of patchy farmland and waste ground, the only building within sight was a tin shack hundreds of metres away. The small boy was lost in the faintly shimmering horizon we had left behind. There was nothing else around us to attract their interest.

'What's this about?' I called over to Aisha.

'I don't know, Paul. I've never seen this before. Our papers are in order. It'll be okay.'

I heard the false note in her voice. The noise of the engine forced us to raise our voices and then the machine hovered, standing off a few hundred feet away from us. I kept my eyes on it as I shouted to Aisha. 'So what do we do? Put our hands up? Act normal?'

The stress was clear in her voice now. 'I don't know Paul. I don't know.'

With a sense of sick fascination, I saw the soldier move and raise his weapon. I turned to Aisha. There was a bright red dot on her chest. She saw my face and looked down.

The dot was remarkably steady. Aisha raised her eyes to me and I saw her mouth frame the words but I didn't hear them. 'I love you.'

I couldn't move, my muscles betraying me as I shouted out her name, the beat of the helicopter engine pulsing in my ears. She glared up at the helicopter, her face a vision of furious defiance, tears streaming down her cheeks as, with equal care, she mouthed, 'Fuck you.'

She glared at them, the dot on her chest, for what must have been ten seconds but felt like ten years before I found myself able to break the spell and move, but as I started to run around the car to her, the engine note of the helicopter changed and the dot disappeared from Aisha's chest. As I pulled her into my arms, the helicopter veered away. Aisha stood rigid and trembling, watching it until the speck had disappeared over the dusty hillside, before collapsing against the car, breathing in great, shuddering heaves and hammering against the roof with her fists.

I put my arms around her and she finally quietened, accepting the tissues I took from the box on the dashboard, wiping her eyes and blowing her nose. She spoke in a hesitant, trembling voice.

'In all the time I have been coming here, in all that has happened to my family. In all the years I have been a Palestinian and forced to watch the repression of my people. In all of this, nobody has ever pointed a gun at me before. Why now, Paul?'

I didn't have an answer for her. I just held her as I wondered the same thing. Was this routine? I hadn't read about it as common Israeli behaviour. Surely if they were in the habit of pointing high powered rifles at people from helicopters, it would have been reported. Why would the Israelis even be interested in us? Could it be something closer to home, something to do with Lynch and Daoud? My money was on Lynch, but I hadn't told him of my trip to the West Bank. So who had?

The thoughts tumbled through my mind as I held Aisha's shoulders and looked into her eyes, as she nodded with a brave little smile and we got back into our car. We were silent, both lost in our own thoughts, but my hand was closed tight on hers the whole way.

We motored through Jenin, yellow taxis dodging around us in the streets of pale stone, modern buildings. Leaving the town, I was amazed at how dusty the countryside seemed. It had been raining on and off for a week in Amman, and yet here we were under hot, blue skies. It might have been summer, except for the greenery that sprouted between the little fields by the farms we passed, olive groves shadowed by the high, shimmering white walls of Israeli settlements. Summers here aren't green, they're brown.

'We're heading for Qaffin,' said Aisha as she watched the countryside go by. 'It's on the way to Tulkaram.'

I remembered the names from news broadcasts. Daoud had told me the farm was in the country between two of the biggest flashpoint areas in the whole territories. I wondered why it had never occurred to me to pinpoint where the farm actually was, how close it was to these places. He also told me the Dajanis' land had been cut by the Israeli security wall, although the whole farm was actually on the Arab side of the 1949 and 1967 lines. The wall did that – it snaked around the old delineations of territory to seize little bits of farmland, grab at water or snatch at green areas.

I was in a state of constant apprehension, trying to calm myself but the checkpoints weren't helping, let alone the incident with the chopper. They were constant reminders of the simmering tension. The land itself spoke of its unease, of the fragility of the peace the Jericho bomb had shattered, of the decades of uncertainty and fear. I kept seeing black specks in the air turning into helicopters before they resolved into birds or, in one case, a black plastic bag caught on a thermal.

We passed through Qaffin. There were children playing in the streets. Beyond the township, a track led off the badly surfaced road and we followed it through the olive groves for perhaps two hundred metres, dipping down and away from the road, virtually out of sight from it before we reached a whitewashed farmhouse. It looked as old as time, almost like an English country cottage, rough whitewashed walls with a terracotta tiled roof. We pulled into the yard, sending a handful of hens clucking away from us.

There, standing in the kitchen doorway, was Aisha's grandmother Mariam. She wore a blue *kandoura*, a housecoat. She was small, bent over a little with the weight of her age but she moved with grace, her hair showing grey under the white *mandeel* on her head. Getting out of the car after the long drive through unfamiliar territory, I hobbled more than she did. Mariam shook my hand, which I hadn't expected. The more traditional women in the Levant won't shake hands with men, holding their hand to their chest instead.

Mariam gripped my hands and looked intently up at me. Her eyes were brown and merry, faded with age but steady in her deeply lined face. She reminded me immediately of Aisha's mother, Nour. Still holding me in her gaze she spoke to Aisha in Arabic, chuckling.

'She says you're not bad for a Brit. She says you've all been nothing but trouble to her.'

Certain Aisha was teasing me, I looked back at the old lady. 'No, she didn't.'

Another burst of Arabic, aimed squarely at Aisha. 'She says I have to translate properly, she doesn't speak English but she knows when I'm being bad, always has done.' Aisha laughed. 'She says you're handsome.'

I looked at Mariam. '*Shukran.*' One of my precious few words of Arabic. She was delighted.

'*Alhamdullilah, Ferriyah, houa etekellum Arabi,*' she said to Aisha.

And I understood her, too – 'Praise be to God, little bird, he speaks Arabic.'

Aisha smiled sadly at me. 'Yes, little bird. You remembered. My father's name for me, given me by Mariam.'

Mariam pulled us inside to drink cool water mixed with lemon juice and honey.

'The lemons grow wild on the hillside here,' said Aisha as we followed Mariam. 'We have a few citrus trees in the yard but it's not always possible to get enough water for them.'

Mariam fired off another burst of Arabic, chuckling.

'She says they keep the water for the olives but try and spare some for the citrus. It's good for her teeth.'

Hamad, Aisha's uncle, was expected back at the farm later on. As the guest of honour, I got to sleep in Hamad's bedroom, while Aisha was downstairs on the sofa. Hamad was relegated to the floor in Mariam's room. The old lady would hear of no other arrangement and had obviously been preparing for our visit. She rooted delightedly through the two bags of supplies Aisha had brought with us, damaged though they were by the inspection and hours rattling around in the back of the car. Almost half the tea had spilled out, mixing with the fish oil to create a noxious paste.

Aisha and I left Mariam chewing contentedly on a liquorice allsort and went out for a walk around the farm as the daylight started to fade. We wandered hand in hand through the olive groves and over the hill behind the farmhouse. The setting sun cast long, spindly shadows from the olive trees in their rows, each smooth-barked and heavy with fruit.

Aisha held out her hand to brush against the leaves as we passed them. 'I used to play in these olive groves as a child. They were monsters or soldiers in my army, sometimes they were courtiers in my court,' she said, smiling.

We crested the hill to confront the shocking scar greyly dominating the green-flecked earthy brown landscape. The Israeli security wall.

I gazed down at the continuation of the olive stands beyond the ugly monstrosity snaking its way through the land, a dust track running alongside it on this side, blacktop on the other. It was built up in huge concrete slabs, topped with barbed wire, immense, incongruous and monolithic.

I was surprised to find myself angry at the sight of it. It symbolised an abnegation of hope, a rejection of humanity. Whatever the rights and wrongs, whatever the history, surely humanity had discovered walls and barriers weren't the answer? We'd knocked down Berlin just to stand silently by while this thing was built: bigger, more sophisticated and far, far more final. Aisha was quiet at my side, holding my hand. She shook herself free of me. I blinked, focusing on her with difficulty.

'What's up?'

She laughed nervously, grasping her hand. 'You're hurting, Paul.'

'Sorry, I didn't realise. This is bad.'

She gestured across the land. 'There's a gate a few kilometres to the left of here, a bigger one past Kirbat Al Aqaba, the village over there to the right. We're lucky to have two so close, the gates are few and far between. Some families have to travel a long way to get to the rest of their land. When they're allowed through of course. It's not always as easy to get through it. The olives don't do well over there, Hamad can't get to them often enough. And the crossings are always shut when they need to harvest. Always. The fruit often just rots on the trees. There is a stream on the other side. It comes from a spring, but we can't get to that, either. Water's scarce this side. The wall always follows the water.'

A perverse desire to get closer to it seized me, compelled me to walk down the hill towards the wall until it blocked out the land beyond, capped with the last of the blue sky and tendrils of dark cloud reaching across from behind me.

Aisha called my name, urging me to stop. I saw the cameras on the wall, the motors whining as they moved to focus on me, the afternoon sunlight glinting off their white casings. I stared up at it, now scared to go too close. It blotted out everything, a surreal barrier above and to either side of me, a show of power, of absolute will made of concrete. I faced it, overwhelmed by the frustration and humiliation of that barrier, locking these people from their land, from the water they needed to irrigate their crops. I turned, shaking my head and walked back uphill towards Aisha. She smiled bitterly as she saw my expression.

'Ah, now you understand.'

Her face was sad and yet proud at the same time, the dying light of the setting sun turning her brown skin golden. I kissed her, angling our faces so the cameras would have a good view. As we embraced, the gathering clouds obscured the sun and the light on Aisha's face was extinguished. I drew back and looked deep into her eyes and I saw myself, falling into her richness.

Raindrops started to fall, impacts throwing up little explosions of dust from the arid land, splashing on the leaves of the olive trees around us, a rich earth-smell rising from the land. A drop fell on Aisha's cheek and I kissed it away. We hurried back over the hill towards the farm, passing between the rustling olive trees, their shaking leaves spattered by the heavy drops. The darkening soil drank.

Chapter Sixteen

We sat talking in the kitchen with Mariam, a strange mixture of English and Arabic, translation and comprehension. We smoked, Aisha and I, while Mariam poured me *arak*, adding water to turn the drink milky white. It was past nine and dark outside when we heard the crunch of tyres on the stony ground in the yard. A few seconds later, Hamad came into the kitchen with the odd, bobbing posture big, shy men have. He seemed slightly taken aback to see us, as if he had forgotten that we were to be there. He shook my hand and smiled bashfully.

'Welcome. Mariam has been look for to meet with you. You like the farm?'

I couldn't help but smile back at him, he was so big and gentle.

'I do. It's very pretty and,' I was aware of how silly it sounded, but my mouth had already formed the word, 'peaceful.'

He laughed at my rueful expression, his quick eyes never quite staying in contact with mine. 'Yes, maybe it is like this.'

I handed him the burgundy tin of pastries from Zalatimo and he took them, dipping his head in thanks, bashful but delighted, putting them carefully on a stone shelf at the back of the kitchen. He sat with us and drank an *arak*, but he had business to attend to in the village and left us soon after, asking me if I would move the car around to the side of the house to make room for his tractor in the morning.

Hamad laughed at my hammed-up reaction to the

temperature change from the warm kitchen as I followed him out. 'It will come more wind, the weather she is change. Better to stay in house and make warm.'

He drove a battered old Suzuki four-wheeler and I waved him goodbye as his tail lights snaked away up the drive to the road, before returning to the warm clatter of the kitchen, where Aisha and Mariam were chattering as they cooked dinner. I sat at the table watching Aisha and listening to her translations of Mariam's comments until Mariam brought the dishes to the table and we ate lamb and rice, spiced with cardamom and dried limes, steaming plates served with fresh yoghurt and bread.

After the meal, Mariam got up and covered a dish of food for Hamad, putting it in the warm oven.

'He will be back late,' Aisha translated. 'He is late often, they have much difficulty with the crops and the border controls and so the men work together, but it is not easy for them.'

Mariam wiped her hands on her apron and chattered brightly to Aisha, who laughed and turned to translate as the old lady lifted my hand and put it to her cheek, smiling, before leaving the room.

'She says she is old and has to go to bed and we are young and have to stay up and that we are to behave and not take advantage of her sleepiness.'

Aisha sketched, sitting cross-legged on the cushion-covered seat built out of the wall. I sipped at my *arak*, growing to like the strong liquorice heat of the drink.

'What happened today with the helicopter? I still can't believe it,' I whispered across the table at her.

She didn't look up from her sketch, the pen flying across the heavy paper. 'I don't know. Maybe they had got a warning or a tip-off and mistook us, I just don't know.' She stopped drawing and looked up at me. 'I was so scared, Paul.'

'A mistake? Not just intimidation?'

She shook her head, focused back on her sketch. 'No, they've never done it before as far as I know. They must have been looking for someone. But I thought it was the end.'

I moved to sit next to her. 'No, don't let that happen. I couldn't bear to be without you. That was my fear, my worst nightmare in front of my eyes. Why didn't they point the gun at me?'

She was drawing a helicopter, dark, brutal and so lifelike it seemed to fly out of the page. She finished it and tossed the pad aside and I kissed her.

We sat in the warmth of the kitchen, kissing and cuddling, playing around and tracing patterns on each other's lips with our fingers before the heat came from within us and our play became passion. Aisha's breast cupped in my hand, her lips against mine, her slow, rhythmic movement against me and her soft, flickering tongue; light kisses turned into deep, reaching open-mouthed ardour. Aisha's hips were moving against my hand on her inner leg when something hit against the side window of the kitchen, startling us. We sat, stilled by the noise for a few seconds. I got up and peered out of the window to see the dark shadow of a tree waving in the wind outside and its branch near the window.

'It's just a tree. The wind's getting up out there.'

Aisha stood. 'Just as well it wasn't Hamad. Come on, *ya* Brit, time for bed.'

I held her face in my hands and kissed her, tasting her sweetness, her eyes flickering between mine, a bruised look on her face.

She gasped and pushed me away, her voice husky. 'Go. For the love of God go before I do something I'll regret.'

I went to bed filled with a sexual tension that could only find one outlet and so I was still lying awake, my breathing slowing, when I heard two cars crunching down the driveway in the early hours of the morning. One parked around the side of the farmhouse near my car, out of sight beyond the shed.

I looked out of the window, but I could only see Hamad's Suzuki. I heard voices and caught the movement of shadows, watching the pale shapes of two faces turn towards me in the scant, blue-grey moonlight before the red flare of a match lit them for an instant, snuffed out to leave two red pin-pricks of light dancing in the darkness. There were muffled sounds of activity to the side of the house, near my car.

I dressed quietly, wearing the darkest clothes I could find in my bag and carefully picked my way across the creaking floorboards, randomising the rhythm of my movement so the sounds blended with the natural sounds of the old house in the wind. With a silent curse for each tiny creak, I inched down the stairs.

Reaching the kitchen, I finally appreciated the situation my curiosity had put me in. Whatever happened outside, if anyone found me outside my bedroom, their immediate assumption would be that I had been with Aisha. They'd make mincemeat of me, let alone the consequences for Aisha. The Jordanians still have honour killings, the families of girls who've disgraced them closing ranks to protect the brother or father who kills her in a rage. What would they do with me, the lone Brit somewhere in the country between two of the most infamous flashpoints in the West Bank? I stood in the dark kitchen, the moonlight shining through the window casting cold bars of light across the wall. I was sweating so much I had to wipe my forehead.

I started moving again, opening the front door with infinite slowness and care and holding it against the sudden gust of wind that threatened to slam it back against the wall. It blew the curtains in the kitchen, making them billow and I waited, a long, heart-stopping pause, for a vase or plate to come crashing down onto the tiled floor before closing the door behind me, the cold air chill against my moist skin. I slid along the wall towards the back of the house with the idea of coming around the other side of the sheds. The ground felt uneven and there were bits and pieces of farmyard equipment lying around. It took me an age to walk those few metres, gingerly pushing my way forwards and shivering with cold and fear.

Aisha and I had stopped here to kiss on the way to the olive groves. Now the wind howled over the roof, the clouds obscured the moon and I could only pick out the vaguest shadows.

I didn't hear the men's low voices until it was almost too late, stopping just in time by the edge of the shed. I could barely pick out the dark bulk of my car. A Toyota was parked alongside it, three men standing between the two cars. One of the men stretched his back, another wiped his hands. Hamad's bulky figure detached itself from the shadows by the house and they talked for a few seconds in low voices before they all shook hands and the three men got into the Tercel, its dark blue paintwork highlighted for a second by the opening of a door. The car made its way up the track to the road, a dark shadow melding into the shadows beyond.

If Hamad went back into the house before me, he'd lock the door behind him. I cursed my stupidity as I stood, shivering and watching his bulky outline immobile against the fading car headlights. Hamad turned, scanning the yard and I moved my head back just in time, pressed against the wall in the cutting wind, waiting and shivering and feeling the coldness under my hands. I heard an outbuilding door creaking open and the sound jerked me into life to grope back down the wall towards the kitchen, the rough surface of the wall guiding me.

I rounded the corner by the kitchen door, scanning the yard for any sign of Hamad before taking my chance and darting into the kitchen, pulling the door closed towards me as quietly as I could, the sound of my breathing harsh in my own ears.

The sight of the candle on the kitchen table brought me to a standstill; I almost shouted out in panic. Mariam's wrinkled features were picked out in the warm, small light of the flame. She shook her head, whispering something in Arabic to herself and waving at me to go upstairs, her finger to her lips, her eyes wide in fear. '*Yalla, yalla.*' – go, go.

Uncertainty froze me for a second before life returned to my limbs and I touched my hand to my heart then my lips, an Arab supplicant's gesture of thanks I had seen before from the beggars in Amman and I went upstairs as quickly and quietly as I could. I was freezing. Shivering, I stripped off quickly and eased myself into the bed, which creaked alarmingly in the silence. I lay in the dark, my heart hammering in my chest. Would Mariam tell Hamad she'd seen me?

The wind moaned softly outside and the house creaked. My sheets were damp with my fearful sweat. I heard the sound of raised voices from the kitchen turn into furious whispers. I imagined Hamad shushing Mariam, pressing down on the air with his big hands.

A few minutes later I heard a gentle knock on my door and Hamad's voice softly calling my name, but I stayed still in the bed, breathing deeply and loudly. I heard his soft footsteps as he walked away across the wooden boards to Mariam's room, then Mariam's slower, lighter steps as she passed my door a minute later. I didn't sleep, lying and listening to the wind and thinking about groups of men huddled together, hidden out of sight of the world in the midnight darkness of the West Bank.

The slow beat of a helicopter's rotors sounded, its turbines' whine steady alongside the rising and falling notes of the wind. It soon died away.

I woke late to sunlight and the sound of birds. Mariam was in the kitchen, Aisha still asleep in the other room, a huddle of blankets and a tousle of hair. I left her sleeping and sat down to a breakfast of Arabic bread, olives and white cheese in blue-decorated dishes laid out on a white cloth.

'*Sabah al khair.*' A smiled 'good morning.'

I had enough Arabic for this, at least. '*Sabah al noor.*'

She asked me a question, but lost me completely and so went through it again, speaking slowly and miming, hands together under her cheek, hands up and a quizzical look. Had I slept well?

I nodded and smiled.

She pointed outside, a warning finger, hands under head, finger on mouth. A touch of the heart, pointing to Aisha and to me before drawing a finger across her lips.

I pointed outside and shrugged, a questioning look on my face and Mariam glared at me, putting her hands on her eyes, her ears and mouth. See no evil, hear no evil, speak no evil.

I caught the moisture in her eyes before she turned to wipe them. She shook her head at me and again I only caught a fraction of what she said, but it ended: '*Enta majnoun, habibi.*' You're mad, my love.

We ate together in companionable silence before Mariam cleared my plate. She touched the thin gold band on her finger and pointed to me and then the living room with an enquiring look. I grinned at her, then, '*Insh'Allah.*' If it is the will of God. Aisha found two happy people laughing together when she came, yawning and fluffing her tousled hair, into the kitchen, Mariam repeating, '*Insh'Allah.*'

Aisha caught my amused expression at her state of disarray and turned to regard herself using the base of a pan as a mirror, which you could get away with in Mariam's spotless little kitchen. She growled at me and shook out her hair. Mariam loosed off a long stream of Arabic which made Aisha laugh.

'She says I'm to teach you Arabic quickly because she's tired of fooling around like a clown trying to get you to understand her.'

'Tell her I'll try, but it's a difficult language.'

Aisha translated, but Mariam just replied if I was such a very clever Englishman, everyone knowing the English were clever and cunning, I'd learn Arabic quickly. That she had the feeling I would learn their ways quickly and perhaps even make allowances for her people. Mariam looked at me as Aisha translated this, a particularly hard stare at the last bit. I got up and looked out over the yard.

Mariam lifted a brass jug she had been heating on the range, pouring strong cardamom-flavoured coffee into little cups.

'How long has Mariam lived here, Aisha?'

More Arabic before Aisha said, 'Since 1945, when she married my grandfather. She was seventeen, he was older. It was his family's farm originally since long back. Mariam came from Sha'ab, a village on the far side of Nazareth from here, quite far away. It's an Israeli settlement now, her family is all dispersed. The farm is all she has.'

I spoke to Aisha but looked at Mariam, a strange triangular conversation. 'How did they meet?'

Mariam looked misty-eyed, gazing out of the window as she talked. 'At a market in Nazareth. The families took a long time to come to terms with the fact they were in love and wouldn't marry anyone else, Mariam says. My father was born here on the farm, in 1946. She says he cried all the time as a baby but when he was two they were forced to leave the farm and my father fell silent. She worried about him, he was so quiet and still.'

1948. *Al Naqba,* 'the catastrophe.' I had turned to look at Mariam as Aisha translated her words, but now I looked out of the window again, the morning light bright in my eyes and my thoughts far away, travelling back to the young couple and their flight from the farm, fear and danger in the night, torn away from their simple life together. Mariam was still talking, recollection making her voice dreamy. She paused for Aisha, who said, 'They came back in 1952, after the border had stabilised but there was a lot of trouble here and they had to leave again two years later and stay in a camp near Amman. They tried coming back many times, but it was too dangerous. Ahmed, my grandfather's brother, ended up on the Israeli side and so became an Arab Israeli. He was a lawyer and managed to protect the farm against them. The Israelis used to try and push against the border, there were raids across it constantly and it was very... I don't have the word, Paul.'

'Fluid?'

Aisha paused to light a cigarette, sliding the pack and lighter over to me. 'Yes, fluid. A lot of trouble. Grandma Mariam and my grandfather finally moved back in 1966, but my father stayed in the camps with his shops and Ibrahim left home and joined him there. For a time they had soldiers staying here from the Arab Legion. My grandfather was killed the next year, in the war.'

I remembered a newspaper snippet from my background research, a biographical article on the Dajanis. 'Wasn't he in the Arab Legion?'

Aisha frowned and sipped gingerly at her coffee as Mariam started to talk again. 'No,' translated Aisha, 'He fought with them but he was a...' She stopped, searching for the word for a second, 'volunteer? Many of the farmers did that, especially if they had guns. Grandma Mariam tried to stop Grandpa but he was angry. She tried to tell him he was too old for fighting, to leave it to the young ones, that they needed him on the farm. He wouldn't listen. He was shot. So she was left here alone with Hamad.'

'I'm sorry,' I said, a platitude. At least I had it in Arabic for her: '*Ana asif.*' Mariam smiled at me, a sad smile and a nod acknowledging my little courtesy.

'The border changed then, the Jordanians lost the West Bank and Jerusalem. The farm became part of Israel. It was a bad time, but Ahmed managed to fight the possession orders and the claims against the land, as he had in the past many times. The Israelis tried being tough, but he was a good lawyer and an Israeli citizen, even if he was Arab. They had to respect his connections and his legal arguments.'

Mariam's eyes were far away and Aisha struggled to

keep up with the flow of her narrative because Mariam had stopped pausing for Aisha to translate. Lost in her past, Mariam wasn't talking to us so much as herself.

'Arafat brought them hope. Until he came, the family were trying to become Israelis, to regularise their position here by gaining citizenship. That was the one time Ahmed failed. They didn't want us. Now she says Arafat is dead and so is his dream of a nation living in peace on the land it has owned and farmed for centuries.'

'What about Gaza? The new peace? Surely there's hope now.'

Mariam changed. I had only seen merriment in her until now, or the sadness of a gentle woman born into terrible times. Now I saw where Aisha's temper, demonstrated so shockingly the day before, had come from. Mariam's face was a picture of loathing as she spat out the words. Aisha translated, her hand on her grandmother's shoulder.

'She says they have no peace. Even Ahmed the lawyer couldn't stop them building their wall through our land. The farm was totally on the Arab side of the 1949 armistice border, but now the wall cuts through it, takes the land from them. She says when she dies, the farm will die.'

I tried to take it all in: the long years of struggle this woman represented, the aching, enduring search for just enough peace to scratch a living, to survive unmolested. An old peasant woman living simply in the face of war after war.

I asked Aisha, 'Does she hate them? The Israelis?'

Aisha shot a sharp glance at me, but translated and the question brought Mariam back from the past, stemming the flow of her reminiscence. She looked at me wide-eyed for a few moments, then at Aisha. Her eyes had tears in them and her face trembled, her lips compressed and her wrinkled skin pulled tight around her mouth. She looked curled in on herself and old. She picked up the tea glass in front of her and started to tap it on the table, an odd, repetitive movement. We both waited for her answer, but she just sat there, staring fixedly at the little gold-rimmed glass she was tapping on the rough wooden surface.

Chapter Seventeen

The night's wind had abated but there was still a thick layer of cloud in the sky, a grey drabness that sucked the warmth and life out of the land. Aisha and I went for a last walk through the olives. I surveyed the concrete barrier slicing through the countryside, trying to remember there were families on the Israeli side with their own tales of loss, with a sense of hurt they too had carried for generations. I struggled to maintain my objectivity, thinking back to the border guard's outburst. If he had endured and lost as much as these people had, I could see how some silly Englishman's use of a word like 'regrettable' would have made his blood boil.

We stood arm in arm for a long time, Aisha's hair soft against my cheek and the misty morning light slowly lightening the rain-cleansed, gleaming leaves of the olive grove around us, a sullen red morning glow washing over the terracotta ground dotted with neat rows of silvery-green leaved bushes.

Hamad and his tractor were nowhere to be seen when we got back to the farm. As we loaded our bags into the boot of the car, I noticed several cigarette butts on the ground by the back wheel. I squatted and inspected the bodywork as closely as I could without being too obvious, but found nothing out of place. Lying in bed listening to the wind in the night, I had let my mind wander with possibilities, with reasons why a group of men would be meeting outside a remote West Bank farmhouse in the cold wind and rain. And none of them were good things.

I embraced Mariam, kissed her cheeks and told Aisha

to tell her I loved her, which made the old lady smile and slap me on the chest.

'She says you're a very bad man,' Aisha translated, adding, 'and she's right, too.'

We left, waving our goodbyes before bouncing along the rutted track to join the Qaffin road. Aisha and I talked about Mariam as we drove through the overcast, drab landscape, stopping for the Israeli checkpoints, a routine I accepted with the same resignation I saw on the faces of the people around me in the queues.

It started to rain again, the morning's red sky coming through with the goods, a light drizzle which kept the dust down and the village children in their houses. In the flat greyness of the day, the villages seemed even more bleak, tired and hopeless. The washed out dreariness ground us down so the squeak of the windscreen wipers and constant drone of the engine soon became the only sound in the car. Aisha opened her window and lit cigarettes for us. It wasn't until the cold air hit me I realised I'd been dozing.

We reached the Sheikh Hussein crossing and this time I asked the soldier if I could go across to the office. He was surprised at the request, paused for a moment before nodding. He walked with me across the floor. I hoped against hope my officer would be there. He was.

'Paul Stokes.'

'You remember me.'

'I tell you, we not get many English tourists here.'

'One of your men told me about your daughter. I just wanted to say I am sorry.'

I half-expected him to hit me. He stood, his lips trembling and his face taut, but his voice was gentle and his eyes were, too. His smile was tight but I knew the bitterness was not directed at me. He reached out and patted my arm and his words, though they seemed anything but gentle, were almost soothing.

'Fuck off, Englishman.'

I dipped my head and left.

I sat on the patio in the cold and damp, watching the rain fall on the garden, drinking warm Chilean wine and smoking. Alone with my thoughts and the sound of the rain, lost somewhere between the two worlds straddling the Jordan. I needed to find a balance, because what was in Aisha's heart wasn't in mine. Although I desperately wanted to be with her in everything, I was a stranger in her conflict and for the most part an unwelcome one. Worried this would always be something between us that wasn't truly shared, I felt alien.

The rain kept falling around me until it became dark and I took the empty bottle and the full ashtray inside, glancing again at the original copy of the Ministry's bid evaluation document on my kitchen table. It had been there when I got back from the farm, placed there by the same invisible hands that had taken it from the chair in the café where I had left it, following Lynch's instructions.

Certain Lynch had intended me to be disconcerted at quite how easily they had broken into my house to return it, I opened another bottle and sat down to read the thing, taking great care not to spill wine on it.

I put the bid evaluation document back on the Minister's secretary's desk early on Sunday morning before going down to my office and starting work on the second issue of the magazine.

The evaluation had been a fascinating read. The committee had suggested the winning bidder might consider subcontracting the Brits for their water conservation and waste management expertise, but this wasn't conditional to an award, meaning Daoud's consortium could effectively ignore the advice. Otherwise, the document was unequivocal – it recommended the Jerusalem Consortium for its technical bid. The last line of the thing effectively saved having to read the forty preceding pages.

The Jerusalem Consortium offer is technically in advance of the Anglo-Jordanian Consortium and offers significant increases in Jordan's water resources through exploration of sources previously untapped by Jordanian stakeholders. We consider the offer and solution as outlined by the Jerusalem Consortium bid to be the only tenable course forward to meet Jordan's water needs for the coming twenty-five years and recommend it be adopted.

The conclusion avoided what Zahlan would have called the elephant in the room – the water the Jerusalem Consortium planned to tap would come from sources which would otherwise flow into Israel. Daoud's bid was based on boring into a series of previously unknown deep springs which rose to feed the massive Lake Tiberias – Israel's hard-won Sea of Galilee. Jordan's gain would be Israel's loss. Daoud was taking back the water.

Aisha came by my desk and we chatted, somehow managing to keep at least a semi-professional distance but both of us aching to touch as she sat at her favourite spot on the side of my desk, grinning and playing with the silver and amber Bedouin necklace she wore over her burgundy polo-neck.

'Lunch, Brit? Vinny?'

Vinny was Vinaigrette, the perennially popular sushi and salad joint in the bustling *Shmeisani* area.

'I can't. I'm meeting up with one of the British Business Group people for lunch. How about later? Come around to mine and we'll go up together.'

Her hand brushed up my arm as she stood, a quick squeeze that thrilled me. 'I'd like to. About five?'

My eyes travelled up her body, from her snug-fitting jeans to the curves under the tight top, undressing her and wanting her, almost feeling the warmth of her smooth skin under my hands as my eyes moved over her. By the time our eyes locked, Aisha's were wide and her lips parted.

My voice came out hoarse. 'How about four?'

She nodded and fled.

I left the Ministry building at lunchtime to meet Lynch, who had picked a busy street café near the Sixth Circle. He was cheery, gesturing me to a chair.

'The falafel sandwich is only gorgeous,' he beamed at me. 'And the strawberry juice here is world-famous, so and it is.'

I sat down opposite him at the rickety, plastic-covered table and took one of his cigarettes before ordering a chicken *shawarma* and an orange juice from the swarthy waiter. The traffic roared and honked alongside, the air reeked of frying and sweet *shisha* tobacco smoke mixed with exhaust fumes and hot engine.

'I hardly need say this, Paul, but you did a great job with that document. It's everything we wanted and more. Good man. It's a shame there aren't more like you about, that's the truth.'

The sandwich came and I stubbed out the cigarette, pulling the tissue paper away from the tightly wrapped round of hot chicken, garlic, pickle and potato chip. I ate while Lynch finished his smoke, gazing benevolently around him. I wiped my mouth, the paper wrap from the sandwich crumpled on the table.

'It's all I'm doing for you.' My voice was flat. I'd rehearsed this scene in my mind many times by now and it was playing out pretty much as I'd reckoned it would.

'Sure, Paul. Let's walk a minute.'

Lynch got up, dropping a couple of Dinars on the tabletop. I finished my orange and followed him up the street. I caught up with him as he turned right into a side-street.

He heard me catching up. 'You were away at the weekend.'

The RFP-returning invisible hand would have reported the house had been empty, the car away. Part of me wanted to make up a lie for him, but I hadn't foreseen this angle developing in our conversation and the only thing coming to my rescue was the truth.

'Yes, I went with Aisha to her grandmother's farm.'

Lynch pulled to a halt and turned to face me. His blue eyes focused on me before skittering away to look around us, his voice insouciant.

'Oh, right. Now where would that be, Paul?'

I hadn't spotted the change in him, even though I had stopped and turned to face him. 'Near Qaffin. The West Bank. By the wall.'

'Why the fuck didn't you tell me you were planning to do that?'

'It didn't seem to matter.'

'Everything matters. You fucking idiot. Have you got no sense at all? Who did you go with?'

'Just Aisha.'
'Who did you meet?'
'Her grandmother. Her uncle Hamad.'
'Anyone else?'
'No.'
'Anyone take the car away?'

I shook my head, puzzled at the violence making him tremble, his lips compressed into a white-edged cut across his face.

'No.'

'Anyone give you anything to carry, any bags?'

'No. What's the game, Gerry? You train in airport security or something?'

He raised a finger to me, his head tilted to one side as he spat the words. 'Don't be fucking smart with me, Stokes. You want to go away for dirty weekends with your Arab bint, you tell me first. You hear me?'

The wave rushed over me, greater anger than I'd ever felt before. It all came to a head, my resentment at Lynch's arrogant assumption he controlled my life, his disrespect for Aisha all channelled themselves in a moment of burning fury. His finger stayed in my face as I found physical release for my impotent frustration. I lashed out at him with all my strength.

He moved with blinding speed to catch my hand and snare my momentum, moving with me expertly with force and precision like a dancer, a whirl of action that slammed me up against the wall with my arm wrenched up my back. The bolt of pain in my shoulder forced me to stifle a scream, grazing my cheek on the rough stone. I felt the rasp of his cheek, our breath mingling as the moment passed and the tension slowly went out of our bodies. But he didn't release me. He spoke in a voice so low it was almost a lover's whisper.

'You move, you tell me. You shit, you tell me. I am looking after you, you ungrateful little bastard and I can't fucking do that if you launch off on daft little tours. You understand me?'

I said nothing and he wrenched my pinioned arm. I cried out, 'Yes.'

He let go of me and stepped back. I turned, rubbing my shoulder and saw the tension in him as he waited for me to make another move. I didn't. His voice was calm, his face impassive.

'I should have left them fucking shoot her when they wanted to.'

I rubbed my aching shoulder and glowered at him. 'What the hell does that mean?'

He stepped towards me and I flinched. I didn't like myself very much for that. His hand rested on my chest.

'You aren't in the UK, Paul. You're somewhere very strange and foreign and you understand very little of what's going on here. I've played it straight with you, but you need to piss straight with me, too. Let me know before you take any more pleasure trips or, so help me God, I'll put you in frigging hospital next time. If you survive any next time.'

He wheeled away from me, stopped and turned. 'Oh, and another thing. If you ever call me Gerry again, you won't even see the fucking lights go out, you hear me?'

He marched away without waiting for an answer.

Aisha and I lay together on my bed, touching and talking in murmurs, the clean cotton sheets rustling under our clothes. Somehow she understood I was still struggling with the aftermath of the journey we'd taken together and it brought us even closer, something I hadn't thought possible. The farm bound us. Our touching became more intense, more intimate and our rhythms increased together, kissing deeply as our hands explored and cajoled, opening clothes and finding warm skin, our hands seeking pleasure. Stayed from reaching the ultimate intimacy by Aisha's reticence, we used our hands, our mouths pressed hard together, until we cried out with a single voice.

We lay in each other's arms, damp heat cooling and the smell of our excitement mingling with her heavy perfume in a rich, lustful stench. The release brought a tremendous sadness upon me and I cried, Aisha crying with me, cradling me into the nape of her neck and softly repeating my name.

I woke in the middle of the night to find she had left, the bed cold beside me. I thought I heard a helicopter, but it was just my imagination playing tricks again in the darkness.

Morning smells filled the kitchen – coffee, toast and butter – the door open to let the cool, fresh morning air into the room, the sky outside grey and dull. I wandered into the living room and flicked on the TV to catch the news as I saw the red text flashing across the screen in its white panel, 'Israel Terror Attack.'

I sat down to watch, finishing my slice of toast and wiping my hand on my sock as I heard the presenter play for time. I watched the news ticker. A bomb, a big one. Fifteen people dead. A busy shopping centre in Haifa.

The presenter cut to pictures of the blast, a home video of a family shopping trip, Grandpa mugging for the camera, giving the thumbs up and Hebrew chattering and laughter on the soundtrack.

Behind the old man, hundreds of feet away, a plume of smoke mushrooms into existence, the street jumps as the corona of the concussion expands in a moment of violence, the black, roiling cloud billowing around a scarlet core. The camera goes wobbly before falling, skittering footage across the tarmac, scattered images, blurred legs. The camera is picked up again, steadies and records wreckage, smoke, dust, blurred people running. A child crying, blood on her frilly pink frock.

Strange details lodged in my mind as the shock of it forced me into slow motion. The name of a shop: Haifa Antiquities. The colour of a young man's shirt: blue, spattered with red. He's holding his hand to his ear, his mouth is open and his eyes are clenched shut in agony. He's staggering in circles. There's someone pointing a phone at him. The report cut back to the newsreader and a blurry satellite linkup to their reporter in Jerusalem.

I held the remote control loosely in my hand. Strange details. Like the small, innocuous car down the street, caught on film behind Grandpa's shoulder, the epicentre of the blast, momentarily there before being rocked and engulfed in the dusty, cloudy explosion. A glint of sunlight on the windscreen before the blast.

I channel-hopped desperately, catching the scrap of video, watching it again and again as my coffee went cold on the floor, catching the instant when the windscreen of the car flashed in the sun before it detonated. A small, dark blue Toyota Tercel.

Chapter Eighteen

Water flicked through the car's open window, lashing my eyes. I raced through the city streets, the engine screaming and tyres hissing on the wet tarmac. I broke out into open country and a vista of cypress-dotted hills and rock outcrops before the road looped back into the suburbs.

I sped around a tight corner in a hilly residential area. The tyres hit a bad road repair and I slid out of control across the smooth, treacherous bitumen. The car spun a full circle before bumping against the kerb, not a damaging impact, but heavy enough to jolt me into awareness of my surroundings.

A pretty street, one of the old ones. Silence, apart from the soft rain falling around me and the ticking of the cooling engine, mist rising from the hot bonnet.

I left the car where it had stalled, impelled by a need for movement, any movement to escape the horror of that piece of video, of the moment before a street in Haifa was torn apart.

At the top of the road there was a small, white building topped with a cupola and a crucifix. I opened the whining iron gate and walked through a pretty garden up to the big door of the church. Inside was warm, the walls and ceiling coloured with rich Byzantine decoration, golden icons hung on the walls, the flames of the candles bobbing as I passed. Pinpricks of light stretched away from me, glowing in the dark comfort of the interior. I walked up to the altar and gazed at the Eastern sumptuousness of it all, my mind empty of everything but the revulsion and shame filling me. I sat down on a cold wooden pew, my fingers tracing the worn lines, the smell of wood and frankincense in my nostrils as my breathing slowed.

'*Pari lou is.*'

A deep voice. I turned to my right and saw a huge white-bearded figure dressed in black, an olivewood crucifix around his neck. I looked at him, opened my mouth to speak, but couldn't make the words come out.

He spoke again: '*Sabah al khair,*' and, when I still didn't reply, 'Good morning.' I nodded.

'Welcome to our Church. I am Father Vahan.'

He smiled, his hands held together either in prayer or greeting.

'Forgive me, but you appear troubled.'

I looked at the richly decorated altar and around at the classical images, glittering Madonnas and Christs on the wooden panels around me.

The priest smoothed his robes, dipping his head to the altar as he bent to sit at the pew opposite me. He inclined his head, a quizzical expression on his face. 'You have suffered a loss, perhaps.'

He waited but I remained silent, looking around at the icons, hangings and decoration. Flickering candles in holders appeared to multiply up into the darkness of the roof above me into infinity. I twisted my hands on my knee, rocking and taking comfort from the rhythm of my movement.

'My name is Paul.' I was surprised at how husky my voice sounded and cleared my throat, the rasping sound echoing in the empty church.

'Welcome, then, Paul.' He waited for me to speak again. And when I did, the words tumbling out of me, he sat motionless and let me relive the months since I had flown through the turbulent desert air into Amman to start my new life and ending up in a cell for helping the hotel driver in his argument with two sneering policemen. I told him about the court case, about my fears for the sentence still hanging over me, of my love for Aisha and my visit to her family's farm. I told him about Gerald Lynch and what he had made me do for him, about Bethany and a lost bag, about Jericho and the bomb. And I told him, crying now, about Haifa and an old man dying on video in front of a car I thought I had seen before, on a cold night in the West Bank.

He listened without interruption until I ran out of words, my tears wet on my cheeks. The double-armed cross on the altar glowed gold in the candlelight and the echo of my last word, spoken clearly, died in the darkness around us.

He waited for me to look up before he spoke. 'You think she made this bomb? Your girl?'

'Yes. No. I don't know.'

'The brother, then.'

'Daoud. I don't know. Maybe. He has reason and resources.'

'But you don't know. There is doubt in your voice now.'

'There were men by my car. Why would they be there in that weather, at midnight, skulking in the dark?'

'You think they hid the explosives in your car.'

'Yes. No.' What did I think? 'Their car was blue.'

His voice was matter-of-fact. 'There are many blue cars in the world, Paul. There are many meetings between men at night in Palestine, because the Arabs love the night. They like to plot and scheme, to talk about ideals and the perfection of the world. Now and then their talk turns to action, but rarely. Mostly they talk and dream, drink tea and smoke *argileh*. It's their tragedy, the

Palestinians, to dream like opium eaters while their leaders fail them. They leave it to others to act and build better houses around themselves.'

'It was close by, just over the border, like the last bomb. Bethany is across the border from Jericho, Qaffin is over the border near Haifa.'

Vahan smiled sadly at me. 'He would have to truly be a monster, this man. To hide explosives in a car his sister would drive in. Is he such a monster, Paul?'

'Convictions make monsters of men, don't they? Enough passion, enough belief, and you have a monster. If you brutalise men, they turn into monsters. Were Sabra and Chatila enough to create monsters? Gaza? Ramallah? Daoud lost his father and brother. Could revenge be a monster? Maybe he's just doing it for God.'

'Not our God, Paul.'

'The same God.'

Vahan shifted his big body to sit more comfortably, his arm hanging over the back of the pew in front. 'So you think she has betrayed you. She is his willing accomplice.'

'No.' I realised I had barked the negative, looked guiltily at the priest, but he remained impassive.

'The Israeli soldiers searched your car at the border.'

'Yes.'

'They are thorough. They use dogs, electronics. I have been through many times to Jerusalem, to our dwindling community there. Do you not think they would have found these explosives?'

'Maybe. Maybe not. I don't know. I know there was a missing bag in Bethany and then a bomb in Jericho. That there were men by my car and then a bomb in Haifa.'

'Ah, but then there are bombs that happen without you, too, my young friend. Are you sure these bombs truly belong to you? The Arabs are very fond of making conspiracies, connecting things to build palaces of supposition in their talk. Are you not becoming one of them, Paul? Are you becoming an opium eater yourself?'

I cast around me for answers I didn't have. I could see myself bursting into Daoud's office, confronting him with it all and his cold, flat voice telling me to get a grip. Aisha crying, my betrayal of her trust tearing us apart. Nour's horrified face: *'How could you, Paul?'* Mariam, a bent old lady in a *kandoura*, tapping her tiny gold-rimmed glass on the tabletop, a lifetime of pain and loss behind her and an unjust wall cutting across her olive groves.

The priest continued. 'We seldom have the benefit of certainties, Paul. It is a luxury we can reserve for our love of God. Maybe you did see the bombers in the night, but this doesn't mean you carried the bomb. Maybe you didn't see bombers. Maybe you saw some farmers asking this man about the foreigner visiting him. Maybe you saw some men planning some other crime. Maybe this car was the same car. Maybe it wasn't. Maybe you are intelligent and have a strong imagination.'

'You don't believe me.'

The priest chuckled. 'Oh, my friend, my fine young friend. I don't think you believe yourself.'

He was right. In the calm half-light of the church, the certainties had left me. I had no answers for him, I couldn't give him anything more than assumptions, circumstantial evidence and suspicions founded on my own willingness to believe in strange things, perhaps because I was adrift in an environment that felt more unfamiliar with each passing day. The child that used to make tanks out of hawthorn hedges and trenches out of ditches. I shuddered as I thought of how close I had come to wrecking everything around me on such flimsy supposition.

The girl who made courtiers out of olive trees as she passed through them, the olive princess.

'You have to be very certain of yourself. Few us of are ever so lucky,' Vahan said. 'You could talk to the authorities.'

'They wouldn't believe me.'

Besides, the only authorities I had been conditioned to trust were represented by Gerald Lynch, liar and thief.

'Then why do you believe yourself? The test of conviction is in being able to convince another. Perhaps you are lacking conviction, then.'

'What do you believe?'

He chuckled again. 'I believe in God, in his will and the goodness he has made in us.'

I listened to his baritone voice resonate in the space of the church. 'And you believe I am imagining this?'

'Perhaps I do, perhaps I believe you are right in your suspicions. There are no certainties. I think you may be right, but then you may be wrong. And I think you are not so certain and you perhaps have been blinded by love. But then perhaps you are indulging yourself in fancy.' He smiled, a wry grin at the floor. 'Perhaps. Everything is perhaps, is it not?'

Vahan got creakily to his feet. 'Perhaps you are asking the wrong person as you sit in this church, in His house.'

I stood with him, but he waved me down. 'Ask Him,' the priest said. 'If you need me, come through the door by the altar. I'll be there.'

He offered his hand and I took it, feeling the warmth of his skin. He walked away from me up the aisle, turning by the altar, crossing himself. 'Paul. Go with God.'

I sat there for a long time, my eyes closed and my hands together, before I finally pulled myself to my feet and left.

I got to work late. Aisha had left a sticky on my screen: 'Your mobile's off. Dinner?' I sat at my desk, going through the motions and turning the images from Haifa over and over in my mind. I read the news reports online, watched the video clip time and again and tried to imagine Aisha deliberately setting out to create that carnage.

I called her on my way back to the Ministry, grinning like an idiot at the sound of her voice.

'Hi Brit. Dinner round at mine? Eight o'clock. Mum wants to feed you up.'

'Great. Is Daoud going to be there?'

'Yes, he's in town.' She sounded a little puzzled. 'Why?'

'Oh, I wanted to talk to him about the water thing.'

'I'm sure he'll be delighted. He's been talking about nothing else for weeks. Paul, are you okay?'

'Yes, fine. Did you see the news this morning?'

'No, I woke late and had to go straight to a meeting over at Finance. What's the problem Paul? What's wrong?'

'Another bomb. In Haifa this time. It killed sixteen people.' I waited for her reaction, hating myself for testing her like this. If anybody had seen me going into the Ministry that morning, they'd have thought me mad. I'd decided if I could make it up the thirty-eight stone steps to the front door in under sixteen leaps, Aisha was innocent.

Aisha's voice was neutral. 'Oh, right. Hang on. Yes,

it's here on Yahoo! So much for Sharon's wall, then. Haifa's near the farm, you know. Just over on the coast. Wait a sec.' I heard her mumbling as she read the news report, 'Haifa, car bomb, sixteen dead. Five children. It says they were all girls from one family. Oh. Their mother too. God be with them, the poor things.'

It had taken fourteen leaps to the door that morning and I'd walked through the big wooden double doors grinning, breathless and certain.

'Catch you later, then.'

'Don't be late, *ya* Brit.'

I sat at my desk, filled with lassitude and indifference to the magazine project. I kept breaking off to look out of the window at the city's darkened buildings, the wet streets capped by the grey skies. I was still daydreaming when the Minister arrived at my desk. I jumped to my feet.

'Your Excellency.'

'Relax, Paul,' smiled Harb Al Hashemi, pulling up a chair. He handed me a sheaf of papers – a printout of my feature on the water contracts.

'This is very good. I've made just one change, where you've talked about the value of the water privatisation and the terms for the bidders. The value is purely speculation until we release the details of the financial proposals from the bidders and I really do not think we're ready to announce it quite yet. But it would be nice to do a... do you call it a sidebox? A view of some of the issues. I'll have Aisha bring you a copy of the original request for proposals as well as the evaluation committee's report and recommendations on the submitted bids. It's highly confidential, but it should give you a feel for some of the underlying issues we're dealing with here.'

'No problem, Minister.'

I couldn't believe it. I'd gone through the heartache of stealing the damn thing and now it was being dropped in my lap.

He got up. 'Good. Look, the Dead Sea Water Conference next month will see the whole privatisation issue settled. It will be the start of a new and important era for Jordan. I think it is critical to cover this in the magazine.'

'Yes, I agree, Minister. It's certainly seems as if it is going to be interesting.'

'I've had you booked into the hotel as a member of the Ministry delegation, Paul. You can talk to all of the stakeholders in the process, they'll all be at the conference. I'd like to establish a broad, balanced view of the issues and solutions.'

'That would be great. Thank you, Minister.'

'A pleasure, Paul. Perhaps Aisha can stay on and act as your tour guide after the meetings.'

'I wouldn't want to put her out.'

He rubbed my shoulder. 'I'm sure she would be delighted at the opportunity. You're a good man, Paul.'

There was no mistaking the presence of a twinkle in his eye as he turned and left. Aisha came down with a copy of the draft RFP and the evaluation document about an hour later. She stood by my desk, holding the document out to me, her face amused.

'Your very own copy of the evaluation. Don't leave it lying around or lose it, now.'

I missed the inference at first, then did a double take and looked at her suspiciously.

'What's that supposed to mean?'

'Oh, nothing. It's a valuable document, is all.'

I quickly changed the subject. 'The Minister knows

about us.'

Aisha's eyes flashed, her hand flying to her mouth. 'How?'

'Don't ask me. But I'm coming to the Dead Sea for the water conference and he suggested I might want to stay over the weekend with you as my tour guide afterwards. I told him I didn't want to put you out and he said you'd be only too delighted to take the opportunity.'

'Oh God. He must have been talking to Daoud.'

'So you're ashamed of me, then?'

She put on a mock angry expression. 'Don't be silly,' she growled, 'Damn Brit.'

'See you later?'

'Later.'

Chapter Nineteen

I took the crystal tumbler of Black Label from Daoud. He sat on the chair by the sofa and I offered him a cigarette. The women were clearing the table after our dinner, laughing and chattering.

'Did you see there's been another bomb?' I wanted to test his reaction, to finally put my suspicions to rest.

'Yes, in Haifa. I heard it was bad.' Daoud frowned. 'I've been trying to get through to my people there, but the lines appear to have been cut. It might just be too much traffic. It's odd, I visited there the day before yesterday.'

I put my glass down and leaned forward. 'You were there?'

Daoud played with the ice in his glass. 'We don't talk about it much. I have two offices in Israel: a representative office in Haifa and another in Eilat. Both offices are highly profitable for our shipping business. I often travel there.' My reaction seemed to amuse him. 'There are quite a few Jordanians with business interests over there, you know, Paul. Stop looking at me like I'm a monster.'

I had never imagined Daoud could actually have business interests in Israel. I realised I had been over-simplifying him to fit my own role for him as a 'vengeful Arab' stereotype. If I took away revenge as a motive, I was left with a Jordanian businessman with offices in Israel and a British with an over-active imagination.

'But the farm, your land. The things you've lost.'

Daoud sipped his drink before leaning forward and looking directly at me, his face still smiling but his voice earnest. 'Life goes on, Paul. One day we will have a proper peace in Palestine, one we can believe in, that lasts. Jordan is at peace with Israel, has been for over ten years. It's not all perhaps quite as polarised as you might think. We're traders, businessmen. You can't pretend Israel doesn't exist, that's something you leave for the dreamers and the extremists. The rest of us, we have to live. Okay, it's not quite love at first sight and most of us don't like to talk about it, but it's a fact of life. There are something like two million Arab-Israelis. My grandfather's brother became Israeli after 1948. He was a lawyer who played a key part in keeping the farm within the family. And he helped to found our business over there, too.'

Aisha came over. 'Coffee? Turkish, medium, yes?'

'Yes, please. Thanks, Aish.'

I watched her walking to the kitchen, her graceful, long-legged step accentuating the curves under her tight cream dress. Daoud cleared his throat and I jumped.

'Talking about the farm, how did you guys get on there?'

Like our agreement to keep the police charge secret, Aisha and I had agreed we'd keep the helicopter incident between us.

'It was amazing, a real experience. I never thought the West Bank would be, well, beautiful. You don't really get shown olive trees and old men smoking *argileh* by the roadside on the television. You just see the violence and stuff. And Mariam is an inspiration, truly.'

'It's a way of life that has all but passed now,' Daoud said, frowning.

I remembered Mariam sitting in the kitchen, her lined face stark in the candlelight her finger held against her lips.

'I met Hamad there.'

'He's a good man.'

'He's quiet. I didn't really get to talk to him, but something puzzled me. He met some men outside in the yard, very late at night. It was sort of odd.'

I could almost hear my heart hammering as I took a sip of icy whisky. Daoud looked directly at me, his frown deepening.

'Really? Why, what were they doing?'

'I honestly don't know. I saw them through the bedroom window. Their car woke me up.'

He sat back, shaking his head. 'The men sometimes meet up and talk revolution and so on, but usually in the warmth of someone's kitchen, where they can share their dreams of freedom and their big talk. Now and then they plot something or another, but it rarely comes to anything. And it's the young ones, not the old ones who are trouble.'

Daoud shifted to sit on the edge of the sofa, his glass held in both hands. 'Damn Hamad. I'll have to go over at the weekend and make sure he's not up to anything stupid.'

He put his hand on my leg and I managed not to flinch.

'Thank you, Paul. I appreciate your candour. It isn't always easy, keeping this family in check. I sometimes wonder if I'm quite old enough for it.'

He sat back and I leaned forward, my inner journalist taking over. 'Your company is sponsoring the Dead Sea Water Conference. Are you so confident you'll win the privatisation bid?'

He smiled at me, a tight little smile. 'You're working still, Paul?'

I shook my head. 'No, just curiosity. I've seen a few

documents that talk of your bid and it seems all very, well, innovative. As far as I understand it, the British approach is about more effective resource management while yours is focused on simply finding more water.'

Daoud winced. 'It's not simple. It's bloody difficult, otherwise half the world would be over here doing it. It's technically very innovative and uses technologies only we can bring to the table. Look, if you're interested I can give you a copy of our bid. You'll keep it to yourself, I know. It's important you do, there are political issues involved as well.'

'Thank you, I'd like to read it. If you don't mind me asking you questions about it all. The Minister wants to refocus the next issue of the magazine on the whole water management thing and I have to admit, I'm on a steep learning curve.' I sipped my drink, frowning as the thought hit me. 'How do you mean, it's political?'

'It's in the Israeli's interests to stop us exploiting new water reserves. They need us struggling with inadequate resources while they get fat on the water they've taken from us over the years. As I told you before, Paul, I mean to take our water back. And as you can imagine, they're not going to be happy about it.'

'What about the 1994 peace treaty?'

'They're saying they don't feel bound by its water provisions. So why should we be? Israel provides Jordan with a fraction of the water they undertook to supply. We cannot go on like this.'

Aisha came from the kitchen holding two tiny cups of strong, cardamom-fragranced coffee, bending to place them on the side table.

'Go on like what, you bully?'

He looked up at her and smiled, sitting back. 'Never mind. We were just talking shop. Listen, I said I'd maybe meet up with Ghaith at Nai. You guys fancy going out for a drink?'

Aisha grinned. 'Cool. We're on. You haven't been to Nai before have you, Paul?'

'Nope. What is Nai?'

'A place for spoiled brats from rich families to behave badly,' said Daoud, his face dark and his eyes on Aisha. 'I'm glad you haven't been there, Paul. It shows you have a pure soul.'

Aisha punched him. 'Come on, I'll get Mariam.'

Daoud turned to me. 'One second, Paul, and I'll dump that file for you.'

I sipped carefully at the hot, strong coffee until Daoud returned a minute later holding a memory key with a Jerusalem Holdings logo on it.

'Here. The Jerusalem technical bid document. There are no financials in there, but it's still highly confidential. It should tell you all you need to know about the problems we're facing and how I believe we have a unique and revolutionary solution to Jordan's water crisis.'

'Thank you, Daoud. That's a lot of trust you've put in me.'

'You already have something far more precious to me, Paul,' he said, laughing. 'My sister's heart.'

I was coming to like Daoud Dajani a great deal.

We bundled into the BMW's walnut-trimmed interior. It smelled faintly of cowhide and cigar. The girls sat in the back and I sat by Daoud as he drove through the dark streets. I held the memory key in my right jacket pocket. I'd already decided this wouldn't be shared with Gerald bloody Lynch and the decision somehow removed a huge weight from my shoulders.

It was past eleven o'clock as we sped through the quiet streets before breaking out into the bright lights of Shmeisani and its bustling restaurants. There was music and laughter in the air, the sweet smell of *argileh* smoke wafting in through my open window as we passed groups of people in the street.

I shook my head in awe at how these people did it. At a time when any reasonable human being would be digesting their food, sipping a scotch and thinking about bed, these guys were starting the evening. I was seeing a different Daoud tonight: he was laughing and joking, high on the enthusiasm washing over us from the back seats as the girls chatted and messed about. I found myself grinning, talking motors with Daoud in the way only an impoverished journalist with zero ambition can talk to an Arab millionaire about fifty thousand pound cars.

We arrived at the nightclub. Daoud threw the keys at a valet and we went down the wrought iron stairs into the thumping music below. It reminded me of The Sheikh of Araby's tent, multi-coloured and hung with beads, drapes and scattered around with oriental lamps and artfully positioned arabesque 'objets.' The club heaved, people dancing, shouting across the packed crowd, vying for attention.

Vodka Red Bull. So many people were drinking it, the place smelled of bubblegum.

'Paul, this is Emma. She works with US AID.' Aisha's hand was on the arm of an American with lovely legs in a short skirt who flashed an excited grin at me. Hard to tell whether she was buzzing on bubblegum or E-ing.

'Hi,' she yelled at me. 'You must be Aisha's English boyfriend.'

Aisha laughed and carried me on through the crowd before I could reply, stopping every few steps to greet a new face, introducing me to a bewildering array of people.

We finally reached the end of the bar and joined Daoud. Aisha left us, calling out, 'One second. Don't move, I'll be back.'

She plunged into the thick of the shifting crowd and was instantly lost in the waving hands and flashing lights. Daoud had ordered cigars. I copied him, snipping the end off with his cutter and lighting it from a splint made from the cedar-wood wrapper. It was strong, inhaling the smoke brought a coughing fit.

'I'm not really a smoker,' I shouted, gasping at Daoud, my eyes streaming.

His hand round my shoulder, confiding, laughing, 'Paul, you're not supposed to inhale the bloody thing. Come, I reserved a table!'

Tables were hard to get at Nai, a few seats lined up in alcove areas towards the back of the bar were empty, with a 'reserved' sign on them. We sat and I people-watched as the crowd moved back and forth to the rhythm of the pumping beats, outbreaks of localised dancing breaking in from the West. Aisha rejoined us, pulling me to my feet and dragging me back into the crowd.

Laughter. A lot of laughter. Aisha on my arm, Aisha by my side. Aisha dancing, all those salsa classes paying off. Elegantly erotic, she moved to the music as if she were one with it.

Paul Stokes, the man at the end of his tether talking quietly to an orthodox priest, was left behind somewhere, a shade in the dim and distant past.

'You must be Paul. Nice to meet you. You're a lucky

man.' This from a tall, thick-waisted young man, maybe in his late twenties. He had teased, curly hair, a precisely cut goatee beard and wore a dark suit and open-necked shirt. 'I'm Ghaith.'

Daoud greeted Ghaith like a lost brother. Mariam danced on the bar, Aisha clapping her on with the rest of the crowd. I went to the toilet, met Aisha in the corridor on the way back into the bar. For the first time ever in public, we kissed, a kiss of sheer exuberance. We walked back into the bar holding hands and I saw Daoud standing nearby, talking to the barman as he bought another Cohiba, our seats empty over at the back of the bar, just visible through the excited throng.

The bomb scythed through them, an awful parabola of concussing violence, bodies flung against the screaming living, glass flying and tearing cloth, biting flesh. The bar in pieces, bottles smashed and drink streaming down the broken wood.

The force hit me, shards flying in the air, tossed me back against the wall. I saw Aisha's hair thrown up in a surreal halo as she jerked backwards and hit the bar with a sickening force that distorted her fine features.

Faux beams falling, a woman crawling towards me as I staggered to my feet, deafened. An awful silence, mouths open, soundless screaming. A man walking, his hands to his ears and blood running down his face like rain, the falling drops spattering on the dusty floor in a steady flow like a broken gutter. I felt wetness on my cheek, saw the blood on my fingers. Aisha. *Aish.*

A woman lay on the floor, her head thrown back and her eyes impossibly wide, her hair fanned out on the wooden boards, her hips jerking obscenely, nostrils flared. The iron tang of blood.

Dust, coughing, thick dust. Ring a ring of roses. I turned, alone. Small fires as the drapes burned up, smoke and dust, choking me. Silence as I turned, gaping, torn flesh around me, open wounds, tangled limbs and open mouths, dresses torn and dead eyes blurring as I turned around, brown flesh, white flesh, red flesh. Brown, white, red. Children playing and mother calling us in from the sun for tea. A pocket full of posies. Whirling madness. Choking smoke and stillness, except for a single dark figure, spinning in the middle of the deadly tableau.

Aisha. Aisha. Aisha.

I'm somewhere white and beautiful, the breeze caressing my skin and she calls out, answering me as I come to a standstill, screaming her name as I double up in pain.

The olive trees are her courtiers, the olive princess.

Chapter Twenty

Aisha sat wrapped in the rough blanket, still shaking and barely able to grasp the Styrofoam cup of sweet coffee I gave her.

The ambulances were still arriving, green-covered forms on gurneys being wheeled past us, but the pace had slowed a little, some four hours after our lives had been transformed by the instant of horrifying force. They were all around us, sitting in groups, lying on the floor, standing by beds or just silently staring. A woman's wail broke into sobs, the nurses shushing her.

Aisha sniffed, wiping at her puffy, bruised eye and wincing. 'How's Mariam?'

'She's fine, just a couple of small cuts. She was really lucky. They've sent her home.'

'Daoud?'

'Still no news.'

'He's here, right?'

'I'm not sure, Aish. The woman at reception says they can't tell who is and isn't here yet. Many of the people they're treating still can't even talk for themselves. And they won't let me check the cubicles.'

'Mum? 'brahim?'

'I talked to both. Ibrahim is coming down here. He's been talking to a contact in the police to try and track Daoud down as well.'

She gazed into her drink, the neon light shimmering on its surface. 'And what... what about everyone else?'

I looked around us. There was no way of knowing how many people had died, how many were injured. The hospital was overflowing, relatives arriving and mingling with the bloodied crowd in the packed A&E. I watched a young man, pale-faced and exhausted, his head against the wall and his hands in bandages, a group near him whispering as they tried to comfort a wide-eyed, violently shivering girl with crimson stains on the bandage around her head.

A nurse stopped in front of us. 'Dajani? Aisha Dajani?'

Aisha nodded. I took the cup from her hand and helped her up. I walked with her, my other hand shut tight on the memory key miraculously still in my jacket pocket along with my mobile.

By the time Ibrahim arrived, Aisha was wearing a collection of dressings, the glass cuts on her arm and thigh stitched and the powerful painkillers making her woozy. I started shaking, too exhausted to even flinch as the sutures entered the gash above my ear and the pattern of tiny cuts down my left side were probed for glass before being dabbed with antiseptic and closed. Aisha's hand on my cheek felt cool and soft, her thumb caressing my hot skin as I tensed with the pain.

Ibrahim wore a beige greatcoat, a scarf around his neck. Aisha caught the desolate look on his face, standing to bury her head in his shoulder. I tried to sit up, the movement creating a sharp tearing pain in my side.

Ibrahim motioned me back, his hand on Aisha's head, stroking her hair. 'Do not try and get up, Paul. You look very ill. Rest now.'

'Have they found Daoud?'

'No. I do not know. We can find no trace of him. The hospital director has been very kind in helping me look through the admittances from tonight. Daoud is not here.'

'The club?'

'No. Civil defence have cleared it now. There are no more people left there. The police have confirmed this.'

The pain returned, sharper this time and making me cry out. The nurse started to prepare a syringe.

I found it increasingly hard to speak, my swollen lips were dry and the stitches painful. 'How many? How many dead?'

Ibrahim grimaced. 'Eight. It is a miracle it was not more, apparently. There are too many injured, some seriously.'

The nurse slipped the syringe into the canula in my wrist. I was still trying to form my next question, my bloated lips refusing to move properly, when the enveloping lassitude lapped over me and enfolded me in darkness.

They let me go home the next afternoon. Aisha had gone earlier, tears running down her face, kissing a finger and touching it gently to my lips.

The ambulance man helped me to make my way up the steps to the house. I went to bed and stayed there through the day until, driven by thirst, I got up and hobbled painfully to the kitchen to get some water. There were missed calls on my mobile from my mother and three from Lynch.

Aisha's mobile went straight to voicemail, so I called the house and Nour told me she was asleep in bed.

I called my mum and told her I hadn't been anywhere near the bombing, that I sounded funny because I had the flu. She had been getting calls from the newspapers. I told her not to worry and to ignore them. Apparently my brother Charles was ill with flu too. I silently hoped, git though he was, he didn't have the same flu I did as I listened to her happy chattering.

I took my water into the living room and settled down painfully to scan the news as it ran footage of the ruined nightclub and told me about the ten dead and eighty-five wounded, twenty seriously. The numbers rolled by on the news channel's ticker and I found myself thinking of how impersonal they were, these tallies of deaths and tragedies, of grieving families and loved ones.

The mobile rang. Lynch.

'Paul. Are you okay?'

'Bit stuffed up, but yes.' It sounded like someone else's voice, harsh and croaky, muffled by my big lips.

'Thank God. Look, Paul, have you seen Daoud Dajani?'

'No. No, I haven't.'

'Well if you do, call me. It's important, Paul. He's a dangerous man. We're now certain he's linked to the Jericho and Haifa bombings and we believe he's behind this one, too. He's disappeared, there's no trace of him. We're really concerned about what he's up to. The man's a terrorist and a smart one at that. Do you understand, Paul? He's dangerous.'

'So find him. Arrest him.'

'We don't have enough to go on yet, Paul. But we're working on it with the Jordanians. You'll let me know if you hear of him, yes?'

'Yes.'

I got a good whack of scotch and a handful of ice from the kitchen and Daoud's memory key from my torn jacket and settled down to read his vision for Jordan's water. Sometime past midnight I finished, stretching painfully and taking my drink to bed with me.

In the blackness, sleep eluding me, I lay wondering what was driving Daoud Dajani. His scheme was breathtaking, his plans meticulously detailed and backed by swathes of research by French experts and Arab researchers who had cut their teeth working on geophysical exploration in the Gulf's oil fields. His proposal claimed to ensure sufficient water for Jordan's consumption to increase by twenty-five percent without breaking into a sweat. It would scale back on currently over-exploited resources and tap into new finds of water deep underground, a system of seasonal aquifers and subterranean reservoirs that had lain undiscovered until Daoud's people had come along with new research based on tracing old Roman water systems. Those deep resources eventually rose up into the depths of Lake Tiberias throughout the winter, drying up in the summer. Daoud wanted to divert and trap the deep water before it got to Tiberias, storing it for use through the dry summer months.

I knew nothing about water, but one thing about Daoud's whole proposal was quite obvious. Jordan's gain would be at Israel's expense and would involve huge volumes of water.

I lay in the dark and tried to reconcile all of the different facets of Daoud Dajani, the brooding presence, the laughing family man, the successful businessman, the visionary with a plan for a nation's water and the terrorist. I was increasingly certain Gerald Lynch was lying to me but I couldn't shake the memory of Aisha's lost bag in the guide's hand down by the Jordan or of the group of men by my car outside a farmhouse near Ramallah.

We're certain he's linked, Lynch had said. I almost wished I could be as certain. I looked up at the ceiling, faint shapes starting to appear as my eyes adjusted. Daoud's plan for Jordan's water could be as divisive as the recent bombings had been. The new peace was in tatters and recriminations were already flying.

Israel's thirst for water had driven land grab after land grab, from 1948 to the insidious alterations in the course of the security wall that curled around springs and aquifers. When the Lebanese had tried to divert the Hasbani River, one of the three that flowed into Lake Tiberias, Israel had threatened war. Israel, Jordan, Lebanon and Syria. These people fought wars for water.

Daoud Dajani was a dangerous man, for sure. I lay in the silence reprising recent events and the people around me. I knew for certain he was no terrorist. He was a water thief, but no terrorist.

I haven't set the alarm. If I wake before ten he's innocent.

Aisha's call woke me. The morning sun's glow through the curtains filled the room with a soft, peaceful light. I checked the clock. Half past nine. She sounded as beaten up as I felt, her voice was dull and she mumbled.

'Hey, *ya* Brit.'

'Aish. How are you?'

'I hurt. I can't believe it. I still think of it as all happening to someone else. I've been asleep since they let me go. What about you?'

'I'm fine, just hurt a bit. How's Daoud?'

'We don't know, Paul. We still haven't heard from him. Mum's in a real state. We've lost...' Her voice broke and I listened helplessly to her as she fought to compose herself. 'We've lost so many friends.'

'We have each other. At least we still have each other.'

'Can you come around, Paul? I... I need you.'

'Of course. Give me a while to tidy up a bit. I'm not pretty right now.'

The hint of a laugh through her tears. 'You never were, *habibi*.'

I cleaned myself up as best I could, but there was a lot of plaster and some fine bruises were spreading across my shoulder, my side and my leg where I'd hit the wall. I had a splitting headache and my lips and eye were still swollen. I drove slowly, turning the wheel was an effort and my cut and bruised leg made braking painful.

Nour met me at the door, dressed in a light blue and gold *kandoura*. She had been crying and I took her in my arms. She patted my back, her touch on my bruised body was agony.

'Thank God you're safe, Paul.'

'Have you heard anything about Daoud?'

'No, nothing.' She held my shoulders as she looked at me, her eyes moist again. 'I believe God will take care of him. I have to believe this. I have lost all my lovely men, I cannot lose him, not Daoud, not the last of them. God wouldn't let that happen.'

Her fierce smile collapsed as she turned to lead me into the house. Aisha sat in the living room and tried to get up when I came in, but she wasn't strong enough. I went to her and settled her back down on the cushions.

Nour said something about dinner and left us. Aisha's cheek was bruised terribly, her arms too. I kissed her gently on the lips, the pain from my own damaged mouth mingling with the pleasure of wrapping myself up in Aisha's softness.

My phone rang. Ibrahim.

'Paul. How are you?'

'Well, thanks, Ibrahim. A lot better.' Aisha raised an eyebrow at me and I shrugged my shoulders back at her.

'Can you come to the Royal Automobile Club? It is perhaps a little urgent.'

'Why, what gives? Have you heard from Daoud?'

'Ask Mohamed at the front desk for me. Thank you, Paul.'

Aisha looked troubled. 'What's happening, Paul?'

'I don't know, Aish. Ibrahim wants to meet me at the RAC. I'd better go.'

We kissed and I touched her breast but she winced so I let her go and left her lying on the sofa. I said goodbye to Nour who had been crying quietly in the kitchen and made my painful way to Ibrahim's club, established by King Hussein bin Talal, long may he rest in peace, and a favoured meeting place of Jordan's terrible, wealthy old men.

Mohamed at the front desk was used to confronting all manner of odd things, his fifty-year tenure evident in his formal greeting as he studied my beaten face. 'Welcome, *seer*.'

'I am meeting Ibrahim Dajani.'

'Certainly. This way please, *seer*.'

We walked through the oak-panelled reception area and up the red-carpeted stairs as they curved gracefully up to the first floor. Mohamed stopped by the double door and knocked gently.

Ibrahim opened the door, thanking Mohamed and ushering me in before closing it swiftly behind me and turning the key.

I stepped forward and Daoud Dajani rose from the heavy, studded club chair and took my hand.

'Thank you for coming, Paul.'

Chapter Twenty-One

I sat down with a little difficulty and looked across at Daoud. He seemed exhausted, moving with an injured precision similar to my own. Ibrahim made me a coffee from the flask on the sideboard. I stirred sugar into it as I looked across at Daoud.

'Nour's very worried about you.'

'I can imagine. I'm sorry for her, but I don't have many options right now. The bomb at the nightclub was meant for me, Paul.'

I sat back. 'Why do you think that? Who would want to bomb you?'

'I don't think it, I know it. As for who, I know that, too. I'm not safe right now, Paul. They would actually bomb a busy nightclub just to target one man. These people are not normal, they don't care for life. At least not Arab life.'

The coffee tasted stewed. 'What people?'

Daoud stared grimly at me over the rim of his cup. His gold signet ring glittered in the light from the chandelier.

'Mossad. The Israelis.'

'Oh, no. Come off it, Daoud. Sorry, that's just mad. I'm not buying it.'

I got to my feet, but didn't really know where to go. Daoud motioned with a finger.

'Sit down, Paul. We have proof. Here.'

He reached across to me with a slim, stapled document. I took it.

'What is it?'

'It's the *Mukhabarat* report on the Nai bomb.' Daoud

glanced across at Ibrahim, who sat quietly on the sofa to the side.

I remembered the story of Daoud's capture on his way back from trying to stop his suicide bomber brother. Ibrahim had engineered Daoud's rescue from the feared *Mukhabarat*, the secret police. *Wasta*. Ibrahim gazed benignly right back at me and I turned back to Daoud.

'So what does it say?'

'It says the bomb did not explode properly,' said Ibrahim in his smoky rumble. 'Only half the charge went off. It is not sure whether by luck or design. These people do not tend to make mistakes. We believe it was meant as a signal, that we were meant to find what we did.'

'And what did you find?'

'The explosive is American. It is from a batch shipped to Kuwait for use by the American forces when they liberated the country from Saddam's army. A large amount of materiel was "lost" and made its way from Kuwait to Israel. There are many documented instances of this. The detonator is from the same era.'

'But it doesn't mean the bomb is Israeli.'

Ibrahim ignored me. 'The explosives were placed in a bag underneath the seat Ghaith Mcharourab had reserved at the club. Daoud was to meet him.'

Daoud's voice cut in. 'Ghaith died in the explosion.'

I had been gazing into my coffee. I looked sharply up at Daoud but his face was remained impassive.

'I'm sorry, Daoud.'

He nodded at me as Ibrahim's sonorous voice continued.

'The explosives were arranged with great precision, using military grade tape. It is quite difficult to make a bomb that will not quite explode. It is very easy to make one that will not explode. It is quite easy to make one that will explode. But to make a bomb that does not *quite* explode. Now this is quite an achievement.' Ibrahim pulled deeply on his cigarette. 'At least so I am told.'

I'd been flicking through the English half of the document and stopped at a diagram which showed the spread pattern of the explosion. Its full force had been directed upwards, but the periphery of its outward arc was a few feet from where Aisha and I had been standing when it happened. There were ten crosses marking, presumably, the dead, all in the arc. I put the report down on the coffee table.

'Okay, say for a moment it was them. Why?'

Ibrahim grunted as he leaned forward to stub out his cigarette. 'Someone called the police claiming responsibility, a group naming itself The Jerusalem Martyrs. The police treated it as a crank call. The group has never been heard of before.'

'And you think they meant it as a reference to the company's name. That's pretty circumstantial, isn't it?'

'They left a one-word message. The caller was most particular it be heard. The word was "water." The police are puzzled by this. Are you puzzled by this, Paul?'

And, of course, the only possible answer was no.

'It's all a bit histrionic, though Ibrahim. Why not just warn Daoud? Why try to kill him? Why involve innocent people?'

Daoud chuckled bleakly. 'There's a lot at stake with the water projects, Paul. They've gone to war over water in the past. Now they're going to war again. Did you read the document I gave you?'

'Yes, I did. And that's the big question it left me with. How will your proposal affect Israel's water supplies? It'll reduce them, won't it?'

'Yes, it will. There would be a significant reduction in

the flow of water out of Lake Tiberias.'

Daoud paused, his eyes scanning my face in a manner disconcertingly similar to Aisha's habit of looking from eye to eye when she was uncertain. He sat forward, cupping his hands.

'The volume of water flowing into Tiberias from the three feeder rivers is actually significantly less than the volume flowing out. It has long been known there are a number of underground springs rising up into the lake from underground seas. We believe tapping these will yield something like a hundred million cubic metres of fresh water a year, mostly during the winter months. That is water Jordan desperately needs.'

'And so does Israel.'

'The difference is, Paul, this water is flowing through Jordanian land into a lake that is rightly Jordanian.

'So, if you're draining a freshwater spring into Tiberias, the water flowing out of the lake to Israel will be more saline.'

'Yes. Yes, it will.'

'So the Israelis don't just end up with less water, they end up with saltier water. Less useful water.'

Daoud didn't answer, his hands clasped together and his knuckles white. As I looked across the table at him, I finally understood how much was at stake in this tug of water – the Jordanian fields would blossom as Israel's gardens withered. Standing in the middle of them would be a great statue of Daoud, Ozymandias with an amphora on his shoulder, tipped to pour sparkling water into a giant irrigation ditch.

I put my cup down. 'And so you think they want you dead.'

Daoud stood, wheeling to walk across the room away from me, Ibrahim ready to push himself up as Daoud turned again and came towards me, shouting.

'I fucking know they want me dead, Paul. This is the third bombing, the third time we have been targeted.

I blinked, stupid in the face of Daoud's passionate outburst.

'Third time?'

Daoud towered over me counting on his fingers, his hands shaking with furious tension.

'Ibrahim's nephew, Rashid, died in a truck carrying tomatoes through Jericho and we all thought he had got involved with the militants, the same way my brother had. He was ten minutes away from our warehouse. Ibrahim and I were waiting for him to arrive. We didn't realise, Paul. You know that? We didn't realise it's about us. We actually thought the poor boy was a bomber. Even when the Hamas people told us he wasn't with them, we didn't believe them. His father went through hell and we still didn't realise.'

Daoud spat the words at me and I dropped my gaze, letting his anger wash over me.

'Then they put a car bomb outside our offices in Haifa. That is the reason I couldn't get a call through to them at the time. The lines had been cut for good. They killed the office boy. You know why, Paul? You know why they killed him and not me? Because I had spilt coffee on my jacket and would have thrown it out, but the office boy wanted it. So I gave it to him just before I left. I had to leave early, before I had planned to and so he walked out of the office onto the street the next morning wearing my jacket when they were waiting for me to appear. And you know what? We still didn't realise. You must think we're really stupid, Paul, no? To cause all that destruction and not even know it's all about us. Not to realise. Well, now we do realise because yet more people have died for no reason and this time they thought to leave us a message. They finally realised, didn't they, how stupid we are. Too stupid to understand the language of violence. The language they thought we understood above all else. Their language.'

I shook my head as I looked up at Daoud. 'But they killed Israelis. Innocent Israelis.'

Daoud had walked away to stand by the ornate dinner table under the chandelier, his back to me.

'What? And the infallible Mossad never makes mistakes? The wonderful Israelis would never harm civilians? Have you never heard of The Stern Gang, Paul? The Haganah? Ain Helweh? Sabra? The history of Palestine since the *Naqba* has been of Israeli killing, of Israeli cruelty and Israeli callousness. Thousands died in Gaza, Paul. Do you think they lost a second's sleep over a couple of bombs and a few dead Arabs? Do you? Killing is a potent drug, Paul. Kill a few Arabs and you'll maybe have less of a conscience at sacrificing one or two of your own.'

A knock on the door silenced Daoud as Ibrahim got up and unlocked it. It was Mohamed, his face apologetic and servile and his hands waving ineffectually.

'*Sidi*, please. The noise.'

Ibrahim ushered him out and locked the door. Daoud filled his glass from the sideboard and returned to his seat by the coffee table. He took a long drink, gazing at the glass before putting it down and looking up at me, sweeping his hand back over his red-rimmed eyes to his forehead.

'I'm sorry, Paul, I don't mean to take it all out on you. I'm a little... nervous right now. I'm sorry.'

'No, that's okay, Daoud. I understand. At least, I think I understand.'

Ibrahim's rumbling voice came through the cloud of a newly lit cigarette. 'We think we need to make this public, Paul. If it is out in the open, we think we might be safe. If Israel has an issue with our scheme for the water, they should take it up with Jordan. Government to government. Not this way, not the killing. They cannot go on this way if people know.'

I nodded, but my thoughts were a storm of conflicting ideas. The voice of the Armenian priest came to me. *'We seldom have the benefit of certainties, Paul. It is a luxury we can reserve for our love of God.'*

'How can I help?'

Ibrahim gestured at the *Mukhabarat* report on the coffee table. 'Take this. It's yours. Daoud has given you the Jerusalem bid document. Use them. You are a writer. Write. Not for the Ministry, for the newspaper. The editor of *The Jordan Times* is expecting your call. You know him already, I think. I am sorry to have been, is it presuming? But I made the arrangement.'

'Presumptuous. But it's okay. Of course I'll do anything I can to help. I'll call him first thing in the morning. I hope it works.'

It seemed like a good time to leave. I picked up the document and walked to the door. Ibrahim's voice from behind me sounded casual as I turned the lock.

'Oh, Paul. Maybe it is a good idea to let your friend from the British Embassy to know about this document as well.'

A thrill of fear, alarm and shame burned through me. I paused and then walked through the door without looking back.

I sat watching Gerald Lynch drink Turkish coffee from a

tiny cup. The nightclub was empty except for the owner, Nadim, who had let me in when I knocked on the garish door under an orange and red striped awning. A fat, sweaty man with jowls and constantly darting eyes, he brought coffees and an ashtray, mumbling and grinning in a subservient dance for Lynch before leaving to sit in his back room.

My head throbbed with the start of one of the violent headaches which had been part of my world since the nightclub bomb. The air smelled faintly of alcohol, cheap perfume, sweat and stale smoke. Lynch sniffed.

'Place is a dump, but it's safe. Nadim's a twat but he knows which side his bread's buttered on. Coffee's good. Try it.'

I took a sip of the strong, sweet coffee.

Lynch flicked ash into his saucer. 'We got the documents. Thanks.'

I looked across at him, his unshaven face was pale and his blue eyes bloodshot from lack of sleep – there was no hint of alcohol on his breath.

'I'm not doing any more for you.'

Lynch nodded wearily. 'Here. Something for you.'

He shoved an envelope across the chipped Formica tabletop. I opened to find an official-looking document in Arabic.

'What's this?'

'Your judgement. Don't bother turning up to court tomorrow. You've been found guilty of affray and have a three-month suspended sentence. The fine of five hundred Dinars will be paid to the court in the morning. Judge Khasawneh will say you were unfortunate and have a good past record and he will hope you have learned your lesson.'

I shook my head in slow disbelief at Lynch's

arrogance.

'So that's it?'

He nodded, his hands deep in his jacket pocket as he sat back on the cheap metal chair. 'That's it, Paul. All over.'

'And what about the Israelis and their bombings?'

'What Israelis, Paul? The *Mukhabarat* report says they found American explosives. They could have been nicked by any old raghead. We've double checked it all with our sources. There's no clear evidence of Israeli involvement in the Nai bombing.'

I swirled the black grounds at the bottom of my cup.

'Daoud Dajani is in danger.'

Lynch glanced around him, his face screwed up in distaste. 'Daoud Dajani? He does stuff with his money we don't like. His brother was a suicide bomber. He spends time on the playground with some very unpleasant little boys. And his madcap water scheme is nothing short of incendiary. There's a very real danger it'll end up pitching this whole region into another stupid war it doesn't need. Whichever way you look at Daoud Dajani, he's bad news. So fuck him actually, Paul. And his safety.'

I frowned. 'He's a businessman, not a bomber.'

Lynch leaned forward, his clear blue eyes fixed on me. He raised his finger. 'You don't know what he is, Paul, and you don't know what he isn't.'

I dropped my eyes as Lynch got to his feet.

'You did a good job getting that bid document, Paul. We thought we had a pretty good idea of what Dajani was up to with the water thing but we'd only scratched the surface. We couldn't work out why the Izzies were going so bonkers over him. Now we've got a pretty clear idea. He's going to pull millions of gallons of water out of the system. Sharon threatened war against Lebanon for splashing about in the Litani River, so imagine what they'll do if the Jordanians award a contract to Dajani and his merry men authorising them to suck Tiberias dry.'

I looked up. Lynch had his back to the stage lights and I couldn't read his expression. 'Try to kill him, perhaps?'

'You've been reading too many Bond books, Paul. Governments don't assassinate people bidding for contracts. But it's obvious Israel will defend its national interest if Jordan starts to drain its water resources. There's a perfectly good British consortium making a sensible bid which will help Jordan to better manage its water without jeopardising regional stability. It's in everyone's interest they win the privatisation. You want my advice? Stay away from Daoud Dajani, Paul.'

Lynch patted my shoulder as he walked past me. I sat looking at the scratched black tabletop in front of me. A shuffle and a high-pitched cough to my side revealed Nadim.

'Some more coffee, *seer*?'

I shook my head and he cleared the cups away. I lit a cigarette and drew the smoke deep into me, tapping the tabletop and trying to work out who I could possibly believe in.

Chapter Twenty-Two

I slipped into Aisha's office and kissed her, stifling her surprised greeting. Her soft lips tasted of coffee. She pulled back with a fearful glance at the door.

I laughed. 'It's okay, there's nobody else out there.'

There was only a faint hint of colour on the side of her face and she had covered up any other remaining marks with foundation. My own pains had pretty much subsided apart from the headaches, although I still had a few scabs from the glass cuts on my side. It didn't hurt anymore to kiss her.

'What are you doing up here, *ya* Brit? Shouldn't you be down in the dungeons working on your magazine?'

'Zahlan asked to see me. What time will I pick you up tonight?'

'Eight?'

I leaned forward and kissed her again and this time we ignored the door and the dangers of discovery. The woody, heady scent she wore made me ache for her with an intensity reflected in her widened eyes. I left her reluctantly and made my way to Abdullah Zahlan's office.

Zahlan was dressed as a young business leader today, his ever-changing wardrobe once again signalling his mood. He smiled, lifting his internal telephone handset.

'Aisha? Can you join us please?'

He gestured to the chair in front of his desk. 'Sit down, Paul. How are you?'

'Well, thanks, Abdullah. What gives?'

He tossed a copy of *The Jordan Times* across to me. 'You have seen this, I suppose?'

I certainly had. In fact, I had written it. Teddy 'Bear' Smith, the newspaper's legendarily foul-mouthed editor, had been delighted with the piece and had even insisted on paying me for it. A growling, chain-smoking Mancunian with a sardonic, grim sense of humour, Smith had whistled and cackled his way through my story. He'd insisted on seeing evidence and grilled me for three hours about every assertion in the piece, finally running it as a three-part special in *The Jordan Times* and its sister paper, the Arabic *Al Rai*. The newswires had picked it up and I was glad I had used a pseudonymous byline. The story was running on CNN.

Aisha came in and sat opposite me. I looked at the paper Zahlan had tossed. The final part of the series was splashed across the centre pages with pictures of the remains of the bombed nightclub.

'Yes, I have.'

'Do you know this Simon Trent?'

I glanced up at Zahlan, but couldn't read his expression. I avoided looking at Aisha. 'No, should I?'

'It's just that you're a journalist. I thought you might have met him.'

I shook my head, gesturing at the piece. 'Sorry, Abdullah, never even heard of him. What do you think of this?'

Zahlan sighed heavily and wheeled around on his chrome-armed black leather executive chair.

'It's obviously caused a huge row. Our government has threatened to break off diplomatic relations with Israel. You know this, right?'

I shook my head and tried desperately to stay calm as the surge of adrenaline pulsed through my body.

'No, I didn't.'

'Yesterday. Israel has withdrawn its ambassador for

consultations. They have threatened grave consequences if we proceed with the privatisation and the Jerusalem Consortium wins. Daoud Dajani is under police protection.'

I was sweating. I'd known this feeling before; it comes with the job. The phone call from the guy whose business has failed because of the article you wrote, the woman whose husband has left her because of your news story. Or, in my case, the head of the borough council you have accused of having an affair with another councillor who turned out to be helping her deal with cancer. End of career.

I had pushed Lynch's warnings to the back of my mind as I got on with the job of documenting Daoud's tale. I had made my decision, sitting there in the stink of the nightclub. But I hadn't considered the reaction would be this big.

Aisha's full voice was bright and neutral. 'The Israelis have denied they were involved in the attacks, no, Abdullah?'

'They have. The Americans are mediating.' Zahlan ran his hand through his hair. 'It's a mess, to be honest.'

He pushed his chair back and went to the window. 'I have just been with Harb. He's spent the morning with the Prime Minister and HM. It's been decided.'

He turned to face the window as he spoke, his hands held behind his back.

'We're going ahead with the privatisation. It's an open and transparent process conducted fairly and to international standards. It's a matter of sovereignty that we have control over the resources and assets of our own country. We will not be bullied.'

Aisha stood, her eyes shining and a huge grin lighting up her face. 'That's fantastic news, Abdullah!'

Zahlan sat back at his desk, picking up a pen and waggling it at us both. 'The Minister would like you both to go down to the Dead Sea tomorrow to be ready for the conference. He has asked if you could write news releases for us as well as working on the magazine through the conference? The Ministry will pay you for the additional work, of course. We want to get blanket coverage for this and explain to the world why it is a critical issue for Jordan. HM's press people and the Petra news agency have both agreed to issue our releases for us. Can you do it?'

'Of course, Abdullah. No problem.'

'Great. Aisha, try and get Paul access to as many stakeholders as you can so he can create as much volume as possible. We need to get our story told.'

We left Zahlan's office and went together into Aisha's, where she closed the door and kissed me and told me what a terribly clever Paul Stokes I was and how much she owed me for helping to save her brother's life.

The knock on my front door came just after I arrived home from the celebratory dinner at Aisha's house. I was thinking dreamily about the next morning's drive down to the Dead Sea for the conference. We planned to take the long way round so I could see Kerak, the crusader castle mentioned in TE Lawrence's *Seven Pillars of Wisdom*. Of the many books I had accumulated in my attempts to come to some sort of understanding of Jordan and its people, Lawrence's account of the Arab Revolt had woven its magic and I had nagged at Aisha until she had agreed to the detour. I wandered over to the door and pulled it open. Lars waited on my doorstep, his face a picture of sick misery and his arms crossed against the late night cold.

'I am glad you're back, Paul.'

The cold and Lars' grim face chased the warmth and laughter out of me. I stood aside and he walked into the kitchen. I got us a beer from the fridge.

'What's the problem, Lars? You look like you've seen a ghost.'

'Yah, maybe I have. I've been busted.'

Lars hadn't opened his beer. Sitting down, I sipped at the froth that welled up from my can.

'How busted?'

'There was an internal investigation at the telephone exchange. They turned up here today and ripped out the IP telephony equipment and terminated my DSL line. My buddies at the telephone company have been sacked. I'm being transferred to Saudi Arabia.'

'Shit. How did they find out?'

He ran his hand back through his thin blond hair, shaking his head. 'That's what beats me, I can't for the life of me work out how they knew. This stuff is pretty much untraceable. But they did. They're talking about fining me thousands of Dinars. My company's getting me out of here fast to avoid the embarrassment. I guess I'm lucky they didn't sack me as well.'

'When are you going?'

Lars laughed, a bitter, short explosion of anger. 'Tomorrow. First plane out. A great deal. No relocation, no weighting on the salary. Go to Saudi Arabia, do not pass go, do not collect the money. Count yourself lucky.'

'I'm sorry. Is there anything I can help with? Anything I can do?' I put my can down on the table carefully as I felt the heat of Lars' glare.

'Don't you think you have done enough, actually, Paul?'

I looked around the kitchen before I finally managed to meet his eyes.

'What do you mean?'

Lars opened his beer with a savage little tug at the ringpull, his eyes still on mine. He held the can up to me, his finger pointing from its lid into my face. 'I think you know exact what I mean.'

'I didn't tell anyone about the telephone, Lars,' I said, looking up at him as he drank from the can.

'You didn't need to, Paul. Did you? Because when they tried to tap your phone they would have found that it doesn't link to any exchange, wouldn't they? You know who I mean, ya? Your friends from the embassy? First they beat me up, then I don't get the message so they do this and have me thrown out.'

I didn't answer him and Lars waited until the silence forced me to look up at him.

His voice dropped to a hushed snarl. 'You're a fucking fool, Paul. A crazy fool. Well, I'm off to Saudi so you're on your own. But you need to get rid of those people, yah? They'll play with you like a mouse now. They're crazy. Don't go on living here with all this shit over your head. Get out, Paul, before something really bad happens.'

I lit one of his cigarettes, my fingers trembling. 'You know I can't leave here now.'

'You have few choices, Paul. You are in a real trouble spot.'

His idiomatic English made me smile. He snapped, 'Stop smirking, you fucking idiot. You don't seem to understand. They will use you until they drop you in the shit and then they will disown you. You're stuck between the Jordanians, the Brits and the Israelis. You're going to get screwed, Paul. You're the little guy. You're the one they'll burn.'

I stared back at him, wide-eyed as he punched the air between us with his finger.

'You think I didn't know? That you have been playing spies with them? That you wrote that damn piece in *The Jordan Times*? What, a dumb Swede won't spot the great journalist's style? What Brits pay you to start a war, Paul?'

'It's not about starting a war. It's about avoiding one.'

'What, you are crusader now? You will save the world, little man with a pen?'

I didn't care anymore, didn't care enough to answer him. But Lars was relentless.

'I know these people, Paul. I knew Andre Sillere, the guy who discovered the damn Roman aquifers Dajani is going to drill into. I know the French guys who are doing the boring work. I drink with them. And I know who your Irish friend is, too. Why didn't you be the one to tell me who he is, Paul? Why didn't you tell me he's a damn spook?'

'I didn't want to involve you.'

'What, Paul? What? I did not hear that. You speak quiet these days, no?'

'I said I didn't want to involve you.'

He hammered the can down onto the rough pine tabletop. 'I am involved now, Paul, no? I am fucking involved. They beat the shit out of me, broke my gear and now they have thrown me out of my house and quitted my job because I am involved.'

'That's not my fault, Lars.'

He got up. 'It is your fault, Paul. It is your fault for being a crazy asshole and for trying to box too heavy. So, I go. But listen to me, one piece of advice for you, asshole. Get out of here. Now. Just get out.'

'I can't leave her, Lars. I can't do it.'

His voice wavered with suppressed passion. 'Then fuck you, Paul. You make your choices. But you think about why someone would want the flat above you empty, Paul? Because they could have acted anytime to stop me stealing some little bandwidth. You get me? This was timed by them, not by me.'

I sat, immobile, looking up at him. I didn't dare speak for fear the lump in my throat would turn into tears.

Lars turned at the door. 'I have got a spare mobile with a pre-paid SIM,' he said. 'I'll drop it to you. Use the second mobile for calls to people you can trust only. Don't use it to call your Brit spy. Keep it for her. Don't use names when you're calling. You'll have a secure line.'

I mumbled thanks, but he waved me silent. 'Forget it Paul, I should have known you were a jerk before. It's my problem for not noticing.'

Ten minutes later, the doorbell rang again and I went over to answer it, but there was just a Nokia box on the doorstep. By the time I got up the next morning, Lars had cleared out.

Chapter Twenty-Three

The early morning sun burnt orange in the blush sky, the rocky outcrops either side of us throwing long shadows across the dusty land as we drove down the King's Highway, the main road from Amman down to the Red Sea.

I pushed thoughts of Lars and his leaving far away. We opened windows, the fresh air filling our lungs, Aisha's luxuriant hair billowing in the wind and her eyes sparkling with the sheer joy of speeding down the desert highway. The old Mercedes bucked as its wheels found the ruts left by trucks in the hot summer months when the tarmac softens.

Aisha had never seen *Seven Pillars of Wisdom*, let alone read the book, and I teased her for not knowing her own history. My enormous expenditure on Amazon had paid off and Aisha's voice was raised above the wind noise, her hand raised, palm upwards and her fingers a splayed cascade of mock anger.

'You pompous Brit. That's your history, not mine. He was a liar, anyway.'

'Who, Lawrence?'

'Yes, your precious Lawrence.'

'How do you know? You haven't even read the book.'

'Everyone knows he was a liar. He liked boys.'

'Unfair. Just like an Arab. Avoid the argument you can't win by choosing one you think you can.'

She thickened her accent as she tossed her head. '*Yalla*, Brit. Live with this. *Ana* I am Arab.'

'He was a great writer.'

She muttered darkly, 'He was a great liar.'

'And a poet.'

'Yah. Right.'

I closed my window so she could hear me clearly. 'I loved you, so I drew these tides of men into my hands, and wrote my will across the sky in stars, to earn you freedom, the seven pillared worthy house, that your eyes might be shining for me when we came. Death seemed my servant on the road, till we were near and saw you waiting, when you smiled, and in sorrowful envy he outran me and took you apart into his quietness.'

She was silent for a while. 'He wrote this?'

'Yup.'

'Why?'

'Does poetry have to have a reason?'

'Maybe. Tell me it again.'

I did, in my finest Olivier voice and she listened, her head bowed and her lips pursed in concentration. I was pleased she liked it: I had always thought it a beautiful piece of poetry.

'What is it? This poem? When did he write it?'

'It's the dedication from *Seven Pillars*.' Aisha looked over at me for explanation. 'You know, when writers have a little note saying 'To Mum' or something in their book.'

'Hmm.'

I enjoyed the fruits of my little triumph (and Lawrence's) silently, opening the window again so the wind whipped along the side of my face. The dedication to *Seven Pillars* is one of the great mysteries of twentieth century literature. I didn't tell her most people think it's written to a boy. No point in giving the enemy ammunition.

'He was still a liar.'

'Aisha.' She laughed, sticking her tongue out at me.

Another silence, wheels on tarmac, wind noise and Aisha thoughtful again, looking out of the window. She turned to me, a look of pure calculating wickedness on her angel's face.

'So who was it dedicated to, this dedication? To his mother?' she asked me, her grin broadening when she caught the look on my face. 'No. This poetry of dedication had a reason. It is written to somebody he cared for, he owed a debt. If he fought for the Arabs, it is dedicated to an Arab. A dead Arab.'

When she learned a new word or a new use for a word, English being full of multi-purpose words, Aisha would try and use it soon after, testing its boundaries and meanings. She felt it helped her put the word in its place. I should have known she'd ask. I thought fast.

'The dedication is simply to S.A. but nobody's quite sure who S.A. is. Most authorities claim it's Salim Ahmed, a young man he worked with before the war when he travelled in the Levant as an archaeologist.'

I was on a roll, having decided on obfuscation as a tactic in my desperation to steal victory away from her. She would have none of it, cutting me off.

'So S.A. was a boy.'

'Well, yes—'

'A dead boy. An Arab boy.'

'Yes, but that doesn't mean—'

'Forget it Paul,' she said. 'Another typical Brit, dressing up his nasty taste for our children in his fine words.'

Sensing I was on a phenomenal losing streak, Aisha was merciless, her voice haughty as she turned away from me.

'You know, the French call it the English disease. Frankly, Paul, I'm surprised I've managed to hold your interest for so long. Surely you must feel the pull of your nation's favourite pastime.'

The car swerved as I punched her shoulder and she screamed 'Bully' at me.

The lobby of the Movenpick Resort and Spa Dead Sea bustled with a mixture of tourists and suits, the bellboys rushing to load the cascade of suitcases, boxes of literature and pop-up banners being lifted out of car boots. We waited at the check-in desk. We had spent all morning clambering around Kerak Castle and I looked dusty and dishevelled with a dark streak of mud on my beige trousers from a slip when we had walked together up Wadi Mujib, a stop on the road from the castle to the hotel. Aisha looked elegant and fresh, untouched by dust or heat. At her feet was the small, round-cornered silver flight case she had brought with her and that she hadn't let out of her sight, a high-end digital camera Daoud had asked her to bring to him at the conference. The police protection team had insisted Daoud stay away from the Dajani house until after the conference.

The desk clerk handed us our card-keys. We were following the bellboy pushing our bags on a trolley when I heard my name called. A woman's voice, an English accent. Aisha hadn't noticed and carried on walking, chatting with the bellboy as I turned to face Anne, smiling as best I could.

'Annie. Wow. What brings you here?'

Her returned smile was brittle. She wore a figure-hugging pinstripe suit and her blonde hair tied back. She gestured at the conference badge pinned to her jacket.

'I'm working with the Anglo-Jordanian Consortium. Do you remember Valentjin?' She took in my blank look.

'Valentjin Steenberg. From the dinner we went to with your friend upstairs. What was his name? Lars?'

Valentjin. Privatisation Man. The disastrous dinner we'd had with Lars just after Anne had arrived in Jordan. Lars and I got drunk while she and Privatisation Man talked international law and sipped iced Perrier. Anne and I had gone home to a blazing row afterwards.

'Yes, yes I remember him.'

'We kept in touch and he brought us in as legal consultants to the consortium because of our experience with large scale utility privatisations in Europe.' She laughed. 'I honestly didn't expect to come to Jordan again.'

A voice in my head asked me how on earth I had ever become involved with this woman, let alone share her bed.

'No. No, I suppose not. Great. Cool. Well, um, good luck.'

Anne put her hand on my forearm which, I realised too late, was crossed defensively. Her touch was dry and I flinched, watching her eyes widen in an instant of exquisite embarrassment between two absolute strangers.

'I actually wanted to try and find you, Paul. I thought you might be here at the conference. Do you have time for a coffee?'

I turned to Aisha, who was waiting with the bellboy by the lift. 'I've just checked in, actually, just have to get the things to the room, you know...'

Anne stared across at Aisha. She turned to me. 'I see. Look, Paul, I just wanted to tell you to be careful. The Anglo-Jordanian bid is strongly favoured by the Israeli, British and American governments, as you probably know. This whole process has become terribly,' she searched for the word for a second, glancing at Aisha, 'political. I know you're tied up with the Dajanis.'

I somehow managed to keep the surge of anger out of my expression, but every shred of me wanted to hurl obscenities at her.

'What have they got to do with a Jordanian privatisation, Anne? It's these people's decision to make, not theirs.'

'Well, there's more at stake than just one country here, isn't there Paul? It's a regional issue after all. Look, I mustn't keep you,' she looked down at my trousers, 'You probably want to freshen up. Perhaps we'll have the chance to chat later on.'

I looked up from my stained leg, but she had already turned and walked away.

We sat on the low wall by the pebble beach together, looking out over the viscous Dead Sea at the last of the stunning winter sunset, the air still warm but cooling fast into night. The still plane of the sea was dark, the last orange reflection seeming to reach out to us. The dark hills across the water were a vignette of terracotta to dark wine as darkness embraced the waning sun. Aisha's sketchbook was closed.

I drank her in, her hair blown back from her face by the warm breeze, her eyes closed and face lifted in exultation, her brown skin catching the last glow of light. The condensation glistened on our glasses and moistened her fingers as she drank. I took her wet hand and put it to my lips.

She opened her eyes lazily, her voice chocolate. 'Flatterer.'

'No, I'm an amateur at that. I'll have to take lessons

from Ibrahim.'

She laughed and sipped her wine. 'I wish this could last longer. I wish we didn't have to do this whole conference thing tomorrow.'

'But when it's over, once the decision's taken and Daoud's safe we've got forever. We can take some time out and just sit on beach. Aqaba, maybe.'

'Why do you think Anne wanted to warn you, Paul?'

'I don't know. I've been worrying about it, actually. I don't know why she'd even want to talk to me. It's not as if, well, you know, as if I behaved well when saw her last.'

Aisha's voice was a touch too light. 'She looked nice.'

'She comes from a different world, Aish. I couldn't understand what I had ever thought I had in common with her. She's like a total stranger to me.'

Aisha stayed silent for a while.

'We have a saying, you know. My brother against my cousin, my cousin against the stranger. Maybe she thought you need protecting from me.' She gave a sly little smile.

I looked out across the dark water, small waves sloshing thickly against the stony shore. 'So are you a brother or a cousin?'

She moved then, getting up in a single fluid moment, sitting on my legs and straddling me, her hand around my neck.

'I am your lover, Paul. Closer to you than either.'

Our mouths opened together, our tongues meeting, our touches slow and rhythmic. We stayed like it for a long time, until the sun had disappeared and the darkness enveloped us. The beach bar had long closed, the waiter leaving us with our bottle and glasses, a single shadow on the wall by the water's edge.

We went up to my room, Aisha carrying her sandals. She sat me down on the bed, carefully padding around the room, turning all the lights off except the bedside lamp. Standing in front of me, she peeled off her black dress, her smooth body shadowed in the lamplight as she revealed black and red underwear. She unpicked the buttons of my shirt and slid it off me, undoing my belt and opening my trousers. I hardly dared to breathe, stilled with the wonder of it all. Still she stood in front of me, close to me. I leaned forward, but she pushed me back. She unclipped her bra and bent, sliding her hands down her thighs, hooking her thumbs into her knickers and pulling them down to her ankles, stepping out of them daintily. She came towards me, took my head in her hands and pulled me into her.

The alarm call woke us at six. Aisha looked startled for a second, then focused her sleepy eyes and found her place, grinned at me and kissed me quickly before getting up and dressing. I lay in bed, savouring our first awakening together, stretching lazily and luxuriating in her scent, the rumpled bed and the lingering musk of our passion.

Watching her, a moment of profound pride and happiness overwhelmed me. I had noticed when we walked together or sat in a bar or hotel lobby together, men's eyes lingered on us. Women would look us up and down, doing that Arab evaluation thing, starting at the head and scanning down then up. I was reflected in Aisha's beauty, somehow becoming more than a sloppily dressed misfit because she was with me. I was proud of her, proud of myself. Just proud.

She stood over me again, almost exactly where she'd

stood the night before, her hands on her hips and her head tilted to one side in enquiry, her hair wild. 'Penny for them.'

I lay back, bare to the stomach, my hands behind my head. 'Truth?'

'Truth.'

'I love you.'

She sat down on the bed then, put her hand on my belly, dark on pale. She was serious, her big eyes on me. 'Truly?'

'Yes. Truly.'

She smiled gravely. 'I have to go.'

'I know. Hang on.'

I rolled out of bed, pulled on the white towelling hotel bathrobe and followed her as she left. I stopped at the door and kissed her before I opened it for her, standing in the doorway as she slipped out.

Aisha's fleeting kiss brought me back to reality for a second as she ran down the corridor to her room. I turned to look at the wreckage of pillows and sheets in the grey dawn light and realised I had used a word I don't like using. I had gifted her my absolute truth.

Chapter Twenty-Four

Aisha's soft touch was a little thrill as I helped her off the conference shuttle bus, the exhaust fumes making me squint up at her as the warm light caught her fine features. It was a hot Dead Sea day and I shifted uncomfortably in the unfamiliar confines of a suit. She glanced at me as her high heels hit tarmac, a flash of white teeth at my discomfiture.

'Come on, let's get you installed in the press office so I can find Harb and Zahlan.'

We walked into the King Hussein convention centre, more buses pulling up behind us as conference visitors streamed in from the hotels along the Dead Sea coast and from the public car parks down the road. The keynote speaker, Harb Al Hashemi, Jordanian Minister of Natural Resources by the Grace of God, was also, Aisha told me, going to announce the result of the privatisation. The evaluation committee had reviewed the financial offers of both bidders and made its choice. Harb would reveal all.

Security was tight, a long queue for the scanners, metal detectors and serious-faced uniforms manning them. Aisha kept setting off the metal detector, taking off her jewellery, watch and finally shoes. A peasant-faced woman in a green uniform grinned at Aisha, tapping herself on her dumpy breasts: 'Wire.'

They took Aisha away, blushing furiously, to be 'checked by hand.' When she came back I got a slap for laughing at her, pushing up my chest and grunting, 'Wire.'

We parted outside the press office and agreed to meet

for lunch before I went in to start putting finishing touches to the conference opening press releases I had pre-written so I could keep up with the flow of news throughout the morning.

After sending off the first release of the day I cued up the second on my laptop. It was the announcement of the winning consortium and all I needed to complete it was the winner's name. Anxious to catch Harb's speech in person, I made my way through the logo-strewn corridors and the smiling suits packing the exhibition area, zigzagging across to the conference hall.

I sat in the back row of the hall so I could get out easily and post my release when the moment came. Although everyone at the Ministry was positive Dajani's Jerusalem Consortium would win, I had to actually hear Harb say the words before I could make the news public.

The huge room filled up quickly, with only a few minutes until the Minister was due to speak. I saw Aisha on the stage fussing over the laptop on the lectern. I stiffened at the voice from behind me.

'Top o' the mornin' to ye. Thought I'd find you sitting in the naughty seats.'

I turned to face a grinning Gerald Lynch.

'Sure, I'd turn back around nice and natural unless you want to advertise our connection, now Paul.' He spoke quietly in the growing hubbub.

'What do you want now?'

'Paul, Paul. Christ, but you are one very grumpy young man these days. Why should I want anything? I'm just turnin' up to hear the great man himself, amn't I?'

If Lynch cranking up the feckless Paddy act was intended to goad me it was certainly working. Scanning the room, I spotted Daoud close to the stage. He had a severe-faced older man with him, a soup-strainer moustache and a brown polyester suit. *Mukhabarat*. Secret police. I'd learned to recognise them from a mile away and Daoud's pal was typical of the breed. Aisha told me her brother had insisted on attending the conference against the advice of the security people. I took care to keep my eye moving through the crowd so Lynch wouldn't notice my interest in Daoud.

The house lights dimmed and people started to settle down, the room not quite full, so Lynch and I were isolated in our back row seats. He leaned forward so his whisper came to me from shockingly close by. 'You know, I should be angry at the stunt you pulled in *The Jordan Times*, Paul. Nice work, though. Jaysus, you've a talent for it, eh? You shouldn't have much trouble getting a job once this is all over.'

'What's that supposed to mean?'

'Oh, didn't you know?' Studied innocence. 'TMG has pulled out of its contract with the Ministry. Shock move and all that. Mister Robin Goodyear felt other markets should take priority, apparently. They picked up a lot of defence-related work in Europe. Looks like you'll be going home soon enough. Sure, that'll be nice fer ye. You must be missin' the old place. Bacon butties, good beer, all that. Porky scratchings.'

The lights dimmed totally leaving only the stage illuminated. The chill-out music died and the room got to its feet as the Jordanian national anthem played out.

Harb Al Hashemi took to the stage. I could hear Lynch breathing behind me but I couldn't turn, couldn't run. I shook my head, denying his insidious voice as the room echoed with applause for the Minister of Natural Resources. Harb was composed, smiling, his hand on the lectern as he scanned the room. *'Bismillah Arrahman Arrahim. Sayidati sadaty. Assalam aleikoum.'*

A murmur ran around the auditorium, *'Aleikoum assalam.'*

'Good morning, ladies and gentlemen. Today is an historic day for Jordan and for our region and I am delighted to be talking to you at the inauguration of what I hope will be the most important platform for our region to share best practices, solutions and strategic partnerships in the development, management and sustenance of the most important resource to our region and its people. Water.'

Harb paused and Lynch's urgent voice filled the gap. 'They're bombers. The Dajanis. They're destabilisers. They're the whole Al Qaeda model. Trigger a war, trigger a conflict. That's Daoud's purpose in all this.'

I half turned. 'Fuck off, Gerry.'

His voice was close enough to my ear for me to feel his boozy breath. 'Is there a problem with that, Paul? Did you honestly never stop to think it all through? The Jericho bomb? The Arafi boy?'

'The problem is acute. The challenge is real. We have to manage and maintain our country's water resources with every tool at our disposal if we are to give our people access to the most fundamental building block of life. And yet we are not alone. All around us, other nations face the same challenge. So we must make the most out of our own resources while bearing in mind the need for our neighbours, our partners, to make the most out of their own resources, too. That partnership is critical for success moving forwards. We must seek mutual benefit from our mutual challenges.'

'Did you think it all a coincidence? That Daoud's a good guy just trying to drive Israel into the ground by stealing their water? Oh, he got you good, Paul. He got you good. Jaysus, but he's a cute hoor, all right.'

Harb was a master orator. The room was silent as he spoke, his eyes like a lighthouse passing around the room, its beam taking everyone in, his voice melodious and paced as he carefully enunciated commonplace phrases and trotted out the language of corporate communication. Now Harb introduced a new urgency, patting the lectern to emphasise his words. 'Partnership means shared responsibility, however. It means recognising the needs that drive us all. It means respect. And it means building trust between partners. The peace we concluded in 1994, the peace that has brought Jordan to the attention of the world as a nation seeking advancement and prosperity for all, was built around this trust. And water. Water for all. A shared challenge and resource.'

Lynch's skin touched mine. 'He tell you he's in danger from the Israelis, Paul? He tell you that? Did he tell you he tied the green ribbon around his brother's head before sending him off to destroy a busload of children, Paul? Or that Daddy raised money for the PLO until he got blown to fuck by the third Israeli mission sent to do for his worthless fucking life?'

'Jordan does not have access to the water resources it needs today, let alone tomorrow. We need to address that issue across every possible stage of the life cycle of this most precious commodity. We need to educate our people to use their water wisely and sparingly. We need to build programmes that help to make agricultural water use more efficient. We need to use our sustainable resources wisely. We need to recycle wherever it is not only feasible, but possible.'

'Well, whatever happens, I suppose you could count yourself lucky not to be doing time in an Israeli jail. You're a lucky boy, Paul.'

I kept my voice steady to deny him the satisfaction of getting to me, but his words had driven cold doubt into every part of me. 'What do you mean, Israeli? They had nothing to do with my dumb court case. It would never have been a problem if you hadn't been involved and we both know it. Get to the point, Gerry.'

'The point? That is the point, Paul. I'm not talking about you going down for a silly assault charge. I'm talking about shipping highly sophisticated Czech explosives across the King Hussein crossing, Paul. I'm talking about bombs that killed innocent Israeli citizens because you helped the Dajanis ship the stuff in your car, Paul.'

I lost track of Harb's words. My tongue felt thick in my dry mouth. The room swam in and out, coming to me through a haze I realised was tears. I suppressed the urge to wipe my eyes. Lynch would see me brush the tears away, but he couldn't see them trickle down my cheeks. Harb continued, drawing applause three or four times before I brought my thoughts back to the here and now of the darkened auditorium. My dry lips pulled apart painfully as I spoke.

'Daoud is going to win this, Gerry. Jordan is going to win it.'

'We also need to find new and sustainable sources of water to underpin our country's development and our people's needs. And it is this element, this crucial element, that has driven our evaluation of the bids for the privatisation of Jordan's water resources.'

'You brought her in your car. She ask you to carry anything here, Paul? Your mo'? Your bird? She bring any presents or cuddly toys for anyone's kids? Any extra luggage?'

'No,' I spoke too loudly, making the woman two rows

in front of me turn because of course, yes she had asked me to carry an extra piece of luggage. A flight case with a camera in it. I clamped my lips shut. I wasn't going to give Lynch the pleasure.

Lynch chuckled dirtily. 'You know what we think, Paul? Ghaith Mcharourab, the kid who died in the nightclub bomb. Remember him? He was the bomb maker. We reckon he was handing a device over and muffed it. That bomb was no more Israeli than I am. We think he'll do it again, Paul, because he needs instability between Jordan and Israel. Daoud wants a war to play with and the way he's going, he's going to get it.'

Harb was smiling, his arms spread. '...have decided to award the management, operation and exploitation of Jordan's water resources to the Jerusalem Consortium.'

The room erupted, the audience taking to its feet and applause breaking out, swelled by cheers.

Lynch squeezed my shoulder. 'Stay away from them, Paul. For the love of God, stay away. This is not over and it's going to turn ugly. I don't ask you to like me, or to love me. But just listen to me. Stay away. I've sent you home, son. So go while you still can.'

I finally summoned the anger and guts to turn and face him, ready to strike out at him no matter how public the brawl would be, to silence his sinister hissing. But Gerald Lynch had gone.

The exhibition area was empty, everyone packed in the auditorium as I strode through the shell-scheme stands to get to the press office and send out the news Daoud had won control of Jordan's water resources. I operated on autopilot, Lynch's skewed version of events too much to allow, too much to even consider. If he was right, everything had been a lie and everyone a liar, including my lover.

I sent the file off to the Petra news agency and the Royal Court public relations people before I packed my stuff into my shoulder bag. Walking back out through the exhibition area, I watched the crowd streaming out of the auditorium and heard the clink and clatter of the china cups laid out across the glass-topped coffee stations. The whole area was buzzing, happy-faced people shaking hands and clapping each other on the back. I looked for Aisha, but she was lost in the throng, her mobile off. I ached for her, for the warmth of her presence and the certainty we were doing the right thing.

I pushed my way into the auditorium, the house lights were up and the massive room was emptying fast, a few small groups of people left behind holding their conference bags and chatting. I reached the technical desk, where Aisha had stood during Harb's speech. The engineer said she had gone back to the hotel.

I made my way out through the crowd in the exhibition area, groups of people knotted around the high cocktail tables, drinking coffee and chattering, the sound of a thousand voices echoing in the high, glass-roofed foyer area. I was almost at the front door when the world went dark, a momentary eclipse. I looked up in time to see the shattered glass opaque above us before the crazed panes collapsed into a scintillating hail, scattering the crowd with tiny bouncing shards skittering on the marble floors. The explosion came a moment later, a bass concussion that shook the ground. I was surrounded by the sounds of breaking crockery, screams and loud, confused voices.

I shoved through the immobilised crowd, breaking through the edge of the throng as they started to flee in panic, people losing their footing and bringing tables down with them, exhibition stands collapsing as the crowd heaved. I ran out into the daylight and heat, up from the driveway onto the road in front of the convention centre. I could see the dark cloud rising above the car parking area, sirens already wailing all around me, cars glittering in the sun, the hot air shimmering over the massed metalwork, flames leaping high in an area of blackened, twisted shapes that had been cars, stick people staggering and holding their heads in their hands.

The police cars started to cordon off the area, an army warthog barrelling down the road towards me and bouncing over the central reservation. Barked commands rang out in urgent Arabic, distorted by the bullhorns. I wheeled away and ran towards the hotel, a few hundred metres to the right of the convention centre.

My laptop bag banged against my hip as I ran, passing groups of stunned-looking people, one guy throwing out an arm as if to stop me. A car had mounted the pavement, the driver standing and looking around him, bewildered. For a second the sound of my own ragged breaths and the pump of my feet on the paved walkway were all I heard before the wailing sirens blocked out all sound. One car slowed, the police waving at me to stop. The distinctive whump of a helicopter beat in the distance as I pressed on, ignoring them. There was a painful stitch in my side and an odd, iron-tang taste in my rasping throat.

Turning into the hotel grounds, I ran downhill and into reception, careening through the pandemonium that filled the reception area, people arguing with staff at the reception area, concerned-looking groups standing around and officials shouting at their walkie-talkies.

Running to the lifts, I slammed against the wall,

hitting the call button. Waiting, the sweat on my shirt cooling and clammy against my hot skin, I bent double and drew shuddering breaths.

The lift took a silent eternity. Reflected in the mirrored wall, I was sweaty, my collar pulled open by the laptop bag and dark patches on my chest and down my sides.

I hammered on the door of Aisha's room. She opened it, the security chain fixed. It shut again before she let me in, walking away from me as I entered.

She had been crying, her eyes were smudged and her face tear-streaked. She looked up at me, her mobile in her hand. I hated her, then, more than I hated myself. Her betrayal of me seemed so complete and profound. She had used me, as cynically as she had used her own self, given her mind and body to me while she was following her own purpose. She had used my stupidity, exploited my vanity, torn me apart and left me with nothing.

We stared at each other. She looked scared, shocked and vulnerable. I burned at how she could look like that, how these deaths could bring her to tears after so many others had gone before.

She lifted a hand to me. 'Paul…'

I stuttered, but then the words flowed. 'Don't. Don't use my name. Don't pretend any more. It's there outside. They told me you would. They told me and I ignored them. You've done it again, haven't you? You used me, Aisha. You're helping him to bomb them, to kill women and children. And you've been using me.'

She shook her head as I shouted at her. 'It was the car, wasn't it? You just got me to drive you around and carry your bombs for you.' I counted off on my fingers. 'Jericho. Haifa. Nai. And now the Dead Sea. The camera box. You used me to kill them and you fucked me to use me and I went along because I loved you and you were laughing at me all the time.'

Her face was in her hands and she shouted my name but I shouted louder, jabbing my finger at her. 'You helped him bomb, you helped him kill. You lied to me. What for, Aisha? For your precious fucking Palestine? For your father? What turned you into a fucking whore?'

Aisha took her hands from her face, screaming at me, mascara streaked across her eyes like stage makeup. She whirled around and I caught a silver glitter, ducking just in time to avoid the flight case as it smashed against the wall, the shower of plaster as the case burst open and the black body of a camera flew out of the foam interior, lenses tumbling to the floor as I lost my balance and fell sideways, hearing her hoarse voice scream, '*Daoud's dead.*'

I rose unsteadily to my feet, using my hands against the wall. Aisha stood at the open door.

'Aisha. I'm—'

Her soft voice trembled and her lips curled down in an ugly grimace. 'Get away from me. Fuck you, Paul. Fuck you.' She took a choking breath, wheeled around and fled, slamming the door behind her.

I slid back down the wall to the floor, exhausted and confused, scrabbling through the pieces of foam and camera parts, the tears streaming down my face.

I picked my way back through the chaos of the hotel lobby and out into the street, past the wailing police cars and ambulances and against the flow of disoriented people walking from the conference centre to the hotels. Some had cuts, others were being supported as they walked. Police were starting to direct the flow and one uniform put out a hand to block me but I pushed past him and he didn't follow me.

There were ambulances outside the convention centre, three covered stretchers by the front door. I stood in front of them, the tick tick tick of the ambulance lights marking the sweeps of light across the shapeless forms under the blankets. I saw blonde hair poking out from underneath the rightmost blanket and in an instant I knew. I stepped forwards but a paramedic had been watching me and stopped me with his arm outstretched. I was numb.

'I can identify her.'

He dropped his arm and I leaned down to pull back the blanket. Anne's blue eyes stared back at me, blood streaked across her pale features. I let the blanket drop. The urge to be sick welled up inside me, the acid in my throat burning.

'You know this woman?' A police officer, important braid uniform.

'Yes, yes I do. Her name is Anne Boardman. She is a lawyer. Was. Was a lawyer. Part of the British delegation to the conference.'

'You have personal relationship with her?'

'No. No I don't.'

I turned away. They eventually found me wandering down the road towards Bethany, apparently, and someone took me back to my hotel room.

Chapter Twenty-Five

I waited for a long time by the car before I finally found the courage to push my legs up to the house. I paused again before ringing the doorbell. Nour answered, blinking in the morning light. She wore a black *kandoura*, the wide sleeves loose at her side. Her face was puffy and pale. She let her hand fall from the door and walked into the house. I followed her into the kitchen where she stood with her back to me, looking out of the window.

I waited behind her until she turned, her face crumpling as I stepped forward. She lifted her arms to me and I held her, as she cried, beating my back and sobbing 'Why?' until she couldn't cry anymore and stood, quiet in my arms. She finally pulled away, holding my shoulders and looking into my wet eyes, her own blurred with the tears that streaked her face.

'He was my boy. First my husband, now my boys.'

'You have Aisha.'

'For how long, Paul? She is hiding from them. How much more can they take from me?'

I didn't have an answer for her as she looked into my face, scanning me for a reaction. She nodded, a little fierce smile lighting up her face for a moment.

'Sit down. I'll make us coffee.'

I sat on a stool at the breakfast bar in the kitchen as she bustled with the brass long-handled jug boiling on the gas burner before she poured the thick, black liquid into two tiny cups.

She lit a cigarette from the butt of her last, drawing the smoke deep down into her lungs. I finally broke the silence.

'Is Aisha here?'

'No.'

'Do you—'

'No, Paul. Ask Ibrahim maybe. I do not know.'

'Have you talked to her?'

Nour looked at me for a long time before she answered, her eyes dropping to her coffee cup. 'Yes.'

The fridge motor kicked in, its faint hum breaking the silence. I took one of Nour's cigarettes and lit it. 'I pushed her away, Nour. I didn't mean to. There have been a lot of lies and half-truths around me. I let them get to me.'

'You had an argument.' Again, she was making a statement. I wondered how much Aisha had told her.

'Yes, we did. It was my fault.'

There was a silence between us. I could feel the accusation, the pressure to unburden myself, to tell her what a shit I had been to her daughter when Aisha had needed me most.

Nour took a gulping breath. Her mobile rang and she snatched it from the kitchen counter, fumbling to find the green key, her voice shaky as she talked, '*Allo, Na'm.*'

I watched Nour as she listened. Her eyes were on me, unseeing, as she nodded dumbly. They widened momentarily as she nodded again, '*Shukran,*' before letting the mobile drop, clattering to the marble surface. I watched her face crumple.

'Nour?'

She looked up at me, battling for control.

'A helicopter. The farm. Mariam.'

I was swept by an awful hollowness. The olive trees, their leaves bouncing in the rain, the water trickling along the baked red soil around their roots and the smiling old lady in her *kandoura* who tended them. Please, Christ, the girl who used to play in them, imagining they were a royal court packed with courtiers. Just like I would imagine the crows circling above were delta-wing fighters.

I went around the breakfast bar to her, letting her cry into me, rubbing her back in automatic, repetitive sweeps of my hand as she grieved. We stayed together in our frozen pose for long minutes until, finally, she lifted her head, brushing her tangled hair back in the gesture I had come to associate so strongly with Aisha. She smiled at me, a terrible, shaky, devastated smile.

'You have better leave now, Paul,' she entreated me. 'Leave me alone with Mariam, yes?'

I knew better than to argue with her. 'Nour, if you see Aisha, tell her I am sorry. That I love her.'

She nodded. 'I know this, Paul. Go. Please.'

Ibrahim had gone into hiding, but I knew where to find him. I waited on the red carpet in front of the RAC club's reception desk as Mohamed made a call on the internal telephone system before leading me upstairs.

The private suite was smoky and Ibrahim looked old and frail, his hair awry. Only when he had locked the door behind me was I aware of the shadowy figure to one side of the room. The *Mukhabarat* man relaxed as I sat down.

Ibrahim sat opposite me, easing himself into the club chair. 'So. Mariam is dead.'

'I was with Nour when she got the news.'

Ibrahim grimaced. 'She would have been upset. It is the way my brother died. These helicopters are their favourite toy.'

'What about Hamad?'

'In prison. The farm has been completely destroyed.

The action is being justified as an anti-terrorist sweep. They used phosphorous on the fields. The olives all were burnt. This I had from Hamad before they came for him.'

'The Israelis?'

'Yes, them.' Ibrahim lit another cigarette. 'You want a drink?'

'No, no thanks. I'm good.'

He grunted and lifted his glass to drink. His hand shook, making the ice tinkle, so he steadied it with his other hand.

I rubbed my sandy eyes. 'What will you do?'

'I will wait. They cannot continue. They have already made arrests, caused much damage. We have lost our offices in Eilat and Haifa and we have lost our farm. But we still have a business in the Arab World. We will survive this.'

Sitting in the ludicrously rich, gilded room, I realised the Dajanis had lost all their young men. Hamad the bomber and Daoud the visionary were dead and Ibrahim and Nancy didn't have kids. Only Aisha could give the family an heir now.

'What about the water consortium?'

'I do not know, Paul. Our government has lost its appetite for this solution, I think. There have been accusations from the Israelis that we Jordanians had a secret agreement with Syria and Lebanon that we would all take more water together. There have been "accidents" in Damascus and Beirut. I think everyone has lost their appetite for water.' He lifted his glass. 'Take my advice, Paul. Take your whisky neat.'

His eyes were closing and I understood how he had managed to retain such composure in the face of his grief. Ibrahim was blind drunk.

I stood. 'Give Aisha a message for me, Ibrahim. Will

you remember?'

His eyes opened. 'I don't forget when I drink. Do you have anything left unsaid to her, Paul?'

I winced at that. 'Yes, I do. Tell her I was misled by the British. They gave me good reason to suspect Daoud was a terrorist. I was wrong to believe them. Tell her I am sorry and I love her. Can you tell her that?'

He nodded and I left him, his head down. The *Mukhabarat* man closed the door behind me.

The rain started at about four in the afternoon. I had spent the day wandering disconsolately around the house, sitting down every now and then, getting up to gaze out of the window or flick through the TV channels. For about an hour I watched cartoons. It was unnaturally dark outside, the garden stark and the trees stripped of their leaves. The rain came, light at first, flicks and diagonal streaks of refracted light across the windows. I sat in the bedroom looking out across the patio as the rain came harder and harder until it was smashing down, splashing on the flagstones, relentless, driving rain obscuring the houses beyond.

I stood on the patio, sheltered by the overhanging first floor balcony and smoked a cigarette, the air wet and cold. I stepped out into the rain and let it fall on me, soaking me. I held my face up to it and felt it hitting my skin, making my eyes twitch with its force on my closed lids. I forced my eyes open and it hurt me, the water and the pain cleansing me. I walked down to the road and wandered the empty streets. I remembered Aisha dancing in the downpour and tears joined the rain streaking my cheeks. The streetlights flickered on and I realised I was walking in darkness. I dragged myself back to the house, noticing lights were on upstairs but too tired and too bruised to care about any new tenant. I dried myself and made another drink.

There was a knock on the kitchen door.

More beautiful than ever, her hair plastered down over her face and her clothes soaked, Aisha was framed by the light from the kitchen. I didn't believe it at first. I stood in the doorway and stared at her.

'I didn't know where else to go.'

I stepped aside to let her in. She waited, dripping on the kitchen floor. I motioned at her sodden coat.

'Take those off.'

I went to the bathroom and got a bathrobe I'd stolen from some hotel and brought it back to her. She was naked and shivering, her clothes over a chair. I rolled up newspaper and laid it under blocks of wood in the stove, then lit it. The warmth was instantaneous and I pulled up a chair by the fire for her.

'Have you eaten?'

'No.'

I pulled some bread from the fridge, made sandwiches and coffee for us both. I spread out her clothes on two chairs by the fire. She gazed silently into the flames.

I brought her coffee and sandwiches and she cradled the cup in her hands, rocking slightly as she ate.

I sat by her. 'Where have you been?'

'Around. Friends. They're watching Mum's house.'

'I know. Have you spoken to Ibrahim?'

'Yes.'

I loved you, so I drew these tides of men into my hands.

'I didn't mean...'

'Yes. You did. You meant everything you said. But I know why you said it, Paul. I've thought about it a lot.'

I was at a loss. I didn't know where we could possibly go from here. But I knew I desperately wanted to be with her again. We were silent together, looking at the fire.

'What about us, Aish? What are we going to do?'

'There is no us. You need to go home. To leave Jordan. I don't know what I will do.'

'There can be an us.'

And wrote my will across the sky in stars

'No. No there can't. We can't undo this. We have been through too much.'

I wanted to plead, to beg her. But she was cold, distant. I took refuge in domesticity, cleared the plates and turned her clothes on the chairs. Her underwear was almost dry.

'Aisha, I love you. I don't want to be away from you.'

She pulled the bathrobe around. Her damp hair formed tendrils on the towelling. 'They have arrested my mother.' I looked up at her. 'They will arrest me,' she added, simply.

'I don't care. I'll wait for you. I'll work with Ibrahim. You've done nothing. Either of you.'

She smiled but there was no warmth in her expression. 'My sister, too. Maybe Ibrahim.'

I had never known myself to possess such resolution, not in a life of wandering and letting the tides of fate carry me, free of ambition or the desire to stamp my will on other people. But now I knew resolution.

'I will be here, Aisha.'

She nodded and reached out, touched my face. I looked into her eyes, put my hand up to her cheek as she asked me, 'Who is Gerald Lynch to you?'

I tried to conceal my surprise at the question, but I failed. 'He works for British intelligence.'

'And so do you.'

The truth, nothing but the truth. So help me God.

'I have done things for Lynch, yes.'

'He pays you.'

'No. Not money.'

'Not money.'

'I got caught up with him. He drew me in. Once I had given him one thing, he asked for another. I couldn't go back.'

She turned away from me. 'The water contracts. The request for proposals. The evaluation. Daoud's bid.'

'Yes,' I said to her back. She had lifted a decorative plate from the kitchen surface and was turning it in the light.

To earn you freedom, the seven pillared worthy house, that your eyes might be shining for me when we came.

'So he knew about us.'

'Yes.'

'Why didn't you tell me about Lynch?'

'I didn't want it between us. I tried desperately to get away from him. I wanted to be free so I could be with you.'

She nodded, picking up her clothes and walking out of the kitchen into the bedroom. I sat looking into the fire for a couple of minutes but she didn't come back. I followed her. She had dressed and was standing in the darkened room, looking out into the rain through the patio window. I spoke her name and she turned. She came to me and collapsed in my arms. I felt the warmth of her, smelled her soft woman-smell.

'I love you, Paul.'

Death seemed my servant on the road, till we were near and saw you waiting, when you smiled

I don't know what stilled us as we stood there in each other's arms, but something made us both animal, alert. The sound of glass breaking and a terrible concussion sucked the breath out of us, making us both scream soundlessly, a high pitched whine in our ears, too loud to bear. The force and sound dropped us both to our knees on the instant before the smoke billowed up around us in choking yellow-white clouds. We reached for each other, coughing, our eyes streaming and bodies shaking.

Shapes in the smoke, tall, dark, bulky alien forms with piercing bright lights for eyes, masks and guns. We clung to each other, touch the only sensation for a second before another concussion forced us apart and I fell. Sound came back, men shouting in Arabic and things breaking. I retched, vomiting on the floor as I crouched on all fours like a dog, choking and drooling saliva in a silvery band to the puke on the ground. Aisha was dragged away, two of them holding her as she screamed to me, reaching out for me. I could do nothing, disoriented and sick, my eyes, nose and mouth burning and streaming. I choked out her name, 'Aisha,' but she had been swallowed by the fog. A bulky shape materialised in front of me, twin pillars of light shining down and a terrible, crunching kick to my stomach and another to my head as I started to go down, falling into my own puke, my lips drawn back from my teeth in pain. My back arched and he kicked me again.

I heard a gunshot. A single gunshot. Aisha's

screaming stopped. I forced my eyes open. The smoke billowed and parted. For a second, her marble face stared sightlessly back at me. Then the curtain of smoke fell and she was gone.

And in sorrowful envy he outran me and took you apart into his quietness

THANKS

I originally wrote this book in four weeks, inspired by a dream of a girl dancing in the rain after listening to George Winston's *Winter Into Spring*. It took a further seven years to become the book you're holding today. It's been a long road.

Travelling along much of it with me has been a merry band of online companions, the 'Grey Havens Gang', so here's to Simon Forward, Heather Jacobs, Peter Morin, Amethyst Greye, Dan Holloway, Sabina England, Robb Grindstaff, Gail Egan, Bren MacDibble, Kate Kasserman, Michelle Witte and Phillipa Fioretti.

Phillipa in particular gave much of her time and considerable talent to working with me on editing the original MS of *Olives* and Robb was its final editor. Any faults in this work are obviously theirs and nothing to do with me.

I have been lucky to enjoy the friendship and support of many remarkable people around the Middle East over the years. The exceptionally talented Lebanese artist Naeema Zarif created the original cover of this book, I chose reluctantly to replace her art with a cover that fitted my other books.

I owe a deep debt of gratitude in particular for the contributions, suggestions and patience shown by my friend Eman Hussein and to the encouragement, friendship and support of Micheline Hazou, Sara Refai, Roba Al Assi and Taline Tutunjian as *Olives* took shape. They have all, in one way or another, influenced the relationship I have with my books and writing. Matthew Teller made some critical corrections to the MS, as did the eagle-eyed Katie Stine.

My wife, Sarah, has been encouraging me in this for something like ten years now. I've long ago lost count of how many times she's said 'Don't give up'. It's terribly conventional to thank your wife for her support, but Sarah has been a rock of remarkable constancy as I have pursued my long career of collecting a quite wondrous number of rejection slips.

Finally, thank you for reading *Olives* – I hope you've enjoyed it.

Also by Alexander McNabb

Beirut – An Explosive Thriller

Shemlan – A Deadly Tragedy

A Decent Bomber

Birdkill

www.alexandermcnabb.com
@alexandermcnabb

BEIRUT
AN EXPLOSIVE THRILLER

ALEXANDER MCNABB

Michel Freij is a powerful man.
But he wants more.
Two hundred kilotons more.

Ruthlessly ambitious Lebanese businessman and politician Michel Freij is slated to become the country's next president.

The son of a bloody Christian warlord, Freij's calls for a new, strong Lebanon take on a sinister note when European intelligence reveals he's bought two ageing Soviet nuclear warheads from a German arms dealer. Cynical SIS man Gerald Lynch battles to find the warheads before they reach Lebanon – and to discover what Freij plans for the deadly weapons.

www.alexandermcnabb.com

@alexandermcnabb